ROT

Book 1
in the 'Necrotic Ruin' Series

ROT

by **Copper & Cobalt**

First published by Iris Copper and Aster Cobalt 2025

Copyright © 2025 by Iris Copper and Aster Cobalt

All rights reserved. No part of this publication may be reproduced, stored or transmitted in any form or by any means, electronic, mechanical, photocopying, recording, scanning, or otherwise without written permission from the publisher. It is illegal to copy this book, post it to a website, or distribute it by any other means without permission.

Without in any way limiting the authors's exclusive rights under copyright, any use of this publication to "train" generative artificial intelligence (AI) technologies to generate text is expressly prohibited. The authors reserves all rights to license uses of this work for generative AI training and development of machine learning language models.

This novel is entirely a work of fiction. The names, characters and incidents portrayed in it are the work of the authors's imagination. Any resemblance to actual persons, living or dead, events or localities is entirely coincidental.
Iris Copper and Aster Cobalt asserts the moral right to be identified as the authors of this work.

Cover and Illustrations by Iris Copper and Aster Cobalt

Line and Copy Editing by Hannah Friedman

First edition

*"You dangle on the leash of your own
longing; your need grows teeth"*

- Margaret Atwood

Prologue

MORNING LIGHT PIERCES INTO THE clear blue of a lake. Complete and utter serenity rules over the shore. A single drop of dew from the nearby weeds falls in. It forms capillary waves that dissolve just before reaching the bank.

On the day of Venus, she emerges from the water. Causing no disruption to the motionless state of its surface, she makes her way to the edge of the lake. Her long black hair covers her back entirely. The remains of her dress stick to her thin figure, the worn fibres ground down to an almost sheer veil from the time she has spent under the waves. Her skin has been washed to a paler shade, one that makes even her youthful face appear sickly.

Stepping on the grass she barely crushes it beneath her feet. Quiet and imperceptible, she prowls deeper and deeper into the forest. Nothing dares to make a sound in her presence—no bird dares to sing, not even the winds dare to swing until she calls them. But the east breeze carries a message, a curious sound.

Her brother has emerged from the waters already, she knows it. She feels it. With no guidance he will be hard to track down, but she needs to find him before he finds her. Resorting to magic might be the only way.

Through thick woods and lissome branches, her feet take her to places unexplored, a duet of crisp voices calls to her from far away. Once the speech is close enough to be intelligible, the sun has already fallen below the horizon, casting moonlit shadows on the forest bed. Two men have found a cavity in the thicket to claim as their home for the night, a pit of fire protecting them from the cold. They speak in a tongue that rings in her ears with familiarity, yet she cannot make sense of it. She studies them from afar. The moonlight glares on a blade thrown carelessly on the ground next to them. When the fire dies down, gradually their words fall silent as they slip into a peaceful slumber. She starts inching closer, as silently as she had moved before.

Looming over one of the men, she lifts the blade off the ground and swiftly slits his throat with it. The cut spits out blood generously, soaking the patch of grass beneath. Red splatters onto the worn white of her gown. He can't even scream for help, choking on his own blood. The helpless gasping seems to have awakened the other one, she can hear his almost undetectable shuffling, can feel him trying to strike from behind but his bothersome presence is quieted with just a flick of her wrist.

Fingers land carefully on the dead man's eyelids before digging inside his skull. The feeling of the empty eye sockets provokes a visceral reaction in her, but she must continue, no matter what the familiarity of the hollowness makes her feel. She closes her eyes and—*nothing*. The man must have died from the blood loss, and he is no longer useful. This magic will only

Prologue

work with someone alive.

She slides her left hand inside the cut and swiftly takes out his glottis, consuming it so fast she almost gags herself. If the still body is of no other use, she might as well help herself. Clearing her throat, she struggles to speak. The words don't come naturally like usual. They are foreign.

She turns to the other terrified man, who is immobilised. He is still trying to speak, to yell, but she has rendered his ability to talk impossible, empty sounds not quite leaving his mouth.

"Talken," she beckons him.

The tight grip of her mental clutch releases him. He starts coughing, gasping for air and stumbling over his words before finally managing to get what seems to be a half-word out.

"Ple—"

"*Ple...*" she repeats after him, testing out the new sound.

"...Please."

"*Please?*" Mimicking his pronunciation is harder than she expected, "Please." Forming her mouth like he does, she successfully imitates the sound but isn't satisfied yet.

"What are you?"

"What are you." She nods to herself, content enough now. Understanding comes slower than the words themselves, but once the other man's glottis digests, the language will be as if she has spoken it this entire time.

Before the man even has the chance to spit out another word, she sends him into a stupor again. Getting up, she looks down to him where he kneels.

"Up." He is quick on his feet now. "After me."

She leads him to a nearby river. Its current slows as they reach closer and closer.

"Lie down," she commands. The man bends to her will, slamming down onto the dirt by the side of the stream.

She kneels down, a water lily floats over to her, its petals tightly clutched together. When it reaches the shore, the petals swirl open, revealing its unusual contents: a dark eye, not unlike her own, torn out of the skull it belongs to. Carefully placing it into her cupped hands, she wraps it safely in her fingers and brings it to her chest, over her heartbeat. All it takes is a calming breath and the weight of it in her hand, and she feels a sense of groundedness. It's not like magic is impossible without it, but it's easier when you have a piece of home with you.

Gently, she holds the eye in her right hand, while her left hovers over the still, terrified face of the man lying immobile on the earth. Winds pick up. In one rapid movement, her fingernails dig into the soft flesh of the man's eyes, pushing them further and further into his skull, until they are mushed together with his brain. Her hair falls off her shoulders as her head tips back, eyes closed, yet the magic grants her a vision all the same:

All the celestial bodies from Hermes to Poseidon align.
The cosmos melts into the crimson waters of a lake.
Vortex spits out a rib bone, left to float on the water.
A guttural scream takes her attention to a golden mane of hair splayed on the ground.

It begins.

Part I

I

Night of Embers

BANE FOLLOWS HIS PRINCE THROUGH the shadow-drenched corridors of the castle. The summer air carries a light chill through the wide-open windows, fresh and brisk. Their successful exit out of the castle walls is secured by the cover of the night, yet Bane still throws worried looks over his shoulder. After all, if they get caught, he is the one who will be punished.

Avgust leads the way in the dark as easily as a cat would. Dandelion waves bounce with his every step, glimmering when hit by the faint moonlight. He had promised a surprise for tonight but has not spared a single hint. Mere minutes ago, Avgust grabbed him out of his chambers and led them into the night without saying where they were headed.

All the secrecy and the suddenness of it make Bane suspicious of Avgust's true intentions. Is he dragging him somewhere to see how he likes it before he takes someone else there?

Almost as if he has heard Bane's thoughts, Avgust turns back to throw him a cheeky look.

"What?" Bane asks.

"You'll like your surprise." Avgust says confidently, coming to a stop in front of him. His hands run at the front of Bane's collar until his arms settle over his shoulders.

"Will I?" Bane raises a brow, Avgust pulls him closer and drags him until his back hits the wall of the hallway. "Avgust... it's not the place..." He makes an idle attempt to put space between them.

Avgust cocks his head, full lips pursed in a pout. He looks at him through long lashes with something between mock confusion and plea. It's hard to resist such a sight; Bane gave up trying a long time ago.

"Have you no shame?"

They jerk away from each other at the sound of the intruding voice. Bane's blood runs cold with the fear of being caught in a compromising position with the prince, here, where anyone could see.

A sigh of relief escapes him when he sees Eden's shadowed figure at the other end of the corridor. She has her brother's best interest in mind—she will keep this quiet.

"And have *you* nothing better to do than to haunt the corridors?" Avgust rebuts, pushing off the wall and away from Bane, with his arms crossed over his chest.

"I have somewhere to be," a knowing look graces her face as her gaze paces between the two of them, "unlike you two."

Her tone is sharp, but playful, just like the light in her green eyes. Her hair is tied back in a braid and stuffed in a hair net. Its honey colour is a shade darker than Avgust's. They have the same curls, but hers are less cared for and much longer. When it comes to their appearances, there are very few things one can point out as starkly different.

"Who says we don't have somewhere to be?" Avgust raises a brow.

"Then you better quit debauching the hallways, because the next one to catch you might not be as discreet about what they stumble upon." Eden's eyes land on Bane. It feels as though she is sending an accusation.

"Oh, you are too kind," Avgust jests, placing a hand on his heart.

"Continue with your quips and you will find the limits of my kindness rather quickly." Eden bites the bait, and they fall into their usual raillery.

Avgust reaches behind himself to find Bane's hand and shorten the small distance between them. He doesn't turn to face him, still engaged in his talk with Eden. Bane breathes in the olive and honey smell that lingers heavily on Avgust's neck.

"I know you like me too much for your empty threats to unnerve me, dear sister."

"Is that all you rely on? My good opinion?"

Ignoring Eden, Avgust looks at Bane instead, squeezing his hand as if to catch his attention. It's unnecessary, his eyes were already set on him. Bane has seen Avgust's face more times than one can count, marvelled at it, memorised it. Still, every time he looks at him it's like the first. The years of staring do not wear off the novelty. Quite the opposite—he can never get enough.

Avgust's hair frames his face perfectly, not overpowering or hiding any of his features but enhancing them, making them even more pronounced. The strong curve of his thin brows, his almost-pointy nose, the defined cupid's bow of his soft lips. Bane's gaze lingers on those lips for a moment more than it should. Avgust, of course, notices and curves them into a wide smile. One would think that all of these sharp features would bring a harsh look to his face, yet they work together harmoniously to create a man so striking Bane often forgets how to breathe.

Out of all of Avgust's attributes, his eyes always lure Bane in for the longest. The emerald green of them is hidden beneath Avgust's long, curled lashes. His irises reflect the sky sometimes and it makes them look a muted blue. Still, Bane's favourite part of them is the dark, star-like spot in his left eye.

"Quit this immediately." Eden's words startle Bane, not realising that silence had fallen around them. She has been left waiting on an answer this entire time.

"Quit what?" Avgust doesn't turn to his sister right away. She huffs and rolls her eyes, defeated and more than eager to leave them alone in the hallway again.

"What's your hurry anyway?" Tone light and curious, Avgust asks, "And where are you taking this thing?" He nods his head to the metal helmet in her hands that she is obviously trying to hide behind her back.

"None of your concern."

"A secret then. Well, it will come to light sooner or later and I will be the one to uncover it."

To that she says nothing but lets a long sigh out as she passes them and continues on her way.

They give her a head start before they take off on their own way, avoiding the grand staircase and going straight down the servant's stairs instead, and out the kitchen door. From there, it's easy. The castle is surrounded by two tall walls: the inner wall around the fortress itself and the outer wall that surrounds both. Between each wall is a courtyard, though they serve different purposes.

The inner courtyard is where the servants find themselves for most of the day going from the kitchens to the small well in the yard or doing other mundane tasks like laundry. The outer wall is where the castle finds most of its visitors, from villagers selling their cattle and produce, to travelling merchants here to trade. Both courtyards are empty this late into the night. The only signs of life are the horses occasionally neighing from the stables.

Avgust and Bane enter the outer yard through a small side entrance on the inner wall. They exit out of the castle through the stables, not daring to get caught sneaking out of the main gate. It's a long walk in one direction before Bane recognises that they are headed towards the village closest to the castle—Starosel. The details of why still escape him.

"What could possibly be in that village that has gotten you to keep a secret from me this long?"

"If I tell you now, all the secrecy will be for nothing, won't it?" Mischief glistens in Avgust's eyes.

Bane hums in agreement, "You can't even give me a hint?"

"Patience and you'll find out soon enough." That bright smile he always wears when he is pleased with himself appears on his face. Bane bumps his shoulder softly with his own as they walk side by side.

Soon the breeze begins to carry voices and music and the smell of fire. The scent brings warm childhood memories to the surface of Bane's mind, memories from his time in the monastery before he was sent to the castle. He almost thinks his eyes are deceiving him when he sees the pile of embers that the people of the village have circled around.

Bane should've guessed, it is the wake of Easter after all, but he didn't know they practice this ritual around these parts of the kingdom. The group that is here to give the blessing must be a travelling one. For all his years here, this is the first time he is reunited with the practices typical to his region.

"How did you know there would be fire-dancing at the village?"

"I heard some maids mention it," Avgust shrugs

nonchalantly, but he looks very happy with himself, "thought you might like to go."

Bane stares at him, surprised. He has mentioned this ritual being held in Kosti, the village he grew up in, maybe a single time back when they were children. Yet Avgust remembers. It's too personal of a surprise to be for someone else. Maybe this outing really is meant for him, and him alone.

The ritual is held fifty days after Easter as a way to sing the praise of the saints and in return be blessed with peace and prosperity, while cleansing the village of evil.

They settle somewhere in the crowd and watch as the elderly walk around the pile of embers with icons of the saints in their hands. A hunched over wrinkled man comes out of the crowd and spreads the coal over the ground with a rake, keeping the fragile fire underneath alive. Music from a heavy drum and a bagpipe gradually picks up pace and intensity, just in time for the dancers to join in. They circle the fire with light feet in an enchanting rhythm before crossing by each other over the hot embers of the coal. Their steps are quick and well-practised, not letting the fire linger on their skin too long.

Bane chances a glance at Avgust to see how he's enjoying the performance and finds the light of the fire beautifully lighting up his green eyes. It's one of these rare instances where Bane catches Avgust unaware of his charms. The plain white shirt hanging off his broad shoulders slopes into the hem of his trousers, hugging his slim hips. That simplicity magnifies his raw beauty. All the jewels and expensive textiles that Avgust adores so much are left at home, to blend better with the village people, and Bane cannot bring himself to miss them.

"Watch the dancers," Avgust nudges him, "you can look at me later."

Bane swallows thickly and averts his eyes back to the performance before him.

A third dancer joins in from the crowd. The two others continue to dance around the scattered coal as the newcomer settles straight onto the fire. Something about her movement is different, unusual—almost unnatural. She stands on the roaring coal effortlessly. Her feet dance in rhythm, but they lack that haste and urgency with which the other dancers escape the scourging fire.

Eyes the shade of amber find Bane through the crowd. They seem to glow with the fire. With the dancer's sole attention now on him, an uncomfortable shiver runs over Bane. He doesn't know where to look, but he feels an all-consuming need to escape her watchful gaze. Something feels wrong. His gut tells him to run as quickly and as far as he can. He looks to Avgust with urgency and places a hand on his shoulder.

"Maybe we should go," Bane says. His voice comes out meek, unable to hide his unease.

"Did the dancing bore you already?" Avgust teases. Despite the question, he leads Bane towards the edge of the crowd. "Personally, I found it delightful."

"No, that's not it." Bane shakes his head, "I loved the surprise."

"Hm, perhaps we can find some place secluded, and you can show me your gratitude," Avgust whispers, leaning closer.

It's one of those suggestions that sounds more like an order than an offer. He can't be sure if Avgust is fully aware of the implications his words can have, being said by a prince to his servant. As with many other things, Avgust maybe chooses to stay ignorant. However, it would be a sure way to get his mind away from the image of the woman. So, Bane does consider it.

They head back towards the castle. A summer breeze swishes the tall grass of the open field as they walk, the trees of the surrounding forest too far to keep the wind at bay.

"How do you think they do it? Walking on fire?" Avgust

asks.

Bane answers without thinking, "The saints protect them."

"Oh really?" Avgust teases, his usual reaction to any mention of saints or God outside of their mandatory studies, "What if I choose to believe it's because they practice witchcraft?"

"Would you rather believe in a lie?"

"If said lie is more interesting than the truth," Avgust shrugs, "then yes."

"Your need to be entertained at all times should be cause for concern."

"Perhaps." Avgust lifts his head high, like he has no shame in it, "Speaking of entertainment, there will be a feast for Eden's and my birthday."

"Isn't it far too early to start preparation for it? It's a month away."

"It will probably be a big affair, guests from neighbouring kingdoms and whatnot." Avgust gestures with his hands, bumping into Bane in the process. "They need time to receive their invitations."

Bane, about to respond with a remark about any ladies attempting to court him, stops him in his tracks as he hears a voice.

"*Come to me.*" A strange voice speaks.

Bane whips around to look behind them, sure someone is following them. There is no one. His hand finds Avgust's hastily and he swerves their path out of the open field and into the privacy of the woods. The feeling of being watched doesn't subserve, but the tall trees create the illusion of safety.

"Are you taking me up on my offer?" Avgust slowly backs Bane against a tree, fingers playing with the thin golden chain that hangs around his neck. It eases the worry off of him slightly, but the goosebumps on his skin remain under what feels like a pair of eyes. Bane tries to shake the feeling away, but he can't get rid of it nagging in the back of his consciousness. His mind begs for a distraction.

Bane responds to the question by capturing Avgust's lips in a kiss. He's only too eager to meet him halfway, soft mouth parting in invitation. Their rhythm is familiar, natural, that of a years-long love. Arms find purchase at the collar of Bane's shirt, a hand running along the skin just under the fabric. Avgust leans easily into him when Bane's hands draw him close by his middle.

"*Find me.*" The words reverberate on the inside of his skull, snapping Bane out of the kiss. His eyes search the darkness of the forest, but the night is eerily still.

"Did you hear that?"

Avgust pulls his lips away from where they had found the pulse point on Bane's neck to look at his face, "Hear what?"

Bane swallows thickly.

"Nothing."

"Are you feeling well?" Avgust's expression shifts into one of concern, thin eyebrows furrowing in a slope over his worried green eyes.

Bane kisses him again. It's slow and deep this time, all encompassing. Avgust's breaths come out in heavy puffs against Bane's lips whenever they part.

"*Find me.*" The voice claws at his mind like an itch. Bane attempts to shake it out of him.

"Are you alright?" Avgust questions again, but Bane can't answer truthfully. He ignores everything in him telling him to run and instead kisses Avgust again, desperate for it to drown out the voice.

"*You cannot escape me; your fate has been decided.*"

Bane's grasp on Avgust tightens, turning them until Avgust's back is the one slammed against the tree bark. A small gasp of surprise escapes Avgust right before Bane's lips find his again. The kiss is hungry and urgent, a pathetic, hopeless attempt at easing his mind.

"Bane..."

How does it know to call him so? How could this foreign voice know the name only his trusted ones call him by? A shiver runs down his spine.

His hands are even more desperate for a distraction when they grip Avgust's shirt and untuck it from his trousers. The skin underneath the white cloth greets him, arching into his touch. The searing kisses do excellently at turning his mind to mush, until the voice rings in his ears again.

"It's inevitable; I have chosen you."

He grips one hand into Avgust's long hair and pulls him in deeper. Avgust begins unleashing his shirt in an attempt to get it out of the way for Bane's hands.

"Find me!" The voice speaks one final time, like a command, and Bane's legs follow before his mind can catch up. He gets one last look at Avgust who is messily dishevelled, lips red from being kissed raw, hair tangled and sticking out in every direction, shirt half-undressed.

The voice doesn't speak again, but the echo of the words pulls him to it, somewhere deep in the woods. He's running before he knows it.

"Bane!" Avgust calls after him, panic stricken. There are footsteps behind him and Bane's stomach drops.

"Don't come after me!" he pleads as his involuntary pace picks up. He has never felt less in control of himself, like a puppet on strings.

Avgust doesn't follow, and despite having to leave him alone and beyond confused, Bane cannot be more thankful.

The further into the forest he ventures, the harder it gets to see through the dark canopy of treetops that hides the moon almost completely. Bane moves where his body tells him to, and it seems to be leading him towards a weak light in the near distance. His legs stop moving abruptly in the middle of a moonlit glade. It's caged between tall trees and thick bushes, leaving a clearing overhead where the stars peer down at him. Every shadow seems to move, every noise seems to whisper.

"I know you better than you know yourself..."

Bane whips around and finds no one behind him. He feels that peering sense of being watched again.

"Your innermost secrets, your shameful desires, the sins you allow yourself," it says. *"Let me give you a gift, one that will let you lead the life you long for."*

Bushes and shrubs crack and rustle as something circles him at such a rapid pace, he can barely make out its shape. Bane turns and twists as he tries to follow the sound of it moving, but his feet are rooted to the ground.

"Show yourself!" he shouts, the fear breaking through in his voice, fingers shakily reaching for the sword he now realises he didn't bring.

"You can't be saved now; you're mine."

Trying to pin the source of the voice seems futile; it sounds as if it's all around him, inside him. With hasty fingers, he pulls out the small cross necklace from underneath his collar and starts mumbling a prayer. Somehow, it doesn't make him feel safe.

There's another rustle behind him and a sharp piercing pain to the side of his neck. Bane fights to keep his eyes open, but they shut tightly in agony. Pain continues to build until he almost keels over, pulse rabbit-quick in his throat, but then the all-consuming sensation is replaced with ecstasy.

There's a flashing bright light behind his eyelids, and when he forces them open there is nothing left of the cold, gloomy field. The trees seem to shimmer around the edges, and the light washes everything around him in a beautiful golden glow. He could be in the clouds right now, in heaven. Maybe this is death.

A figure, tall and majestic, descends before him, emitting its own blinding light. It floats above him, its gown dragging softly on the ground behind it. It could be an angel.

When it kneels before him, he is met with a face he can't quite make out amidst the luminescence. It's a woman whose auburn hair flows in long waves. The eyes that he can't seem to break away from—those same eyes that have been following him all evening—gleam amber. Despite the twisted nature of the woman, her eyes look at him with kindness. She cups his face gently.

"You will do nicely," she tells him.

She cuts the flesh of her palm open with sharp, claw-like nails that feel entirely out of place in the beautifully golden-washed glade. They break the skin easily and Bane winces, imagining the pain of the wound. The image of a bloody, monstrous face covered by darkness flashes for just a moment, and when it disappears, the light blinds him again. He blinks to adjust his vision. There's a thick liquid gathered in her cupped hands now. It shimmers, aureate and rich, a strange undertone of red peeking underneath its shifting colours.

"Drink up, child." She strokes his hair like a mother would. "Quick, before it goes to waste."

His better judgment doesn't seem to rule over his mind as Bane readily laps up the sweet nectar. It makes him feel light as never before, and he draws out more and more, insatiable.

She pries him off herself, and as the light starts to fade, his ears start to ring and the mirage begins to crack.

"Don't fear, my child, I will return to you."

His eyes shoot open. The sky is above him, still a dark shade of blue. He is lying on the grass. There is a foul metallic taste in his mouth, and an aching wound pulsing on the side of his neck.

Standing up proves to be a challenge, as his whole body protests with a dull, sore throb. Bane's head spins and the world doubles for a moment. In search of relief, he lifts his fingers to his forehead. Just as the disorientation begins to clear, a strong wave of nausea hits him, bending him in half. Immense pain curdles from within his body.

A cool stream runs down to his lips and ends up in his mouth. His nose is bleeding, and so are his ears. In a blink, his vision blurs from blood-red tears as he retches and soon begins vomiting a thick liquid that almost chokes him. Dark red pulps and mushy bits uncontrollably fall out of his mouth, accompanied by agony, continuing for too long before it quiets down.

Just when he thinks it's over, it comes again, hurting worse than before. He rolls on the grass, his arms clutching his stomach, failing to stand clear of the puddle of gore next to him. Its revolting, gag-inducing smell only makes him sicker. He turns his head the other way to hopefully avoid spilling his guts again, but it's no use. The retching might have stopped but the pain remains. His throat is scratched raw from the vomit. His lungs feel heavy like they are full of liquid; he wants to rip his chest open and take them out of his body. Maybe he would have if he had the strength, but he cannot even get back up on his feet.

Nothing alleviates the stabbing aches. Curling into himself grants him only anguish yet he doesn't stop until his body gives out, leaving him unconscious on the cold ground.

II

Day of Ashes

THE SUN BARELY PEEKS OUT behind the mountains, yet Bane feels it on his skin like pins and needles. His eyes crack open in slits. They feel dry and tired, as if they're burning in the light. Flies circle around him, like they would a carcass. A putrid smell surrounds the patch of grass he lies on, coming from the pile of gore he had spat out last night. The flies seem to favour it over him, crawling all over the viscous mess. Every bone in his body is sore. His insides hurt. Still, his heart continues to beat, a slow pulse throbbing in his ears—proof that he is alive.

On shaky legs he stands, knees groaning in protest. He has to squint to avoid the penetrating rays of the sun, but the castle waits for him in the distance. Slowly, he starts walking, lifting one foot after the other. His movements are laboured.

Leaning for support on every tree he passes, he slowly

nears the castle. He ends up on the grounds, just off to the side of the kitchens. At this time of day, the well the servants use to bring water into the kitchens should be at its busiest, while the cooks are preparing breakfast, but is not in use now, despite the bustling workers everywhere.

Bane hunches over the well and helps himself to a bucket of fresh water, sensing the confused looks from the servants passing by but not acknowledging them whatsoever. There isn't a single bone in his body not hurting; he can't bring himself to be bothered by the audience.

He peels off the outer layer of clothes from his body before dunking his hands in the bucket to eagerly wash off the grime. Bane pours the entire thing over his head, trying to wash away the reminders of last night. He drops it back into the well and he brings up another full pail. His skin peels under his unforgiving scrubbing, dripping pale pink back into the bucket.

Despite his best attempts to wash it off, he still feels impure in this horrifying, gruesome state of his. He senses it within him, something wrong and not entirely belonging to him. There is only one place that can offer him comfort.

The soles of his shoes track faint crimson stains on the stone floors as he makes his way to the chapel, just like every morning.

Today is different, however. The sins he often finds himself praying away now seem negligible in the wake of the horror he survived last night. His memories spin and turn until they land on Avgust's distraught face as Bane left him alone in the forest.

He feels awful for leaving him behind, and he can only hope Avgust doesn't resent him too much. It's how their relationship is; no matter the offence, they always forgive each other. It's unspoken, never needing an apology—it's what has kept them together so long. But Bane isn't sure he will be forgiven so easily this time.

The faint light of the half-burned-out candles that are left from the laymen who had been here before him glisten with hope. The all-too-familiar smell of incense coats the inside of his nostrils and leaves a heaviness in his lungs as he exhales. Bane doesn't leave a lit candle today. It doesn't feel like something he is permitted to do. Even the icons painted all around don't bring the comfort they usually do. They look down on him from every wall and altar, judging him, like he is not supposed to be here, not in this state. He swallows down the guilt he feels under their scrutiny.

Making the sign of the cross he falls to his knees in front of them, clasping his hands together. His prayers stumble out of his mouth by themselves, as if he has been holding them back. Flashes of the previous night pass before his tightly shut eyes. A pair of amber eyes. A voice that still rings through his head. The revolting smell of decay. He physically shakes the thoughts away. They are not memories, they can't be. How could something like that even be possible?

Bane reaches under his shirt for his cross pendant. Terror washes over him as he fails to feel the chain around his neck. As the panic turns into sorrow, he realises that no matter how many times he pats over his shirt, he won't find it because it's not there. His chest feels tight with the realisation that he has lost the only thing he had left from before coming to the castle. The only possession of his from before the monastery is now gone. How can he ever forgive himself?

Any other day he'd feel lighter after a prayer, but today he feels almost heavier. Bane has questions about things he knows are not natural or real, yet his mind tries to fool him. These memories must be false. They have to be. Visions placed in his head to distress him, to remind him of the wrath of God. It must be his punishment.

The nuns back home used to always say that those who stray from God will be punished. It appears that they were right; they always were. It's no one's fault but his that his priorities have lain elsewhere for a long time now, tightly held in Avgust's arms. Whatever awaits him, he must not tell a soul. It's his punishment and he must suffer it alone.

It would be easy to blame it all on someone else, to say he was tempted into sin, that it was outside of his control. Yet his conscience won't let him convince himself of that. He was always a willing participant when it came to falling for Avgust. Bane chose to walk this path to damnation a long time ago, further and further down to a point of no return. Avgust is not the reason for his fickle faith; he is the very thing that shed light on it, exposing Bane for the man he truly is. The king believes his devotion to be greater than it really is, because Bane's time in prayer is most often spent asking the Lord for forgiveness.

It often happens that when he leaves the sanctuary of the chapel, the world outside is not as kind to him. He prefers to get his armour set up ahead of the other knights, before they even awaken. This morning, however, he won't have the chance. If he hadn't spent that much time trying to wash away the reminders of his shame, he would've missed the throng, but alas.

When he makes it to the armoury, all the other knights are already getting set up, some for guard duty, some for training. His presence doesn't go unnoticed. As he walks through the group, there are several sharp looks aimed his way. It's not unlike any other day when he finds himself at the knight's assembly this late. The looks and the whispers don't get to him normally. Today, however, every sound is maddening, every movement that passes his peripheral vision puts him on edge. He needs to get out of here as fast as possible. Except of course, he is out of luck again.

"How was your little slip away last night, leech?" The foulest one of them, Aleksander, speaks first as per usual. Bane doesn't even bother wondering how he knows about that. Aleksander always has a way of knowing things he shouldn't. Bane doesn't react to his goading in any visible way, but his patience is already worn thin between waking up in his own vomit in the middle of a field and losing his most prized possession.

"We had a visitor last night, asking if you happen to be in the shared quarters. You see, apparently you weren't in *your own* chambers." Stefan, one of the others, speaks.

Bane tries to hide the way his ears perk up. There's only one person in this entire castle that would care to look for him. The manner in which *his own chambers* were mentioned also doesn't escape him. Having a private room is a privilege no one else from the troop has. Bane was given that room when he first came to the castle, long before it was decided that he would join the knights. The room itself is nothing special and yet his peers envy him greatly.

"I had to look the prince in the eyes and tell him that you were not here. He was *really* disappointed," Aleksander says.

Bane swallows thickly, his suspicions confirmed. His stomach churns with guilt. He tries not to imagine Avgust, left all alone in the middle of the night, in the darkness of the forest, forced to go back to the castle all by himself.

"Can't possibly imagine what anyone could need from you, as worthless as you are," Mihai, short but mouthy, says in passing as he puts his boots on.

"Come on, don't be shy, tell us. You must know why he was looking for you," Aleksander tests, a pleased smile on his face.

Bane doesn't typically grace their taunts with a response, but for some reason, the words tumble out of his mouth before he can stop them.

"How would I know? I wasn't here." His tone is rigid and insolent, with a tinge of annoyance he can usually keep perfectly under control.

"And where *were* you?" a tall knight jibes. Christian, Bane believes, is his name.

"Perhaps in the princess's chambers? Covering all the fronts, huh, bootlicker?" Mihai says with sneer.

"Bootlicker." Aleksander repeats under his breath, revelation in his voice. "That is exactly what you are—a useless, pathetic bootlicker." Aleksander shoves at Bane's chest with malice in between every word. Bane miraculously maintains his balance. "The prince's favourite. The king's favourite. What makes you so special?" His breath fans across Bane's cheek, Aleksander's face shoved right in his. "What is it about *you*?" He shoves him again, this time harder. Something in Bane snaps.

It's like he can't control himself when he hits him, as if something else takes over his body and forces his fist to crash into Aleksander's cheekbone.

Surprise and glee appear on Aleksander's face as if he has been itching for this opportunity to present itself. It's not long before he swings at Bane to return the favour. They struggle in a violent embrace, taking turns in who gets the upper hand. The other men egg on the scuffle, encouraging Aleksander, cheering. Something about it makes Bane even angrier. A good punch lands on his jaw at some point, but Bane barely even blinks.

Beneath the noise of the eager cheers and the tussle of their bodies, a set of heavy footsteps approach the crowd gathered around the fight.

"Konstantin! Aleksander!"

It's the third time they call him when he realises that they are calling *him*. Konstantin. The name given to him by the church that raised him, the name of one of the saints of Kosti. He wasn't born there, so it wasn't really his hometown, merely the town he was raised in for a period of his life. The faintest memories still linger in his mind, images of a place nothing like this one. His real home, Bane assumes. He remembers being taken from it, followed by long months on a ship, the sailors yelling at him in a language he did not speak, nor understand. There was only one word that stood out to him, the one repeated over and over again, which made it sound important in a child's mind. He decided it must be his name: Bane. The only name he knew and fully recognised as his own. If he had another one before, he neither knew nor remembered. So, *Bane* is all he has from his past. Konstantin is just the name he was christened with.

Three men are needed to successfully force Bane and Aleksander apart. Despite his swollen bleeding lip and red eye that would soon turn black, Aleksander has that awful, familiar self-satisfaction on his face. Bane spits blood in his direction, while freeing himself from the grip of the man that holds him back. His face throbs and his fists ache, yet he can't find it in himself to regret defending himself.

The two of them stand in front of Viktor like two children about to be scolded by their father, heads lowered, eyes averted.

"This is completely unacceptable!" Viktor tells them, voice stern and sure.

It's impossible to guess that Viktor, shoulders always pushed back in perfect posture, has lived for over fifty years by the way he conducts himself, like a man at his peak. Only his fine, grey hair suggests that he is way past that prime. His face has a few harsh lines that show his age, but not a single scar—a testament of all the battles he won in his youth. If it weren't for his reputation and the stories that travel around the castle, one wouldn't be able to tell how many battles he has fought. Even his lasting injuries he never shows any sign of. He is too proud.

Honour and chivalry—Viktor likes to tell them—is what makes a knight. One without these values is just a foot soldier.

"You two will run three more laps, to have the extra time to properly reflect on why this is unacceptable behaviour between fellow knights. You are not some drunks in a tavern, you are the King's Knights!" Viktor dismisses them with the flick of his hand. "Go now, out, all of you."

The King's Knights is the smallest troop in the castle, with only eight of them deemed worthy enough. All the soldiers either have a title or, in Bane's case, the king's blessing. He is the only one to have received it, which is yet another thing that puts a target on his back. Bane doesn't quite belong here, but for better or worse, he has earned himself the king's favour. It's not like he got to freely speak his mind on the king's decision to put him in the most prestigious troop. He wouldn't say he insists on becoming a knight at all, but the king does. Maybe he has bigger plans for Bane than he has for himself.

When the troop shuffles out into the training grounds like a herd of sheep, only then does Bane snap out of his rage. The sun is shining too brightly in his eyes for him to ignore. That takes his mind off of the violence swirling inside him. What has gotten into him? He needs to pull himself together, before Viktor does it for him.

Running isn't really Bane's strong suit, yet he'd pick it over having to sword fight any time without a doubt. His childhood spent in reading and praying didn't help build up his stamina whatsoever. *'It's too late for him,'* Viktor would say, yet the king was persistent that Bane must be trained.

His late addition to knight training was unpleasant for him and irritating for his peers, who have been preparing themselves their whole lives for this. Unlike them, Bane never had to be a page, he was way too old when it was decided that he should join the troop. *'Holding him back was going to be impractical and unnecessary.'*, Those were the king's exact words. Bane's time as a squire before becoming a knight was so short, it was basically insignificant. In the six years since then, the others hadn't been able to accept him as part of the group and not just an addition; however, Bane didn't blame them. He came out of nowhere, no noble background, no status—nothing. Just the king's blessing, which in fact annoyed them most.

They see him as inferior, and perhaps it is the truth. Bane is clumsy, his endurance is laughable, and he is more often in the way than helpful. He tries to take up as little space as possible, but his stature makes that very difficult. His only saving grace is his brawn, but today, even his armour feels too heavy on his shoulders.

"Get in pairs," Viktor instructs after they finish their laps around the arena—a large, fenced area within the inner castle wall, the ground bare from their constant stomping around. "Konstantin, Aleksander you spar together. Since you want to fight, at least fight like men of honour."

Bane exhales, long and drawn out with annoyance, but steps towards Aleksander with no complaint.

They start to circle each other, Aleksander resembling a vulture ready to feast on a deer carcass. Despite the wide space surrounding him, Bane feels cornered. Aleksander is the first to try to charge at him, but miraculously, his attempt is unsuccessful. Bane doesn't try to strike back, only to defend against Aleksander's attacks, which visibly infuriates him. The more he dodges the more frustration builds up in his opponent.

Bane's headache comes and goes with the sharp movements he must make to avoid Aleksander's skilful jabs. The steady pulsing behind his eyes renders his already less-than-admirable abilities with the sword even more pathetic. The sun blinds him, and he falls back on the ground, face right by Aleksander's boot. Aleksander towers over him, intimidating and hostile, but at least he blocks out the sun.

"You'd do well to remember your place." He leans closer over him. "Eye for an eye, vermin." Aleksander cuts Bane's lip with the tip of the blade, exactly where Bane's fist had split his.

"Aleksander! Help him up! Quickly!" Viktor calls out. Bane helps himself up instead, dusting the dirt off his armour as Aleksander pointedly walks away. Viktor approaches him.

"His Majesty requests your presence," he informs. Bane nods curtly, "Make yourself presentable and go."

Dragging his feet on the way back inside, he quickly changes out of his armour but decides to take the longest route to the throne hall. Passing the dining hall, the pantries, and the solar, he finally finds himself near the garden with the pond. The fresh breeze fills his lungs. He leans on one of the enormous columns, trying to take in the beautiful landscape of the inner garden. A tall oak casts a thick shadow over the peaceful scene. Overpowering greenery rules over every stone encircling the pond in the centre, where lilies float on the still surface of the water. If he could, he would have liked to spend the entire day here, but he is required elsewhere.

The king is expecting him when he arrives. The throne hall is one of the largest rooms in the castle, richly decorated with golden embellishments in the stone walls and complimented by a tall geometrical ceiling and wide-open windows. It is, in fact, so well-lit, his head starts spinning again. He walks the wool carpet then stands in the middle of its length in front of the king's throne, before falling on one knee in a bow.

"Rise."

"You've requested for me, Your Majesty."

"Yes, Konstantin," he speaks, voice calm, "I am expecting to hear your report."

Every week since Bane arrived all those years ago, he has been required to report on Avgust's introduction to the gospel. But over time, slowly and gradually, his reports have become shorter and vaguer, simply because there is nothing new to report that wouldn't have him sentenced.

Is he to speak of the time Avgust *accidentally* dropped his bible in the water? Or the time they couldn't even get through one singular passage before Avgust was dozing off with a loud snore? Or maybe he must report on last night, and the countless nights before that, where the two of them chose a different way to pass the time?

"Avgust's introduction to Christ is going steadily and uninterrupted," he lies. "We began to revise the Old Testament. We are still on the Book of Genesis."

The king nods, pleased.

"You've been injured," he points out. "Are you alright?"

Bane's hand flies to his busted lip. "Nothing worth your concern, Your Majesty."

"What happened?"

Bane is hesitant to answer but he knows Viktor will probably report the scuffle between him and Aleksander anyway.

"It was just a misunderstanding, My King."

"If there is someone unfit to serve in the King's Knights, someone causing trouble, you should hold no reservations and inform me right away. You know I trust your judgement."

"No, no, nothing of the sort, Your Majesty, you mustn't worry yourself." Bane dismisses quickly. The last thing he needs is the other knights' opinions of him to deteriorate even more. "We dealt with it between ourselves."

"Good. I count on you to keep everything there in order," the king says, and Bane preens under the praise, though he knows it's undeserved. "Your faith makes you a reliable and responsible soldier, son. Don't let that be wasted."

"Thank you, Your Majesty."

Bane lowers his head in another bow, laced with the shame that comes with not being worthy of the trust the king puts in him. He excuses himself and is more than ready to leave as he turns.

"Konstantin," the king calls again.

Bane turns around, startled.

"Wash your face; don't walk around the castle all bloody. People will worry."

"I'll see to it."

He bows again before finally making it out of the hall. The cut on his face hurts so little, he hadn't even realised he was visibly wounded.

Once he is back in the inner court, he takes a look at himself in the reflection of the pond. He reaches into the water, bringing his dampened hand to his mouth and uses his finger to wipe the blood away.

When the ripples clear, and he looks at himself again, he sees no wound at all.

III

The Ladies of The Court

AVGUST LIES SPRAWLED OUT ON the large bed in a room he feels far too comfortable in, despite it not being his own. The wooden canopy above stares down at him. Groaning for the thousandth time that day, he buries his face into a pillow that muffles his screech.

"He loathes me so; he can't even stand to look at me! I'm certain," he concludes after summarising the events of last night in unnecessary detail.

"Trust me, he finds it difficult *not* to look at you," Eden states confidently. "It appears to me there's not much else you do besides look." *And touch.* But that goes unspoken.

"Do you even talk?" she asks.

Rarely, when they're in public and there aren't better things to do.

"How does this matter right now? He is missing! What if

he never comes back?"

"Have you even tried to look for him?" she scoffs at him.

The "*no*" is loud on Avgust's face.

"You're quick to make your conclusions, but you haven't even spoken to him. You will worry yourself sick over nothing." Eden's dismissal does the opposite of easing him, but he leaves it at that. Maybe she is right to think so.

Avgust gets off the bed in one swift motion, taking a spin around the room. The furniture in Eden's chambers is made from rich, dark wood, crowded in her modestly sized bedroom—modest for a princess, at least. The room is bright, which is a nice contrast to the dark colours of the tapestries lining the walls and the mismatched rugs overlapping on the floor. Faint streaks of sunlight make their way through the fabric of the curtains that swish gently in the breeze coming from the large windows on one wall. The heavy wooden desk where she sits is littered in tomes and loose papers that threaten to fly with the wind were it not for the inkwell holding them in place.

Avgust steps closer to Eden's large dresser table on the other end of the room. Opening the top drawer, he runs a careful hand over the luscious jewellery displayed in it. Golden and pearlescent jewels jingle under his fingers with a rich beautiful chime. He singles out a silver headpiece engraved with emerald stones.

"Since you carry around my helmet, perhaps I can take some of your jewellery," Avgust suggests, half-jokingly, "to make things even."

"You can take all of them for all I care." She shrugs him off like it's nothing, as if such beautiful pieces are not worth her attention.

If it were up to her, Avgust knows she wouldn't go for the type of jewels that were bought for her. He doesn't quite understand it but adornments have never really been her thing. Avgust has his own jewellery, of course, chains and signet rings. The pieces he is forced to wear are bulky and severely lack the elegance of the more feminine pieces.

Avgust studies the diadem in his hands, turning it to look at every little detail on it. He bets the jeweller's hands have to be as elegant as the piece to make such beauty. Subtilty is something his jewellery could definitely use more of.

Eden now rests on the cotton covers of her bed, long honey hair splayed around her head. Avgust returns the circlet back to its place and joins her with a dramatic bounce onto the mattress.

"What did you do with it anyway? The helmet?"

"Well," she says, "If I tell you, I would have to kill you."

Avgust gasps dramatically, "Kill your own brother? My, my—Is this what you're training for whenever you sneak out?"

"Yes. And I'm sure one day it will come in handy."

"Are you really not going to tell me?" Avgust asks playfully, hiding the hurt he feels, "It's impressive you have managed to hide it so long without raising suspicion."

"Hiding it from your nosy self has been difficult, yes. But the less people who know, the better. And as it stands, no one knows." Eden sighs. "I'm not afforded much freedom as a woman, and if this secret spreads, it may jeopardise what little of it I get."

Avgust gives her a hum in understanding.

"I wish we could swap places," Eden says with a heavy sigh. "You would get to play dress up as much as your heart desires and I would be free to do whatever I please."

"I'm not as free as you think."

"But you were born with a purpose, while I..." There's a long pause after she trails off. Just as Avgust starts to think she's not going to finish her thought, she continues. "I don't even qualify as your spare. The closest I get to having value is to be married off."

There's a defeat in her voice only Avgust truly understands.

"What I wouldn't give for you to be king in my place."

His words suck the air out of the room. Avgust winces at his own tone, which came off far too serious, far heavier than he intends. Still, it rings true in the silence.

"Avgust..."

Eden's expression is one of concern and sympathy. There are pages of unspoken words exchanged in their glances, and it feels safe to know he isn't alone.

"Well, you seem closer to being a knight than a king." He lifts himself up onto his elbows again.

"Maybe..." She hesitates to confirm it, but Avgust knows he has gotten closer to the truth of where she goes at night.

Avgust grins. "Can I come with you the next time you sneak out?"

"Absolutely not!"

"Wherever it is you go, you won't even know I'm there! I have an excellent disguise in mind..." He snags the bedding from under them and puts it over his head. "I can be an old crone." Hunched over, he walks around the room with a fake limp.

Eden laughs, sitting up on the bed. "If I'm a knight more than a king, you are closer to a jester!"

"I can even pretend to curse your opponents." He twists and wiggles his fingers in her face. "Or maybe...curse you!"

"Come on, old crone, out, out!"

After pushing him across the room all the way to the door, she stretches an expectant hand. "I'll need those back, too."

Avgust straightens himself, reluctantly taking the covers off his head and hands them over. He watches her from the door as she throws them back onto the bed before stepping to her dresser. She takes the same silver headpiece he was looking at from the drawer.

"It may not fit around your massive head, but here, have it."

Avgust gives her a wide smile. "You may not be much fun, but you do know how to bribe."

"Alright now, off you go. I'm probably late already." Eden pushes past him through the door and sets off down the corridor.

"Where are we going?" Avgust follows like a lost duckling.

"*I* am going to join the court." Eden places a hand on her chest before flicking her wrist in his direction. "*You* can go wherever you please."

Avgust struggles to keep up with her quick strides as she surges ahead.

"I shall be coming with you, in that case."

Eden swivels around and sends him a look. "Suit yourself, but I am not responsible if you get thrown out."

"Thrown out? The ladies love me!"

When Eden opens the door to the great chamber, Avgust lets himself in after her.

Four heads snap up in unison. The ladies leave the embroideries in their laps forgotten in favour of greeting them.

"Oh, Prince Avgust!" Lady Roza exclaims, "Will you be joining us today?" She has her dark hair in a snood, one of the highest fashions with an intricate weave to its pattern. Its light colour complements the green of her dress.

"Ladies." Avgust bows slightly with a smile and preens at the giggles it ensues. He can almost hear Eden's eyes rolling. She assumes her spot in the middle of the crescent shape the ladies' chairs are arranged in. Since he is nothing more than an uninvited guest, Avgust doesn't have a designated seat; so, he brings himself a footrest chair and plops down next to Eden without complaint.

"Tell me, what have you been using your talents on, ladies?"

Lady Maya perks up. "Would you like to see? I have been working on improving my natural motifs, what do you think?" She turns her embroidery hoop around and shows him the garden of flowers she is making.

"How can one improve upon perfection, Lady Maya?"

She giggles and brushes her mousy brown hair behind one ear, before returning her attention to her work. Avgust sneaks a peak at Eden's hoop and the mess of yarn she is trying to poke through it.

"Now yours, on the other hand, leaves much to be desired."

Eden kicks him only lightly, but it hurts badly enough.

"Avgust, I think you are far too busy to dull yourself with

our company," Eden says.

"Nonsense, dear sister. I am delighted to be amidst the most beautiful court of the castle. And yourself, of course."

"You are aware your face is merely an unfortunate copy of mine, yes?" Eden gives him a look of irritation through her brows, but Avgust can tell she isn't all that annoyed with him.

"I, for one, am glad you have joined us, Prince Avgust," Lady Roza says, with a bat of her lashes, hazel eyes sparkling at him. Out of all the ladies in Eden's court, she is always the happiest to engage with Avgust's antics. Her sympathies for him are no secret to anyone. Her obvious interest is flattering, and he willingly indulges it.

"The sentiment is shared, my lady. After all, where else can I enjoy such well-mannered company?"

"You are very welcome to join us anytime you please. Our company is yours to enjoy," Lady Maya says, nodding at him politely.

Eden holds her tongue, but she gives him a shake of her head in disapproval of the lady's invitation. Avgust bites his cheek so as not to laugh.

The women go back to their respective tasks, leaving Avgust bored in the silence. He looks around, in search of ways to entertain himself. Soon his attention lands on one of the girl's dresses and his eyes trace the intricate stitching and craftsmanship of the fabric.

"Lady Irena, I must say, that dress is a perfect match for the colour of your eyes."

"Oh, Avgust, ever the sweet-talker." Irena hardly ever falls under his charms, but there is a slight tug at her lips. It feels like a triumph anytime his words do crack through her cold exterior. Avgust plays up his compliments often enough, but he does usually mean them. Irena's midnight blue dress *does* compliment her stormy grey eyes. It's beautiful. The sleeves drape from her wrists in a fashionable manner and the neckline stretches enough to display her shapely bosom.

"Why are you carrying this around?"

Avgust turns to see Lady Georgiana looking at the diadem he has carelessly placed in his lap. If Irena is hard to charm, Georgiana is impossible. The times he has gotten a laugh out of her can't be more than a handful. Avgust sometimes thinks that her clever eyes see right through his false bravado. Fortunately, she never cares to call it out.

"Oh, this old thing." He picks it up and tucks it under his armpit, not allowing anyone the chance to inspect it. "I saw the miserable state of it in Eden's room and I couldn't help myself. I have to take it to the jeweller for polishing. It's a shame to let such beauty rot."

"I see," Georgiana says, but something about the squint of her eyes makes her look unconvinced. She would be right, of course—that is not at all why Avgust finds himself in possession of the precious diadem.

"Oh, Prince Avgust, you are so thoughtful," Roza exclaims with rapture, "Not many men notice things like that."

"It's not so much about noticing, my lady; it's that most men are unable to appreciate such beauty." Avgust puts on his most charming smile, gaze not leaving Lady Roza's. "And I for one, have an eye for it."

She blushes under his attention.

The door to the great chamber opens.

"Ah, ladies, glad to see you have gathered." Nurse Vila walks in, interrupting their chatter. Her greying hair is tied neatly into a practical bun and her kind smile greets the myriads of ladies. "Care to explain why there's six of you?"

"Nurse Vila—" Avgust starts to plead his case, but the woman cuts him off with a quick lift of her hand.

"Your Highness, you are distracting my ladies."

"A worthwhile distraction I hope." Avgust winks at the court and enjoys Lady Roza's secret smile and Maya's quiet chuckle, all while ignoring Eden's unsubtle shake of her head.

"Now, time to excuse yourself, young prince, my ladies need some quiet," Nurse Vila says calmly, but it sounds more like a scold.

"Well, ladies…" Avgust stands up, and fixes his clothes. "It pains me to do so, but I must say farewell." He bows ceremoniously to all the ladies and sneaks a look at Lady Roza.

"I will be in the garden if any of you happen to need me."

It doesn't take long before his mind wanders back to the events of the night before as he strolls through the castle corridors. The stone keeps the fortress cold even on the warmest days, but the chill is unwelcome against his frost-bitten heart. Bane has never left him like he did last night. Vulnerable and still wanting. Whether intentional or not, being left in that state sent a message: *Bane doesn't want him.* Avgust hadn't realised how much of his confidence is dependent on Bane's attention. And now, when he is unsure that he is what Bane desires, he needs someone else to fill that void. Someone more than willing to express their interest.

The Ladies of The Court

Avgust paces slowly, swaying from wall to wall just to make his stroll longer. He passes through cold, empty hallways and ones full of servants taking care of rooms. He wanders down to the floor below through a narrow staircase, away from the main entrance. Hastily, he walks out and continues strolling, until he makes it to the garden with the pond where he sits by one of the columns, which separates the garden from the halls, and waits. Lady Roza is not usually one to refuse him, and sure enough, after a few minutes pass, she makes her way towards the inner court.

"Prince Avgust. Was I correct in assuming this was an invitation meant for me?"

"More than correct, my lady. You are just who I was hoping to see."

The rosiness of her cheeks is present whenever Avgust goes out of his way to speak to her. It eases him into his charming persona when he knows his advances are desired. Bane never affords him the courtesy of confirmation. For all Avgust knows, he merely tolerates them.

"We shouldn't be sneaking in secret like this all alone. It's a scandal waiting to happen."

"Maybe so. We can go somewhere more populated, if you so wish?"

Lady Roza's nervousness whenever the two of them are alone is always obvious. Her cheeks colour easily, her eyes are shifty, anxious to not get caught.

"No." She looks at him from underneath her lashes. Despite her hesitation to be left resisting Avgust's charm all by herself, she does enjoy his private company. She tells him so. Avgust, beaming under her pleasant attention as it is, never had the intention of taking it further than secret conversations. But she seems to expect him to act on his promise of romance. Maybe that's why she keeps agreeing to meet him like this.

Lady Roza's clear interest is a great thing when Avgust is left doubting his value, but it holds very little weight when she isn't the person he needs to receive it from. Bane rarely spares compliments. He doesn't like to say things he doesn't mean. Maybe that's why they spend their time tangled in each other, compared to the quieter company Lady Roza offers.

Lady Roza is a beautiful woman, one of a prestigious lineage, smart, kind. But she is so keen on letting her interest be known, that she seems to agree with Avgust on even his most outrageous opinions. Bane never lets him get away with any ridiculous claims and is always the first to challenge him on all of his intentional misconceptions about the world. That's what makes choosing to believe in the supernatural over any God fun in the first place—to see how people try to convince him otherwise. Lady Roza seems to want to hear his mind on all matters just to blindly believe him, which removes the thrill of the argument that usually ensues whenever Avgust brings up such beliefs to Bane.

"I can't stay much longer; Nurse Vila will come looking for me," she says, "but I will request your company when I can sneak away for longer."

"Well, I shall expect your signal and join you whenever you please, my lady."

Avgust upholds the pretend secrecy around their meetings because it makes Roza feel important, special. Maybe it's cruel to encourage those feelings when he knows the drastically different endings his secret meetings with Bane have.

Lady Roza takes her leave, sending a shy smile his way, tucking a strand of hair behind her ear. Avgust stays in the garden for a while longer, enjoying the colours in which the setting sun begins to paint the sky above.

After wasting the rest of the day away, Avgust makes it back to his room. He dreads being left to his thoughts when they all end up wandering to Bane.

Despite the warm glow of the lit chandeliers, his room feels cold. It's too big for the sparse furniture he has—a dresser, a desk, a mirror and a bed—all scattered along a different wall with too much space between them. The fireplace rests unused with the remaining charcoal from the last cold days of spring. His room lacks the cozy warmth of Eden's room, with nothing decorating the empty walls, no patterned rugs to keep his feet away from the stone floor, just the vast feeling of loneliness. It's only bearable being in this room when Bane is here to warm the space.

Avgust forces himself away from his door until he stands staring back at his reflection. His mirror is the biggest, most lavish in the entire castle, with golden embellishments all around the heavy frame. He had begged for it like a child and despite his father's reluctance to indulge him in his vanity, he had granted his wish. Now, Avgust gets to stare at himself wearing jewels that don't belong to him—that shouldn't ever belong to a man—and face his flaws where he can't hide from them.

While everyone has a passion, a calling of some sort that

fulfils their days, Avgust is stuck waiting for the inevitable to happen. Eden thinks he has a purpose, when all he has is an obligation.

He kneels beside his bed and adds the new piece to his secret collection of jewellery (all stolen from or willingly given by Eden), kept in a small wooden chest. Avgust then shoves the locked chest back under his bed.

Itching for a distraction, his gaze catches on the hairbrush on his nightstand. He grabs it and runs careful fingers over the wood. It's a beautiful thing and like many beautiful things that end up in his possession, it was taken from his sister.

The chipping paint on it is thanks to the negligent care Eden bestows upon most of her possessions, but Avgust loves the beautiful carvings that curl and twist in a floral pattern underneath the blue colour.

Standing back in front of the mirror, the methodical mindless movement of the brush up and down his hair provides little comfort, if any. Inevitably, Avgust sinks again into those dreadful thoughts he can't keep at bay anymore. His hair, often his most cherished physical attribute, now feels dull and colourless against the bristles of the brush. The face it frames seems to twist uglier with each passing moment as it stares back in the mirror. Avgust is shamed often for his vanity, but when nothing else about him manages to impress, he has no choice but to care for his looks.

It feels in vain, now that he holds nothing but doubt that he truly ever was as beautiful as he liked to believe. Bane is one of few people that did not seem charmed by his beauty, and last night was nothing but a bitter confirmation of Avgust's worst fear. There is very little that can be done to console him out of thinking his looks have already begun to spoil.

He keeps brushing, although it's no use. It won't make him prettier.

His attention snaps to the knock at the door. Once, twice, followed by three more in rapid succession. It's a familiar sequence that sets his heart drumming in his chest. The only person who uses that knock is Bane.

Avgust hesitates. He isn't sure he wants to see him. He isn't sure he wants to be seen. There is a fear that Bane will run away again at the sight of him. Hurt rings deep in his chest at the thought, but his heart has already started leaping at the promise of seeing Bane.

He swings the door open in such a rush he almost catches his nose with the edge of it. They come face to face. Bane is tired, his eyes droop heavily with every blink, and there's a smear of dried blood on the bottom of his chin. His warm brown skin appears ghostly. He looks drained and sickly, as if he hadn't had a proper meal in a while.

Avgust tries not to show his concern.

"Good evening, my prince," Bane greets with a raspy, worn-out voice. Avgust chews on his lip, conflicting emotions crashing within him. He is indescribably happy to have Bane crawling back to him, but his heart still lies in his chest bleeding.

Despite the tangled mess that is Bane's hair and the red stain around his mouth, Avgust is still glad to see him. He hesitates but his hands can't help but grasp Bane's fragile jaw, tracing his stubble with gentle fingers, concern overpowering his detriment. Bane leans into the touch, a shared relief passing between them when his nose digs into the palm of Avgust's hand, as if trying to bury himself into the skin. Avgust turns the pliant face in his hands to have a better look at it. He doesn't seem to be injured and there's no apparent source of the blood smeared on his chin.

"You look like hell," Avgust informs him.

Bane hums simply.

"You need rest, but you need to change out of those muddy clothes first." Avgust steps towards his dresser and digs through his clothes to find something that would fit Bane's broader shoulders. He finds a shirt that had originally been Bane's but has found its way into Avgust's belongings. It's not the only of its kind in his trunk so he doesn't feel too regretful returning it.

Bane takes the shirt and turns around before undressing. Taking the hint, Avgust looks away. It feels strange, avoiding each other so when they have seen each other bare more times than is appropriate for an unmarried pair.

"What happened last night? You were very eager to run from me," Avgust finds himself asking, back turned to Bane's undressing form. If he chooses to lie about it, Avgust doesn't want to read it in his eyes.

Something shuffles behind him and Avgust chances a look over his shoulder. Bane has fully changed into the clean shirt and shed his heavy leather boots.

"I...I'm sorry," he mumbles, looking like a scolded child.

Avgust is desperately trying to meet his gaze, but Bane won't look at him. He is fixated on the stone floor. The furthest that he would allow his eyes to lift is to the collar of Avgust's shirt.

"I just need to know if you are alright," Avgust says. He swallows down the hurt that still tears at him. Bane didn't deny wanting to run, almost as if trying not to offend him with what he already suspects is true.

"I am—" Bane clears his throat. "I am, just tired."

His eyes roam all over Avgust like he is trying to soak him in just as he is, yet still not meeting his gaze. It sends a tingle through his stomach, followed by confusion. Bane steps closer shyly, until he's close enough to touch again. His hands trace along the back of Avgust's nightshirt, featherlight and barely touching, but his hold lifts the fabric just slightly until air brushes along his hot skin. Avgust fights the urge to flinch away.

Their breaths sound heavy in the quiet room. Avgust's shirt hangs slightly off one shoulder; Bane grazes the exposed skin with his fingertips first and then brushes a gentle kiss against it. Avgust shudders as Bane raises the fallen collar back into place, tucking the kiss under the fabric to keep it safe.

Bane finds the loose strings of the shirt, retying them with care, covering Avgust's chest; he is keeping Avgust's skin out of sight. Although it does nothing but break open that bleeding wound inside of him, he will take what he can have. His arms wrap firmly around Bane, crushing their bodies as tight as they could go. He is surprised to feel Bane's hands tightening around him in return, as he buries his face in the crook of Avgust's neck. He noses along the skin and breathes him in deeply. Maybe he missed him, even if he can't stand to look at him.

"You are asleep on your feet; let us get you to bed."

Bane doesn't protest and follows without resistance as Avgust leads them to the other side of his room. Avgust watches as he stops to look at himself in the mirror. It's a habit of his, every time he ends up in Avgust's room, he fixes his appearance. Tonight, his reflection elicits a small gasp. Quick hands run through his black wavy hair trying to untangle the knots, before he finally notices the smudged stain on his chin. He turns his back to Avgust, trying to hide his reflection as he wipes at it with desperation.

They end up lying side by side on the bed sheets, both staring at the ceiling. Bane tosses and turns with soft whines and moans, like he's unable to find a position where his body doesn't hurt. After what feels like forever, his breaths fall even, and the sheets stop rustling.

Avgust turns to look at him, only to see him peacefully fast asleep curled into a ball, facing him.

They don't often get to rest in each other's presence so innocently. Time not spent under each other's warm hands is time wasted, as they only have the nights for their private enjoyment. Avgust is afraid of the moments they don't spend wrapped in pleasure. Pleasure is safe, something known and well-rehearsed. Anything outside this is uncharted territory. Now, that they find themselves lying together in the quiet without having so much as kissed before bed. Avgust doesn't know how to read into Bane's intentions. It's possible he isn't looking for companionship, let alone with Avgust. They haven't talked about it and Avgust is too afraid it will change things between them if he ever dares to bring it up. But he knows they like each other's touch; Avgust is willing to give that as long as Bane keeps coming back for it.

It's a way of living that kills him, but at least he gets to have him.

Avgust stares, eyes tracing along the pronounced hump on the bridge of Bane's nose. Feeling braver now that he is asleep, he dares to run a finger over his thick, furrowed brows, smoothing the tension. His stubble prickles under his fingertips, as Avgust chances a slow caress down his jaw. Gently, he rubs his thumb against Bane's mouth, his top lip jutting out ever so slightly further out than the bottom. His profile is handsome, brow bone pronounced, jaw tight with tension. Avgust worries about where he disappeared to last night, what happened that left him so empty of life. He finds himself neglecting his own feelings, in favour of making excuses for Bane's unusual behaviour.

Avgust hates how he has already forgiven him.

IV

Knight Out

PASSING THROUGH THE SEA OF people, countless hands pat her back and shoulders, wishing her luck. Eden's heart beats in her ears, not unlike every other night she duels. Despite the secrecy that surrounds these types of gatherings, word always gets out and people from the nearby villages join more often than not. An audience is always welcome, as long as word doesn't reach the wrong ears. There are few rules in these types of fights and the only thing strictly prohibited is murder. That has never been a problem for Eden, she isn't here to maim and harm, nor for the money prize. She enjoys the art of the fight, the rush it gives her, the unpredictability. No duel is ever the same as the one before.

If she could compete in a real tournament, she would, but that's not an option for a woman, let alone the princess.

Eden remembers going to one such event as a child. She

remembers the thrill of seeing the armour-clad men for the first time, the sprint of the horses, the rush of the fight...But there are no lances in this kind of tournament, and the only horses here are the ones tied to the fence waiting for their owners to return. Well, she has to make do with what she can get, even if that means competing under an alias.

A man perched on a hay bale yells in efforts to overpower the noise of the crowd, announcing that the duel is about to begin. Eden waits by the edge of the ring, the gathered audience behind her.

"I've placed a lot of money on you, lad," an old man says to her with a confident smile. She has made quite a name for herself around here, people know and trust that her skill will earn them some money and they don't shy away from betting. Of course, she isn't unbeatable but her past triumphs seem to shape her reputation. Whether it's luck or wishful thinking, the odds often seem to be in her favour. She has developed a taste for confidently being expected to win.

The man atop the hay bale calls for the duellists, before he jumps down and blends in with the crowd.

Eden takes a steadying breath as she reaches the arena—a circle scratched in the dirt with a stick. She drops the long burgundy cloak off her shoulder to reveal what once used to be Avgust's new shiny chainmail, now her scratched up version of it. A child not older than twelve, comes and collects the cloak from the ground, scurrying back to the mass of people lining the ring.

Her opponent tonight is a large man, which doesn't intimidate her—in her experience, bigger men are clumsy and sluggish when it comes to their attacks. When she gives him a more thorough look, she sees his chainmail is worn and torn in multiple places. The difference between their suits of armour is like night and day.

He wears a clearly well-loved set of armour, probably handed down from a relative. The metal rings that hang together are chipped and rusted in spots and the shirt he wears under the chainmail is just plain cotton.

Eden's—well, *August's*—armour is top class and recently made with new metal that appears far sturdier than her opponent's. A sturdy iron chest plate protects her front, a luxury not even most knights have for their armour. She wears thick padded gloves, and high strapped boots. Her undershirt is made of thick leather, which in the warm summer weather is sticky and uncomfortable but does well in protecting her and making her silhouette more square and flat.

While her entire head is hidden under a helmet, only her mouth is uncovered by the metal visor. The man doesn't have a helmet on or even a chain coif, leaving his head of greying hair unprotected. He is either not too bright or thinks too highly of himself, and judging by the look in his dark eyes, it is more likely the latter.

As Eden analyses her opponent, tearing into every possibility of weakness, she finds him doing the same. The man has a complacent smirk on his face, his teeth peeking from within his thick, dark beard. He is underestimating her. Forming opinions off of her visibly smaller build. Eden welcomes it.

They get into starting position. With flail in one hand and longsword in the other, he starts to circle her like a predator.

She mirrors his movement, and they fall into an unfriendly dance. Eden runs at him in an attempt to attack, but he dodges as he leaps to the side. They switch places, continuing to circle each other, taking turns in swinging, neither of them successful in landing a hit.

He lunges the flail forward and its chain wraps around her sword, trying to pluck it out of her hands. For a moment she loses her balance as he yanks her forward. Eden quickly recovers but not for long. Her opponent strikes again, this time with his sword. Still shaken, Eden almost fails to escape his jab.

Leveraging her weight while holding onto the handle of her sword, Eden reaches for the narrow point of her blade with her other hand before delivering a solid kick right to the middle of the man's stomach. He drops the flail and when it hits the ground she sends it further away from his reach with her heavy boot.

The audience cheers loudly, a chant of her name: *Lord of Steel, Lord of Steel, Lord of Steel!*

Eden tries to stay focused, but an all-too-pleased smile rises to her lips under the thick shadow her visor casts.

The point of her sword is at his neck, but he thwacks it away with his own. As he swings it at her, she manages to grasp the blade of his weapon in her free hand. That catches him off guard, leaving a perfect opening. In one swift movement, she jerks his sword back, poking him in the stomach with its handle, then plucks it from his hand before he can even realise. Now with two swords, she cages his throat between the two blades until the man calls for mercy. He should have worn a helmet.

The crowd is silent. The announcer comes to the centre of

the ring, declaring that the duel is over now.

Stepping back, Eden releases her opponent from her clutch. The announcer comes between them, taking one hand from each contestant in his own.

"We have our champion!" He raises her arm up in the air and her chainmail rattles with her victory.

The crowd has never been louder. All the applause and the adoration soaks into her skin and she lets herself bask in it, taking her time.

***

It's not out of the ordinary for Eden to find herself in the local tavern after a duel. It's packed tonight, every table occupied, the air heavy with the leftover heat of the day. She is all too familiar with the wooden interior, the short stools, the creaky kitchen entrance door, the scent of mead and roasted meat that gets overpowered by the smell of sweat and humidity as the night progresses.

Nonsensical chatter goes in and out of her ears. At least it distracts her from her own tedious thoughts. She stays in the tavern, out of courtesy, to give back to the people who have faith in her by sharing her reward in the form of drinks. Her generosity has made her a favourite out of the other contestants that frequent the tournaments, or so they tell her. Eden also stays out of complete reluctance to go back to the castle. She truly cannot stand it there. The stone walls and the seemingly endless corridors nauseate her, but most of all she avoids going back to the meaningless life she despises.

Any attempt from the drunken men around to include her in their conversation is met with indecipherable grunts. They don't seem to notice or care. After a few tries, they usually leave her alone, but she stays prepared for the rare cases in which they don't. Avgust's constant chatter is good for one thing, as she can imitate his voice well enough to deceive the drunks around her. It's a good enough imitation to pass in the already noisy tavern where people are barely able to hear each other, but she knows it wouldn't hold up anywhere else. Drinks keep being ordered for her, which somehow always end up in the bellies of the men around her.

"To our champion!"

Toast after toast is raised in her name, the cups crashing into each other, spilling beer all over the table. "May God give you good health, long life and the strength to defeat many more, Lord of Steel!" She only nods, but the praise pleases her.

There are a lot of rumours surrounding her persona. They judge by her custom-made armour and her luxurious heavy cloak and say she must be a wealthy Lord coming amongst the peasants to fight in secret in seek of thrill. Or that she is a soldier disfigured in battle who is now forever forced to hide his hideous face.

Eden has heard it all. Sometimes she wishes the stories were true, they are far more interesting than the reality she lives in.

"Incredible victory tonight." Marten's scrawny frame crashes into the empty space on the bench next to her. "Your cut." He drops a small bag of coins on the table.

Marten is responsible for the trivial things around the duels that hardly interest Eden. He agitates people to gamble on her, collects her pay and signs her name down for duels. She met him one fateful night after her first successful fight. He sought her out, first to congratulate her, and ended up advertising his services. Eden pretended to need a moment to consider it, so she didn't seem incompetent, but the second she learned of the hassle that comes with the duels, she was already too eager to leave it all to someone else to manage.

Eden lifts the pouch with her fingers, measuring the weight. He always gives her the bigger cut. '*You do most of the work,*' he always says whenever she brings it up, so she stopped trying to argue and instead treats everyone with the money.

"Buy a few more rounds for the table and keep the rest, I'm leaving after I finish my ale." Eden lowers her voice when she speaks, sliding the bag across the table.

"Oh, you are far too generous, Stranger."

Marten never called her a lord, or any of the other ridiculous things the villagers came up with. He is one of the few who don't believe the rumours.

"And you are far too used to handling my money," she says jokingly.

His smile only widens.

"Another round, please!" Marten shouts at one of the passing waiter boys, "Our champion's treat!" he announces and elicits a loud cheer from the table.

The drinks come on a large tray that can barely fit all cups at once. The waiter boy spills a bit of ale as he struggles to hold it up. Cheers and laughter boom around the table as the men around her enjoy their time and free drink.

"Do you even hear yourself?" someone yells from a table

nearby, that can't disrupt the cheerful group around her but it sure catches her notice.

"Demonic creatures are roaming around...I'm telling you!" another man says, almost whispering. Despite its ridiculous nature, that is by far the most intriguing conversation she has heard all night. Her interest is piqued, and her ears home in on whatever else that man is about to say.

"This morning, they found one of them in its lair, stricken it down in its sleep." He lowers his voice even more. "They say its blood was pitch black."

"What did it look like?" the third man at their table asks.

"Just like a woman, only its monstrous teeth gave its satanic nature away..." He takes a sip from his cup, "That and its burning eyes...piercing your soul with their yellow glow."

She scoffs to herself—the ravings of a drunk. It's all nonsense, but at least it provided some form of entertainment. The state of her table's conversation is not much better, only far less fun. It's mostly yelling and drunken singing, and Eden doesn't even see the point of listening.

She is monotonously tracing the ridges of the wooden table with her finger when she feels a wave of anxiety coming over her. There's this uncomfortable feeling of being watched. Eden thinks it's just the tavern packed full of people; some are bound to stare. She even looks about the table but finds everyone engaged in their own talk. It starts to feel like a physical touch on the back of her head the more she concentrates on it but is unable to pinpoint the source. Making subtle movements, her eyes swing from one side of the tavern to the other, until she spots a cloaked figure tucked in the corner of one lone table.

Eden readjusts herself in her seat, self-conscious under the gaze of the stranger.

She brushes it off, deciding it's likely the roaring cheers in her name that are gathering attention. But it doesn't subside. No matter how much time passes, the feeling of eyes on her persists.

It's worry that gets to her first. She fears being discovered above all else. Her anonymous identity in this social circle is precious and best kept secret. Does this person know who she really is? Do they know she doesn't belong here? Eden's eyes bore into the cloaked figure, trying to steal a glance under the hood and dreading the possibility of recognising the face underneath. Their gazes meet for one split second, a dark pair peeking from the shadow of the cloak, just as a hand comes to the side of Eden's face. The man sitting next to her makes an attempt to lift the visor of her helmet. Her quick reflexes snatch the offending wrist, and she grips it in her gloved clutch.

"I strongly advise against that." Her voice comes out raspy and deep, her eyebrows so tightly furrowed she can barely see through the slits in her helm. "If you want to keep that hand." The man swallows. Eden brings a hand up to make sure the visor is secured down. Moving without thinking, she stands from the table. This was too close of a call for her liking.

When she looks back at the shadowed figure, it's gone, no longer in that secluded corner. Eden looks around the tavern frantically, people upon people hunch together in joyous laughter, a rugged barkeep yells to the drunkards at the bar, while a group of young boys count their coins at a table. Miraculously, Eden spots the very edge of a black cloak just as it exits out of the tavern. Her chair scrapes the floor in her hurry to follow them. Clasping her dagger, she weaves her way through the crowd, shoulders and elbows mashing at the people she tries to pass by. It feels like she's crossed all seven seas before she makes it to the door.

The cool night air threads through her chainmail, offering a pleasant change from the stuffy tavern. Out of the corner of her eye, she catches a glimpse of the cloak as it slips around the corner of the tavern. Eden's pace picks up out of desperation to find out who hides under that cloak. When she catches up to the figure, she is quick to snatch an arm, pulling them back and against one of the tavern walls. They stand next to one of the tavern's windows, yellow light casting over them. Eden's dagger digs into the tender muscles of their neck, but the hood remains on their head, mocking her. She finally yanks it down and is met with...a woman? Not a royal guard sent to snoop, or even Avgust as she had briefly hoped it was, but someone she has never met before.

At full height, the woman reaches just past Eden's shoulders, but despite her small stature, there's something threatening in her presence. Intrigued, Eden uses the blade placed under her chin to tilt her face towards the light. The stranger's wide, hooded eyes are framed by pale lashes that match her almost translucent eyebrows. Her long black hair falls like silk over her shoulders, blowing softly in the breeze with an enchanting rhythm. Dark irises shimmer as they latch onto Eden's through the slits of her helmet. There's a certain glint beneath that gaze, under the startled expression, almost like she is studying Eden. Something about her seems out of place. Like she doesn't belong in this run-down tavern. Eden supposes the same can be said about herself.

"Who are you? Who sends you?" Eden demands.

Curious fingers reach up to Eden's helmet. She allows it to happen, fully aware she had almost broken a man's hand over this mere minutes ago and lets out a long breath into the night air as the visor is lifted up. The woman stares, her eyes dance along Eden's face in that same curious way. She isn't sure when it happened, but her knife is no longer threatening to spill the woman's blood, and instead, her hand rests on her collarbone.

"I asked who sends you?"

The woman slightly cocks her head to the side, her gaze now on Eden's lips. She stares insistently, watching as her mouth slacks open in confusion. The woman brings her fingers to Eden's jaw, tilting it towards herself while her eyes continue to stare, unbreaking.

Stumped by the action, Eden doesn't move. She finds herself suddenly nervous, in a way she doesn't think she has ever been made to feel before. There's a sudden twist in her stomach.

"What are you doing?"

The woman watches the words form on Eden's lips, and appears to mouth them herself, repeating.

The sound of something breaking inside the tavern steals Eden's attention with a snap of her head. There's a yell and a holler, and when her eyes return to the woman, she is nowhere to be found. Only the phantom feeling of her touch left to haunt her. It's as if she slipped through her fingers like water. Almost like magic.

V

The Woman in The Lake

THE WARM BREEZE SWISHES THE grass, tickling her skin as she lies down. Eden and Avgust enjoy the pleasant weather in peaceful silence for a while. Her hands aimlessly pluck at the grass beneath her fingers, busying herself.

They find themselves within the inner wall of the castle. The courtyard is empty around this time of day, the kitchens are busy with lunch and all the other workers keep themselves cool within the fortress. The day is calm, but Eden's mind isn't.

"Do you believe in phantoms?" Her words break the silence. It has been bothering her, the mysterious stranger from that night, the way she had vanished into nothing.

"I haven't thought about it to be honest…" Avgust muses, "I suppose I do. Why?"

"I read something." She shakes her head quickly,

swallowing around the lie. Avgust raises himself on his elbow, eyes searching her face in interest. She pretends she doesn't see him.

"Oh, you read something, did you? Liar!" He bumps her shoulder with a playful hand. "Now I must know, tell me!"

Eden lets him hang without an answer for a long moment, thinking about how she should phrase this. Or if she should say it at all. Even if she ends up sounding crazy, it's just Avgust; he cannot judge on that account.

"The other night, at the tavern, I think I..." she begins, humming to herself and decides to start over. "There was this woman—"

"Hold that thought..." Avgust's words trail off as he looks at something in the distance, panic overwhelming his face, "I think I have to go be...elsewhere." He gets up so quickly his feet scrape at the mud beneath the grass, as he speeds towards the castle like there is a pack of wolves coming for him.

"Avgust!" Eden yells after him, but he only quickens his steps.

"We will finish this later!" he shouts, not turning back to look at her.

A shadow raises over her, covering the patch of grass she is sitting on.

"Kaledena." A familiar, stern voice startles her. That name sounds like a screech to her ears.

"Father," Eden greets, blinking up at his large figure. She gathers herself off the ground and scrambles up to her feet. His usual disappointed face stares back, and she isn't even sure what she has done this time.

The Woman in The Lake

The king is a tall, big man. Despite his thick, prominent eyebrows, the frown lines between them are the most defined feature of his face, making him appear permanently angry—and he usually is. She rarely sees him smile. He has always been like this, even when her and Avgust were little, even when their mother was still alive. Always angry and cold.

"Walk with me," he says like it's a mere suggestion and not the demand they both know it is.

They walk and walk and walk in complete silence, until they have nearly made a full circle around the courtyard. Eden knows her father's intentions aren't to enjoy his daughter's company on a beautiful summer day. He has something to say, he wouldn't bother to seek her if he didn't.

"Your brother seems to be acting strangely as of late," he finally states. "Don't you think?"

"I haven't noticed."

"You didn't notice him leaving the second he saw me coming? I believe he has been avoiding me."

Well, that's not in any way a surprise.

"No, he isn't." Eden suddenly regrets not following Avgust away from here. "I can assure you he must not have seen you." It's a lie—a bold, obvious lie. She gulps around the lump in her throat, not quite sure her father believes her.

"I see," he says, nonetheless. She can tell he isn't convinced, but she'd take his pretend calmness over whatever he is really feeling.

"He has been neglectful of his duties. Would you happen to know where he spends his nights?"

Eden freezes.

"No, Father. He hasn't told me."

The king continues silently studying her face, waiting for her to crack and tell on herself. Eden might have done that when she was a child, getting herself and Avgust in trouble with her honesty more times than she can count, but over the years her self-preservation has overpowered her conscience. The stern look in his eyes leaves her feeling like she wants to cry, one thing she hadn't quite outgrown, but she remains calm despite her heart trying to raise up to her throat.

"You look tired, are you not getting enough rest?" the king asks in what could easily be mistaken for fatherly concern.

"Yes, plenty of rest," Eden lies again, "I simply didn't sleep well last night."

"That's concerning. Is there something bothering you?"

"Definitely not," Eden blurts out, and a sudden wave of panic overwhelms her. "Nothing out of the ordinary, Father."

"How are you fairing in your court?"

"Great...Speaking of, I have to go, Nurse Vila must be waiting for me."

She strides past him, bypassing the labyrinth and heading straight back to the castle with a quick stride. Eden doesn't often stumble over her words, but whenever she does, it's usually in the presence of her father.

Eden ends up in front of Bane's door within the minute. His room is tucked into the very end of the servant corridor, and it's nothing grand, but she knows the other knights envy him. Avgust would be here, since the first place their father would look would be his own room. This isn't much of a hiding place, but she supposes it would prolong the king's search by a fraction.

Her fist meets the heavy wood. There's rustling on the other side and hushed, whispered words before the door opens.

"Your Highness?" Bane's brows furrow in confusion.

Eden takes a peek behind him into his room and finds a bed with rumpled sheets, but no Avgust. She almost thinks she might have assumed incorrectly that he would be here, just as he jumps out from behind the door with a sigh of relief.

"Oh, it's just you," he says and goes to sit on the bed where the sheets were already moulded to his sitting form.

Bane steps aside to let her in, and she closes the door behind her. Bane has gone to join Avgust on the bed, their legs tightly pressed against each other. Bane's hand rests on the bed behind Avgust, who leans into the closeness. It's not as subtle as they probably believe it is, which is the issue. She averts her gaze and looks Avgust in the eyes, suddenly serious.

"Father is onto you two."

"What?" Avgust almost jumps up to his feet, but Bane catches his hand and keeps him seated.

"You should be more careful from now on," Eden warns, "No sneaking into Bane's quarters at night."

Avgust blinks a few times, "He sneaks to mine, mostly."

Despite being the one to bring it up, she doesn't appreciate the confirmation of who goes where at night. But now she's not sure how the king has caught onto them in the first place.

"You should be cautious nevertheless," she says, chewing her lip, "Please be safe."

Avgust is left staring at her in shock and disbelief as Bane gives a curt nod. She knows she can at least trust *him* to heed her advice and keep out at night.

It's not unreasonable to believe they can live without each other's intimate company. It seems it is nothing more than a pleasant way they have found to pass the time. If their safety is under threat, she expects them to put a stop to this whole thing without much difficulty. It doesn't serve them well anyway; they end up in a fight half the time. Maybe it would be better to let it all stay in the past for the sake of their friendship.

***

The metal of Eden's armour clanks loudly as she crashes to sit on the hay bale next to Marten. The next match has already begun, and the crowd is enthralled with a new set of loud chants. Under their noise, Eden dares to seek conversation without fearing her voice will give her identity away.

Marten pats her shoulder. "Head up! One loss is nothing on your reputation, Stranger."

"Easy for you to say. You aren't the one disappointing everyone who roots for you."

"No, I'm just the one getting threats for taking their money." Marten leans closer to whisper, "Besides, you were good out there. The other guy was just better."

"You're blind as a bat. Are you sure you even saw the fight?"

"Ha, ha. I see well enough to know you tried your best," he says, "Anyway, let's go cheer you up. The tavern awaits its beloved champion."

"I'm not in any mood for idle mingling. I think I will head home."

Marten's face wears his concern obviously, brown eyes involuntarily squinting trying to read Eden's expression through her helmet. "Is it wise to be left to wallow in your loss?"

"I will be alright."

Marten looks like he wants to protest, but he decides to trust her judgement. Eden's gloved hand lands on his shoulder in a friendly pat, but his slim frame sways under the weight of it. They exchange goodbyes.

And so, she leaves.

The shirt under her chainmail sticks to her skin with sweat. As much as she hates having to return to the castle, she is excited to change into a fresh set of clothes and take a much-needed rest. It's not often that she competes several nights in a row, but she has been feeling far too ill at ease to just sit home and restlessly turn as she attempts to sleep.

Eden had participated in today's tournament and the one from the night before, and she would have gone two nights ago too, had there been one. However, in trying to avoid suspicion, the gatherings don't happen every night. Tonight, just like last night, Eden lost. It wasn't that her opponents were stronger or more capable; in fact, she finds it quite embarrassing that she didn't come out victorious in these particular matches.

Despite what Marten claims, it wasn't that her opponent was better. Eden's mind is elsewhere and has been for the past few days. And nights. And any waking hour. Every thought that isn't spent worrying over Avgust is consumed by the strange woman she had threatened with a knife. The way the woman had vanished wasn't all that had captured her attention, like the strange way she was repeating Eden's words under her breath or studying her face with otherworldly curiosity. She wishes every night that the woman would come back and give Eden some much-needed answers.

Her boots, caked in mud, weigh heavier than usual. Each step feels like a chore as Eden strides through the woods on her way back to the castle. Afraid to have anybody follow her, she takes a bit of an unusual route, straying from the forest path to avoid it being obvious that the castle is her final destination.

Starosel is long behind her now, the yellow lights no longer visible through the trees. Ahead of her is just forest. She knows the castle's outer wall should be in sight in a short while, but it feels like the forest swallows her deeper.

Something in her periphery catches her attention. An unnatural glow comes from between the trees, as if a mirror is placed there, reflecting the light of the moon back at her. Eden feels drawn to it.

Her legs take her closer, until she hears the quiet rumble of the nearby water. The moonlight dances on the surface, glistening, hypnotic. The night casts onto it, a deep blue seeping onto the reflection. Faint fog drizzles over the grass, obscuring the view ever so slightly. There's movement somewhere to the side of the pond. And that's when she sees her: the very same woman from the tavern.

Eden is surprised that she didn't catch her attention right away. The woman looks at peace, away from any people, content with her own company. Eden simply observes.

Long black hair falls to the surface of the pond as the woman bends to cup water in her hands, lathering it onto her pale skin. Her back shifts with the motion of her arms as she submerges her hands in it again. She washes her body with wet hands, sighing deeply, satisfied. Eden leans, trying to sneak a look at her face, but instead stumbles like an idiot.

The woman's eyes snap to her as Eden's muddy boot squeals under her weight. She feels pinned beneath her gaze, but a thrill of excitement runs up her spine. Dark eyes look at her over a slim pale shoulder, as if beckoning her closer. Eden's mouth falls slack, struggling to form a single word.

While her tongue fails her, the woman jumps into the water, submerging herself fully. Her hair floats on the surface until it sinks deeper, and her faint form dissipates entirely. Eden leans over the pond, frantically looking for her outline, but it's like the woman has dissolved. Like the water has reclaimed her.

"Wait!" Eden calls out, but all she is met with is the calm sound of the wind grazing the surface of the water.

VI

Family Ties

MUDDY WATER SPLASHES AS ANOTHER cart drives through a puddle on the road leading towards the village. One pair of eyes watches as it passes by, hidden in the shadow of the trees. Many villagers pass through the road, and she uses the opportunity to study them from where she can't be seen.

Interpreting the vision and the ties it has with her brother has proven to be a challenge. When she dared venture into the village with the intention of finding any trace of him, she was caught snooping in the tavern with a knife to her throat. She has decided on a more distant approach since then.

There's talk in the town of a plague—people dried of life, dropping dead with no previous signs of illness. She knows that to be no ordinary plague. Her brother lurks somewhere near, but she has failed to trace his energy to any one particular place. It's like he's everywhere and nowhere all at once. There are too many signals clashing with his, scattering the signature of his magic that she cannot seem to pinpoint.

Her eyes track the village man with the horse cart as he fades into the distance, hoping to witness one such peculiar "*plague*" death. The man disappears, disappointingly alive, and then everything is still again, leaving only the sounds of the birds singing and the leaves swishing from the wind to keep her company.

"It's you." A voice startles her, making her head snap to the side. Her brows furrow, she thought she was better hidden than she apparently is. It's the woman from the tavern, the one that wears the metal helmet at night, standing right behind her with her arms crossed over her chest. She is now wearing a flowy dress that, despite fitting her perfectly, doesn't quite become her. In contrast, her own dress is just plain and white, stolen off of some villager's clothesline.

She doesn't grace her with a response, hoping the woman is just passing by and will leave. Unfortunately, she speaks again.

"What is your name?"

"Lemana," she finds herself answering.

"Well, Lemana, I'm Eden. I find you in the forest again. You sure seem fond of it."

Lemana doesn't have time for pointless conversations when signs of her brother have been appearing more and more. She moves further into the treeline of the forest, threading deeper in hopes the woman will leave. Instead, she follows.

They walk for a while, as she tries to rid herself of her human shadow. Lemana, having no interest in making conversation, lets them roam aimlessly further into the forest in silence.

"Where are you headed?"

"Anywhere."

"You're threading closer to the castle. I must ask you to keep to your forest and not infringe upon the castle grounds."

Lemana continues walking, her steps heady and determined, despite having no clear direction of where she's going.

"I have no interest in your castle," she says.

The woman replies something Lemana doesn't care to catch, stopping in her tracks. Tiny red drops that have freshly dried on the stones on the forest floor catch her attention. She bends down and takes one stained pebble in her hand, then clutches it. She feels the faintest pull of energy beaming from it. Lemana had only dreamed that she would happen upon such a lead. This woman must have been born under a lucky star. She appears and solves in minutes what Lemana has been trying to solve for days.

"What do you have there?" The woman's voice startles her again.

"A pebble. I collect rocks." The lie slides off her tongue easily.

"Is that what you keep in your bag?"

"Yes. There are plenty of extraordinary stones around this road, that's why I come here." Lemana doesn't even bother to sound sincere as she throws a hand on Eden's shoulder and turns her the opposite way. "You should go look for some, I'm sure you'll find a lot of good ones over there." She points to where they came from, closer to the road. This idle attempt to distract her only earns her a concerned look. The woman doesn't so much as turn to look at where the supposed rocks could be.

Lemana hurries on ahead before the other woman gets the chance to say anything. Following the trail of red drops, she is finally able to put some distance between herself and the woman. It's just a few steps, but that's as far as she seems to let her get away.

With this small sliver of privacy, she hovers her free hand over the pouch that hangs to the side of her body. Lemana closes her eyes shut. Moments later a red liquid springs from the ground, starting where the drops were, forming a thin stream that leads ahead. It disappears deeper into the forest, dodging between trees, twisting like a furious river.

Lemana leaps to follow it.

"Wait!" The woman catches up to her rather quickly.

Lemana wonders if she has seen the trail of blood-red liquid yet.

"There is something that's been bothering me about you," the woman says. "The other night, I saw you jump in a pond, and you never emerged again."

"How are you so sure I didn't come out after you left?"

"I waited for you."

"Not long enough it seems."

"I suppose not." There is a note of doubt in her voice, but Lemana knows she won't bring it up again, regardless of if she actually believes her.

They venture deeper into the woods, following the thin red stream. Lemana doesn't bother worrying if it has caught the attention of the woman or not, far too invested in where it will take her. For a long while, it weaves itself around trees and bushes seemingly with no direction, looping onto itself and in circles. Then, something rustles beside them, hidden behind the row of trees where the stream flows. It sounds like footsteps, careful and slow, light feet stepping onto the forest floor.

Lemana locks eyes with a woodland creature so injured and damaged she feels her tongue tie itself useless. The creature, a wolf, stares back motionless. She can feel the recognition in his single eye, a sorrowful familiarity.

A quiet gasp snaps her out of the moment as she looks to the woman whose already wary expression has hardened, afraid. Lemana doesn't see the need for fear.

"Don't move." She holds out an arm in front of Lemana in a protective manner.

Lemana ignores her and steps closer. Even after everything that transpired between them, despite herself, she still feels that kinship. No amount of hurt that they inflict on each other can erase that bond. Seeing the creature in front of her, in this fragile state makes her mournful.

The wolf is sick. He is dying.

With a gaunt frame barely holding onto its bones, he begins dragging himself to her with incredible difficulty. Her eyes meet his bloodshot, pale-blue one. She feels a need to be near him, almost instinctually. Lemana moves even closer, still holding his gaze.

The wolf growls. He is the first to break away their locked eyes, the muscles in his empty eye socket twitching with the movement. Lemana clutches her pouch to her body, knowing that's where his attention has gone. He has always been smart, he knows what's in there. He probably feels the presence of the eye—after all, it belongs to him.

The wolf lunges for it, fragile body flying across the distance to try and snag it from her, but she can't let him have it. Before she can even grab the pouch tighter, she is already on the ground, tackled with wet grass under her and honey locks above her. She finally makes a connection she should've made a long time ago. Lemana has found the *golden mane* from the vision.

Wide, accusatory eyes look down at her, as if the woman isn't the one who tackled Lemana.

"Why didn't you dodge?" she asks as she rolls off of her, stretching out a hand to help Lemana up.

"He wasn't going to attack me." Lemana accepts the offered help, and clasps their hands, letting herself be pulled to her feet.

She grumbles, dusting her dress off with rigid movements. Lemana turns to where the wolf used to be, the space now empty. The thin red stream she conjured earlier follows the faint tracks he has left behind, into the woods.

"It's a wild creature. How can you be so sure?"

Lemana doesn't answer, a smile threatening to rise to her lips. She scarcely fights it. That was no wild creature. It was her brother.

VII

The Spotted Fawn

THE SUMMER SHOWER THAT THREATENS to become a pouring storm any moment has put a spoke in the wheel of their plans. It is Bane's last day before he is set to go visit the monastery in his hometown. They were supposed to spend it looking for his lost cross pendant, but alas the rain interfered. *'We should wait it out'*, Bane had suggested, sure that it would stop soon. But it has been hours now.

Avgust lies back on Bane's bed. He's being made to listen to Bane read out loud from one of his holy books, the one with the chipping black leather binding. The faint sounds of the rain provide ambiance for it. There is a perfectly good chair prepared for him to sit on, right across from the one Bane is occupying, but tossing around on the sheets seems more appealing. Avgust can't help but hope that maybe later when Bane retires to bed, he'll smell his scent caught in the fabric and think of him.

Boredom finds him easily with nothing to entertain him but the monotonous drawl of Bane's otherwise lovely voice, and Avgust gets to his feet to prance around the room. He toys with a half-finished wooden figurine of an elk left on the nightstand next to the bed but gets tired of it right away. He moves over to the chest that stands at the foot of the bed and studies what's inside. Bane is very pointedly ignoring him, but even through his level reading pace, one can tell with certainty that his attention is still entirely focused on what Avgust is doing.

The chest holds a few folded garments, most of which Avgust is intimately familiar with, but on top of one pile lies a cordate-shaped holy book he instantly recognises. A smile tugs at his lips seeing that Bane did keep it after all. He has never seen him read it.

Avgust closes the chest and takes a couple of paces closer to the chairs, moving to stand beside Bane, who continues reading out loud. Avgust's fingers find Bane's collar easily, tracing featherlight touches over the skin of his neck. It makes him stutter in his reading, but he keeps his attention focused on the Bible in his hands. Thunder rumbles outside. Avgust's hand persists, moving to the small curling strands of hair at the nape of Bane's neck, waiting patiently until his resolve snaps. Hoping for it, welcoming it.

Avgust's fingers trace across Bane's back as he moves to face him. His reading pace grows uneven between sighs that Bane tries to pass off as ones of annoyance. Avgust knows better.

He slides a knee on the chair in between Bane's thighs, yet

he still doesn't react, at least not in the way Avgust wants him to. He cocks his head to level Bane's eye with his and caresses the side of his face gently. Bane shivers under his touch, finally giving into it. The rain outside begins to pour, heavy and spitting.

Avgust isn't one to control his urges usually, but this is a deliberate tease, done precisely to get a reaction. He needs the confirmation that Bane still wants him, that this isn't a flame that has been slowly dying out.

For as long as he lives, Avgust thinks he will desire Bane, and it kills him to think it might not be a returned feeling.

The Bible thuds to the floor when Bane drags Avgust's weight onto his lap, with a hand on his jaw, their lips connecting. Avgust's fingers tug at Bane's dark hair in return, tilting his head back, bringing him even closer. Bane, clearly craving the same, lets his hands find purchase at Avgust's back, pulling him in until their hearts beat next to one another.

Despite his belief and moral values, Bane unravels under Avgust's fingertips easily, like a flower in the sun. It feels like it should be more difficult to make him put aside his virtue, but Avgust rarely needs to try.

It's so raw when they crash into each other, like a confession of its own, whispered through the cloth that separates them. Their bodies move in splitting waves, chasing something that can only ever be satisfactory when they find it in each other. Avgust's flesh burns for the bare touch of hands, but Bane's steady grip on his hips draws his thoughts away from the need for it. Want flows through his very being as they share every sharp breath they tear from each other.

The Spotted Fawn

Bane leans back in the chair and tries to run his hands under Avgust's shirt. His blood freezes over. Letting him proceed holds the terrifying possibility of Bane leaving him again. That's a risk not worth taking. Not when Avgust has him secure in his arms.

Panic-stricken, he finds Bane's hands and brings them to his chest, holding them down where he can see them, putting distance between them in the process. He arches in desperation to make them whole again, but this can only mimic the real thing. The sudden coldness from the now severed touch, two pairs of hands separating them, leaves Avgust feeling as if living meat is being torn out of him. Yet, he will take what he can get. He'd gladly sacrifice closeness if that means having Bane for longer exactly where he is.

Not trying to free his hand from his grip, Bane only seems more eager to press himself into Avgust.

A knock tries to interrupt their rhythm. They both ignore it at first but when it repeats Avgust snaps his head to the door. Bane still desperately clings onto him, not yet realising that there is someone at the door. The next series of knocks brings him back to his senses.

"Yes!"

"I carry a message for His Royal Highness! I was informed that he is here."

"A moment please." Avgust stands up. He takes a second to make himself presentable, smoothing out his hair and attempting to straighten the wrinkles out of his clothes before opening the door.

"A message from Lady Roza." A little girl that he

recognises as Lady Roza's maid hands him a scroll secured with a bow before quickly disappearing down the corridor.

When Avgust turns back, Bane is still where he left him, looking out of breath and dishevelled.

Avgust undoes the bow, and the scroll unravels with a delicate scent filling the air. He starts reading, but not out loud, so Bane can simmer in his curiosity.

"What does it say?" He comes to where Avgust is standing, still catching his breath.

"She will be very *pleased* if I join her in the courtyard as soon as the sky clears," He looks to the window and finds no clouds in the sky. The only indicator of the rain that poured mere moments ago are the drops falling off the tree branches, "Which may as well be now."

"Are you really going to go?"

"Why not?" Avgust shrugs innocently. "I enjoy her company."

Avgust holds his breath in anticipation. The words *"don't go"* seem to be on the tip of Bane's tongue and nothing would make him happier than to hear the plea. Bane's anger is quickly rising, but he has always been able to contain it. Avgust hopes today is the day he might get it to spill out.

"Do you, now?" Bane says under his breath. "What is this smell?"

"Rose." Avgust brings the scroll to his nose and lets Bane sniff it. "The paper must be scented with it." He appreciates the effort Lady Roza is putting into her courting. It's something Avgust would do.

"Isn't that a little bit too on the nose?" Bane is barely

able to stop his eyes from rolling and Avgust doesn't even try holding back the grin that rises to his lips.

"If I didn't know you as well as I do, I might think you are jealous." A hand finds Bane's collar then travels up onto his clean-shaven face. "But you needn't worry, you already keep my heart in your chest." He places a chaste kiss on his lips before he leaves.

Reaching the courtyard of the inner wall, he spots Lady Roza immediately. She is fixing the long sleeves of her dress, fussing over her appearance. Even from a distance, Avgust can tell that she's wearing a beautiful gown. Today she has let her long, dark hair flow down, topped with a beautiful diadem reminiscent of two twisting branches. Rubies glisten, dangling from her ears, matching those embedded into the circlet. Avgust sees the effort she has put in, and loves being the cause.

When she notices him approaching, she immediately stiffens into perfect posture, her hands clasping together in front of her body. Avgust takes them in his, then brings them to his lips to greet her.

"Lady Roza, to what do I owe the pleasure?" His eyes wander up to the tower behind her. She certainly doesn't know that the place she has chosen for their meeting is perfectly visible from a certain chamber. Avgust couldn't be more gleeful about it.

"Good day, Your Highness." The red flush that rises to her face does nothing but stroke his ego, glad to see that his gestures of courtesy can cause such an effect even when not entirely sincere in nature.

"I'm sure you have other important business to attend to,

I don't want to hold too much of your time."

"Oh nonsense, let us take a stroll." He offers his arm for her to lean on as they walk. "It's a beautiful day." He leads the way, heading to the labyrinth positioned not far from where they are in the garden.

To her, his choice to wander about in the labyrinth might seem like one of someone seeking seclusion in the thick green of its walls, but privacy is the last thing that Avgust is looking for. If the place of their initial meeting is visible from Bane's window, the labyrinth is front and centre of his view.

They walk an easy pace, following the path created between the high hedges without much thought. Avgust doesn't try to initiate anything or even start a conversation as they venture deeper and deeper, nearing the centre.

"I was wondering…" she finally musters up the courage to begin, "if you would save me the seat closest to you at your birthday feast and perhaps a dance or two later in the night." She bats her lashes at him.

"Unfortunately, the arrangement of the tables is outside of my control." He hates having to disappoint her so. "But my first dance of the night is all yours."

Avgust watches as the excitement leaves and comes back to her eyes, like waves crashing on the shore. She quickly hides it away, maintaining her pristine and polite demeanour. They continue their stroll. Avgust looks up to the tower again.

***

Avgust stands by the entrance of the castle's chapel, back

pressed against the cool stone wall. It rarely has visitors who aren't Bane or the priest during the day. The only person who might threaten to destroy the solitude of the hallway is the king, who has a private entrance of his own into the chapel directly from his quarters. But Avgust knows his father to be a man of God who doesn't find time for worship.

Bane must be in there. If not, it means that he went to search for his cross alone. After peeking inside the door of the church left ajar, Avgust's guess is proven correct. Bane kneels at the altar, quietly praying.

"You know God welcomes you in, Your Highness." The voice of the priest startles him. Avgust gathers himself quickly.

"I do, I simply wanted to give Ba–uh...Konstantin some quiet," He lifts his head, and nods in greeting. "I'll just wait out here."

Avgust doesn't turn to look, but he hears the doors creak as the priest strides into the chapel. He doesn't feel the need to go inside, because there is no reason for him to be in there. He is not going to say a prayer and he most definitely has nothing to confess. If God really does see everything, He should already know if he has sinned. Avgust doesn't understand why one would tell on themselves if He happens to have missed it.

Avgust also knows how Bane feels about his confessions. It's something private for him. If he were to join, he would spoil that.

It doesn't take much more waiting until Bane makes his way out through the creaky chapel door, greeting Avgust with a look of confusion. He didn't expect to be found here, it seems.

"Wasn't the *tryst* entertaining enough? The lady must have

grown bored of you if you're back already."

The venom in his voice is not as much a surprise as it is a delight.

"Oh, we were both more than entertained!" Avgust exclaims, glad to see that Bane is still affected by it, "But our plans hold priority. Shall we go?"

He doesn't say anything, but Avgust feels the sharpness in his eyes disappear. His cross pendant isn't going to find itself.

The hall echoes with their conversation, as they walk the short distance to the main entrance, exiting out into the inner yard.

"How did you even lose it? You never take it off," Avgust asks.

"The chain broke," he says but doesn't seem entirely certain.

Their destination is somewhere in the forest, and to get there, Bane must lead the way. Avgust doesn't want to bring down the mood by pointing out how highly unlikely it would be to find such a small necklace in the vast forest.

Bane takes them through the thicket, around the same place he had left Avgust a few nights ago. They stride towards the woods, tracing his steps from that night. He looks to be having trouble figuring out where to go, seemingly trying to find his way by trial and error. Avgust wonders if he even knows where they're going. Bane doesn't seem to remember exactly.

"It should be somewhere around here," Bane mutters at one point. Avgust notices that they are now passing by that same strange, angled rock a second time.

Soon they find themselves in a forest cavity. A rotten

puddle, sunken into the grass, makes itself present by its reek. Avgust can smell it all the way from the shade of the trees, hands desperately clutching his nose in a futile attempt to keep the stench away. Flies and maggots squirm all over and a crow enjoys the feast, pecking away at the crawlers.

"What is that? It looks like something died here."

Adam's apple bobbing, Bane swallows thickly, his mouth in a tight line, "Probably an animal…"

"Should we try to bury it, that smell is foul!"

"Let's just leave it alone." Bane stops him from nearing it with a hand to his chest, "We won't be long."

They spend what seems to be eternity searching through every bush, inspecting every undergrowth around every tree, but still, there is no sign of the pendant. Their labour might prove fruitless.

"I don't see it anywhere." Avgust speaks loudly so Bane can hear him from the other side of the glade.

"It has to be here. We have to find it; I can't leave without it."

Avgust has tried his best to forget that Bane is leaving for his hometown tomorrow, but the constant reminders make it hard to ignore.

"I know, I know," Avgust says. He swallows a lump in his throat before asking, "Do you have to go?"

Bane turns to look at him, brows furrowed. The longer the question is met with silence, the more Bane's expression softens. "You know how dearly I miss home. It will be just a short visit, I promise."

It's not meant to hurt, hearing that, but Avgust itches to

remind him that this is his home. Here, where Avgust is. He had always wished that he would be enough to make this place feel like a new home, but he never seems to be.

"Let's keep looking," Avgust prompts, turning away to search a patch of grass nearby.

Avgust doubts that they'll be able to find it, but he cannot share that with Bane. He doesn't want to dishearten him. That cross is the only thing he has left from the home he had even before the monastery. He seems to have worried himself sick over losing it. He has looked ill for the past several days.

Maybe that's why he left him there the other night. He realised it was gone and went to look for it. Avgust wants to laugh at himself for how deluded the excuses he is trying to make for Bane are starting to sound.

He is about to give up and start thinking of a way to tell Bane it's a lost cause, when the sun gleams over something shiny that catches his eye. It's near what he assumes is an animal carcass, almost in the pile itself.

Maybe they've been out here long enough that the sun has moved, exposing the cross's hiding place. Of course it might be something else. God knows what is in that pile.

Upon closer look, gleaming from within the rot lies the cross pendant covered in red chunks.

"Unbelievable..." he says under his breath. Avgust plucks it out with two fingers, and rubs it clean in the rain-wet grass. "Bane!"

"What? Did you find it?" Bane rushes over to steal a look at what Avgust hides in his hands.

"Close your eyes, give me your hand."

The Spotted Fawn

Bane looks at him deadpan but obeys. Just as he is about to place it in his hands, Avgust notices that the chain is unbroken. He doesn't mention it. Instead, he decides to put it around Bane's neck, seeing that it's all intact.

"As good as new." Avgust's fingers linger a bit too long on the chain.

Bane's hands clasp Avgust's over the pendant, holding them against his chest. His dark eyes, wide and shimmering, look into his. Bane captures Avgust's hands and brings them to his lips to kiss them, eyes unbreaking.

"Thank you."

Maybe it's a coincidence that he chose this specific gesture of affection or maybe Bane really did look out his window when Avgust hoped he would. The birds start their song again, almost like a response to Bane's obvious forgiveness over Avgust's gestures towards Lady Roza.

The glade in the forest starts to look more and more familiar now that the pendant has been found. Fully taking in their surroundings, Avgust realises where they are.

"Wait, I think we are nearby..."

"Nearby what?"

"You will see."

He tugs on Bane's hand with a giddy smile, leading them deeper into the forest. They find the tight clearing easily, and draw to a stop before a lake with waters of rich red. It's impossible to tell if the depth causes the colour to be so opaque or if it's just naturally this bloody.

"Do you know the legend of the Lover's Sorrow?"

Bane shakes his head.

"Let me paint you a picture." Avgust gestures wildly with his hands. "Many, many years ago, there was a man and a woman, star-crossed lovers. But just when their love prevailed, the woman got struck by illness. Despite his better judgment, her lover sought out the help of a witch, who promised him that in exchange for his soul, his lover would be healed and never fall ill again. Desperate, he agreed, but it was soon after when he realised that a trick had been played on him. His lover only grew weaker and weaker, steadily fading away right in front of his eyes." Avgust nods to confirm his story, seeing the disbelief taking form on Bane's face. "This exact valley is where he took her corpse to bury. When he placed her body to rest on the ground...she awoke! Rose from the dead! Or that's what he thought, only she wasn't dead at all, she was turned. She had become *undead*—a monster feeding off the blood of the living. A vampire!" Avgust gasps theatrically at his own words.

"In the ecstasy of being reunited with her lover, even beyond death, she held him close in her embrace, but the scent of him unleashed that new monstrous nature of hers. Her teeth grew big, her mouth began to water with the sweet, sweet smell of her lover's blood pumping in his veins. Her teeth sank into his neck, taking and taking until there was no life left in him to take..." He shakes his head pouting his lips. "And then, realising what she had done, she cried. Her tears slowly turned from clear to blood red, filling the entire valley."

Bane looks at him unblinking for a long while before he speaks. "It seems such a waste making you a prince when you would've excelled as the court's jester," he huffs.

"You might be standing in the exact place she was..."

Avgust points with a shaking hand, feigning fear. "It's perfectly normal to be frightened."

"Oh, quit it."

"I'm telling it to you the same way it was told to me," he says keeping his tone as serious as he can, "If you drink from the Lover's Sorrow, her curse will befall you...You will become that same, blood-sucking..." Avgust snaps forward. "Demon!"

Startled, Bane trips backwards, almost landing in the water. He catches himself just in time, taking in a sharp breath.

"What happened to her after?" Bane asks.

"The sun took her; these kinds of monsters fear the light."

"I see..."

There's a rustle of leaves just behind the treeline. Avgust jumps and finds himself clutching at Bane's arm, drawing himself closer.

"Did you hear something?"

Suddenly, the forest is still again as if nothing had ever moved in the first place. Another sound comes now, closer, like footsteps crushing the grass beneath. Out comes a wolf, large and menacing, but raw-boned. Avgust yelps in surprise, before feeling Bane stiffen in his hold as he pushes Avgust behind himself.

It bares its enormous, yellow canine teeth as it snarls at them. One glowing eye glares while the other empty eye socket leaks tear-like, murky liquid. The gaping hole brings a nauseating feeling to Avgust's stomach. The eye isn't the only thing it is missing—its guts hang out of its exposed ribs, trailing half a step after the creature as it makes its way to corner its prey. It's a miracle that the thing is still breathing. Avgust can't be sure if that's even a living being at all. If hell demons exist, this might be one.

Avgust locks eyes with the creature. Its pale-blue eye stares back at him with an intention that he can't quite understand. Yet he feels it in his entire body, as if he is being examined. From head to toe, from outside in, from his mind to his soul. The target is laid on him. Bane is of no interest to this being, Avgust alone is its prey. He is paralysed but it's not from fear, the wolf's gaze has him pinned in place, unable to break out of its hold.

Forced to stay under its watchful eye, the nausea returns. He doesn't know what's more unsettling, the empty socket oozing pinkish gunk or the foreign feeling demanding him to stare back at the wolf.

Just like it had appeared, the wolf disappears back into the deep, dense forest, leaving no visual trace behind, like it was never there.

But it has clawed its way into Avgust's mind.

VIII

Rupture

INK MEETS PAPER, CURVING WITH the shape of a letter at the tip of his quill. Avgust sits at the desk in Sofron's study, tasked with writing out yet another horribly boring document. His pretty handwriting put him in this unfortunate situation of having to write pages upon pages of logs and records. The chore falls on him because the paper is precious, and they don't trust just anyone with the private royal documents.

Avgust has considered ruining a page on purpose, just so they would never ask him again, but he fears his father's wrath too much. He cannot deny it, his letters are even and legible; however, there are a thousand other things he would rather be doing. Granted, there isn't anyone to do them with now that Bane is away, but Avgust is sure he could stand his own company for a while if he must.

Sofron sits on a comfortable chair behind him, shuffling something in his hand and looking out into the distance. Avgust has known him all his life and hasn't noticed any changes in his appearance at all. His thin hair was always this exact shade of grey, and the same streaks of white remain unchanged in his brows and beard, neither thickened nor spread. He was always a little bit hunched over, but despite it he didn't appear short.

His old age has rendered his eyes useless, yet he could immediately tell when Avgust stops writing or if he had translated more ink to the page than he's supposed to. It's like the old man could make these assumptions by smell alone, and he was somehow always right. It freaked Avgust out a little.

"It needs to be done today," he reminds him every so often, without even turning to look at him, at which Avgust only rolls his eyes and silently continues to work. He must admit this isn't the worst thing he could be doing; he finds peace in the art of writing.

"Easy!"

Avgust hears yells and a horse neighing out in the distance. Instinctively, his head turns to the window to investigate what's happening outside.

Two men—guards—are circling a horse outside trying to calm it down. The beast continues to neigh, distressed, going up and down on his back legs and stomping at the men trying to tame it. It has a saddle on its back and luggage on its sides, yet there is no rider to attend to it. When the men do succeed in taking hold of the reins and manage to restrain it in its disrupted state, Avgust has the chance to look at it more carefully. The slight difference in the dark colour of its body compared to the legs, the well-kept mane and tail. He knows this horse—it's Bane's.

"You've ruined it!" Sofron says, snapping Avgust out his spiral of thoughts.

"What?" He looks away from the window to find his inkwell splashed all over the paper. "Oh, I didn't mean to."

"...Wasting good paper like it's nothing," Sofron murmurs under his breath.

"It wasn't on purpose!" Avgust tries to vouch for himself, but the old man won't have it.

"Start again, daylight is running out." It's not even noon yet, but Avgust sees no use in arguing.

His attempts to talk Sofron into letting him go for a bit are unsuccessful. *'My wrist feels stiff'*, he claims, but the old man is determined that it should be done now and won't have it any other way.

It itches away at him. He needs to know what happened, but Sofron has him starting the page anew. Avgust's leg bounces as he writes, and as much as he tries to pay attention to the words, his mind wanders.

Avgust can't even rush it because he knows if he doesn't do it properly, Sofron would have no issue making him start *again*. He wouldn't hear the end of it if he ruins any more paper.

The task takes him longer than usual to finish one single page, let alone the two dozen he has been ordered to write. But after what felt like forever, Avgust places the last page on top of the pile with the rest of them.

"I'm done." He stands up abruptly, and before Sofron can even check if he's telling the truth, Avgust is out of the door.

Hurried steps take him to the floor below and he opts for the east-wing hallway to shorten the distance to the stables. The guards are probably long gone from the scene, so his best bet is to go ask around the grooms. He is so very close to the exit when his stepmother spots him from across the corridor.

"Avgust, dear, where are you headed in such a rush?" Her kind hazel eyes look at him with worry. Maybe the anxious impatience shows on his face. "Aren't you meant to be transcribing with Sofron? Your father was adamant about you enhancing your penmanship. You know he sees it as a rather disciplinary task."

"I have finished for the day." Avgust holds off the urge to bounce on the spot with urgency.

"Already?" she exclaims, blinking owlishly. Her rich brown hair is tucked under a beautiful glistening net, which Avgust would find himself jealous of if he had the time.

"Yes, Your Majesty, the task was very enriching and I'm grateful to have the opportunity to learn from Sofron." He is left surprised by how sincere it came out of his mouth. "Will you excuse me?"

The queen's eyes trail after him as he bows and turns his back to her, continuing on his way down the hallway. Avgust waits to turn a corner before his steps pick up in speed, rushing to the horse pens. It doesn't take him long with this pace, but it's not like he hasn't missed the commotion already anyway. The hurried speed is more for his increasing need to know.

When he gets there, Avgust is reminded why he doesn't like going to the stables. The strong smell of animals tickles his nose and burns in the back of his throat with the threat to choke him. He shakes away the slight nausea and enters with determination despite it.

The only person there is a stable boy, probably at least half Avgust's age. He is sorting wheat straw and animal feed with a pitchfork too big for his size.

"Your Highness, are you planning to travel out?" he says as soon as he sees Avgust walk towards the stable, with a courteous little bow. "Should I prepare your horse?"

"No, no, that won't be necessary."

Avgust looks around, Bane's horse stares at him from the first pen like it recognises him.

"May I help you with something else then?" Noticing Avgust's hesitant stance, the boy tilts his head in question.

"I saw from my window that there was a situation with one of the horses," Avgust says, feigning nonchalance as he worries his lip between his teeth. "My curiosity got the better of me, so I decided to come check if everything was resolved."

"They found the horse roaming around the outer wall. It got home by itself." The little boy leans on his pitchfork. "Very capable creatures, horses."

"And it's Konstantin's horse, correct?" Avgust asks in a rush.

The boy nods.

"Is he somewhere around?"

"I can't be sure. I might have seen him, but I can't recall when it was," the boy says with a hum. "Was it a few days back... or maybe today? I can't be sure."

"Would this help you recall?" Avgust holds out a gold coin in front of his face. He always carries a few around with him;

one can never know when they might prove useful. The boy's eyes light up. He quickly grabs it and puts it away in his pocket.

"I haven't seen him here. If he is back, I couldn't know," he says, looking worriedly at the horse in the first pen. "But if he was, don't think he would leave his horse outside like that."

"No, he wouldn't," Avgust says under his breath. "You haven't heard anything else then?"

"I hear a lot of things, I don't know if any of them would be of your interest, Your Highness."

Avgust takes out another coin to untie the boy's tongue. He takes it with a wide grin, showing his missing front tooth.

"A villager came by the gates. I saw him while I was picking apples for the horses. He seemed to be in great distress. I don't know why, but a few guards have gone somewhere with him. It looked urgent."

"When was that?"

"A little after the horse was brought in."

"I see," Avgust says. "Thank you, boy."

"You're welcome, Your Highness. I'm always happy to share what I know."

Happy to receive some coin for it, more like, but Avgust isn't one to judge.

Avgust leaves the stables, mulling over what that distressed man from the village would need guards for. The news has stuck a lump in his throat that he can't seem to swallow away.

When he arrives back at the courtyard, he witnesses three bodies being dragged in. All three are clad in chainmail—knights. Avgust's heart drops to his stomach.

Before he can think, his feet are taking him running across

the yard, trying to see whom it is they're carrying. He crashes into a guard that tries to keep him away. A small, shocked crowd of maids and servants has gathered around the three dead men.

"Your Highness," the guards carrying the bodies greet him solemnly.

"Who?" Avgust feels a sting pricking behind his eyes, as his vision begins to blur with unshed tears.

"Mihai, Stefan and Christian of the King's Knights, Your Highness," one guard states as they pass by him. "Villagers passing found them near the forest path."

His lungs punch out his next breath with relief. Three men are dead and all Avgust can feel is thankful it's not Bane.

He doesn't know what to think now. But there's hope in not knowing.

IX

Reticence

AS EDEN LETS HERSELF IN, the wooden door groans. The kitchens are mostly empty at this time of day, too early to begin preparing lunch. She's avoiding the possibility of running into her father, and also avoiding Nurse Vila, who must be looking for her. Avgust might be as bored as Eden, she might go look for him. There are hushed voices coming from deeper in the room. Eden stops in her tracks, sliding behind the wall that hides the servant's staircase from the rest of the kitchen.

"He is marked–marked I tell you!" A woman, short and stocky with an apron tied around her waist, gestures wildly to her own eye. "Marked by the devil himself." She huffs, shaking her head. "There was always something wrong with that boy."

"Yes, yes ever since he was a child. The incident with that little bird was telling enough. Truly evil, butchering a creature so beautiful." The other woman, younger yet still Eden's senior by at least a decade, gives a grunt of displeasure.

They're talking about Avgust. Eden remembers that incident, and how could she not, to this day people won't let him forget it. They couldn't have been older than nine years old, their mother was still alive. The two of them had been fighting over something so stupid, she can't even recall now. Avgust had shouted and Eden had jumped to bite and scratch him until they were both blue and crying. She remembers telling him she hated him. Avgust was red in the face, tiny eyebrows scrunched together as he stormed off by himself into the woods. When Eden finally calmed down and told her mother where Avgust had gone, it was already nightfall. They found him with a dead swallow at his feet, blood covering his tiny hands and cheeks from where he tried to wipe his tears.

No one believed him.

They thought he had attempted to tear it apart with his teeth. Even if it hadn't been for the countless times Avgust had tried to defend himself, crying and trying to explain what happened, Eden still wouldn't believe he had done it.

'I was trying to help,' he would say, in between chokes and sobs. The memory alone breaks Eden's heart. They claimed he had done it in rage, but she knows it not to be true. It makes guilt swoop to her gut—if only she hadn't fought with him or purposefully said things to hurt him, he might not have run away.

They separated them after that, at their mother's insistence. Put Eden in a different room with the argument that they were too old to share a room now, but they all knew what the real reason was.

Avgust never received an apology for the way he was treated by his own mother while she was still alive, and he never will since she is no longer among the living. Instead, he is doomed to carry the weight of what was done forever. No apology can save him from the stained opinion of the servants.

Her hand grips the corner of the wall that she's using as a steady tool to eavesdrop, and that makes her realise she hasn't been listening almost at all, lost in thought. Her ears home in on the hushed words again, catching the middle of a sentence.

"...died in their sleep, all of them."

The other woman gasps quietly at her words.

"I won't be surprised if *he* has something to do with it." She looks around, making Eden instinctively retreat further behind the wall, before she leans in to whisper, "You didn't hear it from me, but the prince...he is not one with God."

"A heretic?" Her voice raises ever so slightly with shock.

"Shh, shh, keep your voice down."

"And that boy, the one always following him around like a dog, to *'preach to him.'*" She shakes her head disapprovingly. "A charlatan! No real servant of God should be a knight. Makes me think they went through all that effort to bring him to the castle for nothing."

"And here we were, hoping he might be able to remedy the prince of his vices, while all that was done was find the pot to his kettle."

"Hello." Eden confidently strides into the room, plucking an apple out of a large bowl that was probably going to end up at the stables later.

"Princess." The two women blink owlishly at her, wiping sweaty palms on their aprons.

"Oh, don't let me interrupt your chat, it seems very important." She tries to keep her calm demeanour, but inadvertently, she snaps, "Do you think this is the proper manner in which you should speak of your future king?"

"It's just the town's gossip," the younger woman tries to defend, gulping nervously. "We don't actually believe any of it."

"Town gossip has no place inside the castle walls," Eden says, her back already turned to the women.

There are a few mumbled apologies behind her as the door leading from the servants' quarters to the inner-wall yard creaks as it shuts.

She hates having to play the high and mighty princess, hates people cowering at her feet, but sometimes she is glad she has that power. Avgust is not only her brother *and* the crown prince, but he is also Eden's favourite person. No one else understands her like he does, even her most queer of quirks. The least she could do for him is tell off a few servants to defend his honour.

The way to her room is uneventful, fortunately. No one tries to speak to her or bother her. She hasn't seen Avgust all day, but he will eventually turn up, he always does. Today, of course, is no exception, as he is already in her room when she arrives.

"Don't you have a room of your own?" Eden strides into her chambers, shedding off the thick upper layer of her dress that suffocates her in the warm weather. Avgust gives her a quick look before looking away again. He had dragged himself a chair to sit next to the window.

"Bane should've been back already," he states, lip quivering just slightly, eyes almost empty. Not a trace of her brother's usual wits. "His horse came back without him the other day, did you hear? All his luggage on it too."

"Maybe—" Eden tries to calm him, but he interrupts.

"How is he to come back without a horse? Did he even reach the monastery at all?"

"He is very capable, he…" Eden doesn't have the heart to dismiss his worries, this isn't one of his usual self-inflicted overthinkings. Avgust is right to worry. But if Bane doesn't show up soon, he will worry himself sick. She doesn't even want to entertain the possibility of him not coming back at all.

"Father won't let me go look for him, nor send a search party or even word to the monastery. He said I *'worry over nothing.'*"

Eden is unable to find the right words, afraid she will see tears well up in his eyes soon enough. So, she just moves closer to stand beside him by the window, a hand on his shoulder. Avgust turns and clings to her. She lets him, wrapping her arms around his back in return. As she rests her chin on top of his head, he clutches even tighter to her dress, like she would disappear too if he didn't hold her down in place. A sob tries to choke out of him, but he doesn't let it out.

"He will be back." She pets his head. "It will be alright."

Eden can't know if that is true, she can only hope it is.

✳✳✳

Reticence

The battle turns out how you would suspect, the bigger guy won. Eden isn't participating today, instead watching from the side of the ring. Her armour is at home where it belongs, save for her helmet, and she's only draped in her heavy burgundy cloak. It hides her form well, but she didn't dare show up without the leather under-armour that flattens her.

Marten stands next to her, counting the coins in a small pouch that had just been handed to him by a member of the audience. The bets for upcoming battles were always heftier when Eden had skipped the previous few.

"I think you should drop out of the next match, Stranger," Marten says, voice tight. The coins continue to jingle as he returns them to the pouch one by one.

"What?"

"I have a bad feeling. Some men were in the village yesterday asking strange questions."

Eden's heart drops to her gut.

"What questions?"

"About a noble man with blond hair and green eyes." Marten watches her carefully as it all settles in.

Eden swallows thickly. "That could be anyone."

Marten shouldn't know what she looks like.

"Of course. But it's better to be safe than sorry."

There's a long silence, filled with the clink of metal and the coins in the pouch.

"You know I can't drop out. You've already started collecting the bets," she speaks again.

"I'll manage." His tone comes off as casual, but the worry is there.

"No. That's your livelihood; I can't do that to you," Eden says firmly, "I'm fighting."

X

Repellent

THE CRIMSON LAKE—OR THE LOVER'S Sorrow as the locals have named it—makes itself present at the end of the blood trail Lemana followed the other day. It looks as if it was taken straight out of the vision she had. The water is still, with not a single ripple. It is certainly missing a spitting vortex, but it has to be the same one.

It seems to be the source of the energy Lemana has been feeling, an energy not too foreign, repelling her. The first step to understanding why she feels it was discovering its source, but now a new problem has arisen. She can't go near it, let alone in it.

An invisible force field is pushing her back, like a physical shield over the water. Something is hidden in there, right at the heart of the lake. Lemana can sense it. She knows it has something to do with her brother; it has his signature all over it. His familiar sapping energy oozes from the centre of the lake, untouched. Who knows how long it has spent in there, waiting to be reclaimed—whatever it is. Ursedius's signature has changed with the decades, and his core that used to call to hers now repels her.

In her search for him, Lemana couldn't follow the traces of his magic. Creatures loom and lurk nearby, muddling his pull with their own energy. This, however, lying at the bottom of the red lake, emits that old, pure pull she recognises as her brother's, from all those centuries ago.

Ursedius always had an affinity for transactional spells, and his favourite currency always stayed the same—sacrifice. Although it may vary in its severity, in its core it is the same every time: eye for an eye.

A barrier like this one, with such strong protection around it, would likely require an offering to be opened. But how is she to make an offering if she can barely step near the lake?

Lemana looks around for something to use, a puddle or a pool of water anywhere on the forest floor, but the blazing rays of the summer sun have dried them all since the heavy rain.

Then, she notices that there is morning dew still clinging to the blades of the grass around her. She swings her hand gently over the ground, collecting each and every drop on her skin. The eye in her bag rests under her palm, familiar and calming, as she clenches her fingers together letting the dew drip.

With every drop, the liquid runs thicker and thicker until it starts solidifying into a sharp, glass-like blade.

Despite being capable of doing magic on her own, she had only practised it with her brother. Lemana is so used to his presence that she almost feels unable to do it without him.

Ursedius's case is different. Unlike her, he can't do any magic on his own. She acted as a catalyst for him, letting him channel his power through her. Their strongest spells were always the ones they did together. Until something changed.

To this day, she doesn't know how he found a way to do magic by himself, all she knows is that one day he was suddenly stronger than her. But it didn't last long, the last time she saw him she could barely feel him.

The shield is so strong, Lemana is barely able to stand over the lake. Resisting against the force, she manages to hover her hand over the water and with effort takes the icy blade and cuts her palm open. She squeezes her hand into a fist. Nails pressing into the wound so it won't close right away. Blood starts pouring down in a trickle, but just before it's about to drop into the waters, it bounces back, pooling right above it. Levitating. The lake won't accept it, and the blood is left floating in the air near its surface.

"Curious…" Lemana says under her breath.

Despite hoping that might work, she isn't really surprised it hadn't. This isn't one of the childish tricks they used to do as kids—she can't cheat her way in. It is calling for a real sacrifice, and so she'll give it one.

***

Lemana spent the next hour hunting. Now, she has both her test subjects lined up, silent and pliant, laid out on the grass by the shore of the Lover's Sorrow. Unfortunates she lured off the road that passes through the woods. Shepherds, judging by the strong smell of cattle clinging to their clothes.

The lake has named a price greater than she is prepared to take from herself.

She calls one of them to her. He follows obediently and they stand at the edge of the lake where she pulls her blade and slits his throat. His body drops in the water, bubbles rising to the surface as he sinks further and further into the red abyss.

A few moments pass with no indication that this offer has been accepted by the lake. The body has long disappeared into the depths when she tries to enter the bloody water, only to be sent back by the repellent magic. The shield remains undamaged. Lemana falls to the ground defeated, her efforts proven in vain. A small growl of frustration bubbles out of her as she grabs a stone off the ground and hurls it towards the lake. She grunts, running a hand over her face before she notices the rock hovering over the water, its surface unbroken once again. She rises to her feet to look at it as it floats over the lake. Blood colours the stone crimson. She looks down, the pebbles at her feet are also patterned with her blood splattered all over them. *Of course.*

"Come to me." Lemana turns to the other subject, now armed with a new theory. When he reaches her, she hands him the blade. "Cut your hand and let it spill into the water."

The man does as he is told, eyes glazed over yet still full of fear as his mind bends to her will. His blood flows, dropping directly into the lake with no resistance.

Her brother seems to have designed this spell so she, specifically, is unable to claim the prize that the lake keeps safe...

"Go in there and bring me whatever lies at the bottom of it."

The man steps in, navigating his way into the water with no issue, passing through the invisible shield effortlessly. When he reaches the centre, he dives in and descends deeper until Lemana loses sight of him. Soon the water is still again. She is left to wait.

Minutes pass that turn to hours, yet the water's still surface remains undisturbed. He doesn't seem to be coming out of the lake any time soon. As the sun starts to go down, Lemana knows that he won't come out at all.

Two sacrifices made and yet nothing has been received in return. Maybe this was never a transactional spell, but to ward off what is hidden at the bottom so impenetrably is unlike her brother. There has to be a way she can get to whatever it is he is trying to protect.

Lemana will get to the bottom of the lake even if it's the last thing she does.

XI

Resurrection

BANE'S EYES FLUTTER, UNABLE TO open with a foreign weight keeping them shut. His lungs burn and he realises he can't breathe. The desperate gasps for air leave him with a mouthful of something grainy and foul, flaring up into a cough instead.

Soil. It's soil he tastes. It's soil filling his lungs. It's soil all around him.

He is buried underground.

Panic pangs in his chest. No matter how much he runs out of breath and how little air is left in his lungs, nothing happens. Bane remains alive. He tries to move his body, but its weak state doesn't do much against the heavy pressure he feels covering his entirety, confining him to one position—lying still, arms pressed against the sides of his body.

He can't know if it's the lack of oxygen or fatigue that

leads him to fade out of consciousness. It doesn't matter. When he wakes up again, it's much the same. Still dark. Limbs still compressed to his sides. Air still failing to reach his lungs. The only difference is that now there's a sound coming from somewhere above him. Muted, like it's behind several walls, but it feels like a deep rumbling, and he swears he can hear water splashing. It tells him nothing about his surroundings overground, nothing useful at least.

Bane wakes up again, not sure when he had passed out, not really having a way to measure time in his early grave. His fingers twitch and he realises he can move with a newfound vigour, yet still it feels like he's moving through thick butter. His hands tunnel through above his face and he starts clawing at the ceiling of his confinement...only to have it crumble more and more with each dig. His nails are raw. It feels like he has been doing this for ages when light finally begins to poke through.

Digging his way to the surface, he comes out above ground to a familiar forest. He takes a large gulp of air. Immediately, he starts coughing up the dirt he had inhaled. A cloud of dust spills from his mouth as he chokes it out, clutching at his chest in a futile attempt to ease the burning pain. He still finds it difficult to keep his eyes fully open, all the dirt that had gone into them and the sudden glaring light irritates them greatly.

Bane crawls to what he thinks is a body of water nearby, dragging himself limply and with great effort. The water feels nice in the palms of his hands; he brings it shakily to his lips, gulping handful after handful. He pays no attention to the peculiar taste of it, he could be drinking from a swamp for all he cares. Still with cupped hands, he washes his head and face of the dirt until he feels cleaner. A deep breath of relief lets itself out of his lips, as he tips his head back in content. He licks his still dry lips. Only then does he recognise the iron taste of the water. Only then does he realise he had been buried by the shore of the Lover's Sorrow.

The rich red colour of the water he drank stains his face, hands and clothes. He backs away. Having gotten rid of the pain in his chest, he is hit by a sharp ache in his head to replace it. It might be due to the time spent underground, but the sun feels like a knife stabbing his eyeballs, and a thousand needles piercing his skin. He tries to blink it away, covering his head with his hands. It doesn't do much against its strong rays. Bane pulls himself on hands and knees to the thick shadow of an old oak.

His hand reaches for the chain around his neck, the metal cold under his touch. It's there.

Despite his lapses in memory, Bane knows he never made it to Kosti. Another testament of that is the fact that he is a walking distance away from the castle. His horse is nowhere to be found, and he can only hope the creature has found its way back to safety.

Wracking his brain for the memory of what exactly happened, he comes up short. Confusion and agony swirl in him as he brings himself up to his feet. They feel unused and weak, which leaves him wondering how long he has been buried for. He touches his face, no stubble had grown, maybe it hasn't been that long, but still he hadn't shaved a couple of days prior to leaving and his face remained with only a shadow of a beard.

Resurrection

His body tells him nothing either, he feels no hunger, all he feels is a thirst that he knows he can't quench. He doesn't dare go near the water, afraid he might be tempted to drink again. Avgust's tale really got into his head. He has a way of speaking with such confidence that makes everything he says feel true.

Bane begins to stride in the direction of where he hopes the castle is, but the sun proves to be a bigger obstacle than he anticipated. It feels like it's melting the meat off his bones. He cannot bear it for long without hiding in the shadow, so he ends up under another large tree. He decides it's smarter to wait out the day and begin moving again at night.

Exhaustion pulls at his limbs as he sits down against the trunk and rests for a while. His eyes close, heavy with sleep.

When Bane wakes up, he is underground again. A neatly compacted dense layer of earth on top of him, weighing on him, suffocating him. It's all black, his eyes shut tightly, but not by his own will. The struggle to release himself is fruitless. He keeps digging and digging, each attempt more desperate than the last. Soon he realises he is digging himself further down.

Bane gasps, his eyes opening abruptly. He is relieved to find himself under the shadow of the tree, above ground. It was just a nightmare, but the burning in his chest is real.

The sun has fully set, but there is still light lingering in the sky. It's time to go, yet Bane doesn't move, staring up at the darkening sky blankly.

After a few more moments he brings himself up on his feet, hands aiding him on his sore knees. He takes off and the time spent between the rustling trees flies by faster when he stops counting each step he takes closer to home.

The lapses in memory gape like holes in his mind. He feels them itching on the tip of his tongue, so close to the surface of his conscience. He remembers a face...several faces. He thinks they hauled him together—pretty sure he recalls being dragged with great struggle. Somehow the vague outlines of the faces feel familiar. People he knows.

Then it clicks. His memories rush back all at once and slot into place in the missing spots in his mind.

The hooves of his horse thumped against the ground, suddenly joined by the sound of feet. Bane turned around to see three figures catching up with him in the distance. Their speed should not have been possible, especially not dressed in heavy armour sets. He clutched the reins tighter and whipped them once to set the horse running faster. The distance was not able to prevent the attack.

They reached him faster than he could escape, dragging him off the horse violently. He thrashed and fought but three bodies against one was unfair to begin with, and Bane had never felt as tired as he had in the past days.

Still, he was far from pliant, refusing to let them carry him away. But they had come prepared. A knife rammed into his stomach, the wet sound of skin being pierced loud in his ears.

The horse ran and Bane wished he could have followed.

Bane's teeth clenched in agony, but he didn't stop trying to fight off his attackers. When the second stab came, he finally took a look at their faces. Christian and Stefan restrained him; Mihai held the knife.

Bane's hand was weak as he tried to grab Mihai's wrist and pull out the knife. As he bled, he felt himself grow tired. His eyes were heavy, and he fought against the need to close them, but he wasn't strong enough.

It was Aleksander's lackeys that buried him alive. Only,

Resurrection

Aleksander wasn't there, leading them like usual, instead the other three seemed to have unanimously decided to act together, like a hive mind. Which wasn't unusual, but their lack of leader definitely was.

He can still feel the blade of the knife in his gut, like a memory, but he feels no pain. His hands come up to clutch at his middle where he should have been bleeding still, only to find no wound at all. Did he imagine it? Could he trust his faulty memory?

There are holes in his shirt, torn in straight lines from the tip of a knife, stained a rusted red around the cuts. But the skin under remains intact, although paler than it should be.

Bane tries to shake the dread he feels, knowing people want him dead, and decides to ignore the fact that he will have to face them tomorrow. If he makes it back, that is.

✳✳✳

At the sight of the castle in the near distance, Bane's legs buckle with relief. He feels the sore exhaustion settle into his bones. The imposing towers on the two sides of the outer gate make it into view first, followed by the tall walls of the keep. Strangely, the cold, grey stone of the fortress makes him feel at home. The castle itself is cast in the darkness of night, but there are a few windows still glowing despite the late hour. He finds himself looking for Avgust's window, and his eyes pick it out almost instantly. Not only is the light on, Avgust is resting on the sill, chin in his hand, looking out into the night sky. He looks so beautiful.

Avgust's head turns in Bane's direction, as if he knew he was there, as if Bane had called to him. Bane lifts a hand to greet him with a small wave, which Avgust doesn't have time to return because he jumps to his feet and rushes away from the window. He misses the sight of him as soon as he's gone.

The main halls are dark, the castle asleep.

Bane hears him before he sees him running down the hallway, before he even turns the corner. Avgust is all wild curls and wide smiles, rushing towards him dressed only in his smallclothes as if plucked right out of bed. His thin linen shirt exposes the bare skin underneath. Bane gulps, drinking in the sight.

Avgust crashes into him with unbridled urgency. He doesn't even let Bane get a word out before his lips meet his, messy and fast. Avgust is the first to break away.

"Oh, to hold you in my arms after all these days!" Avgust draws him in a quick embrace again before cupping Bane's face with his hands. "When they brought in the bodies, I thought the worst had happened..." Tears start forming in his eyes, but he blinks them away quickly. "But you're here. You're alive."

"What bodies?" Bane asks.

"Men from your troop."

He doesn't need to hear more, he knows who it is. A feeling of ease fills him, knowing that God's punishment has found them. But another feeling overpowers it, a guilty satisfaction over the fact that he is not the only one to suffer. It's a bitter feeling of cruel relief to know they got what's coming for them after what they did to him.

Avgust gently caresses his face, "I should never let you

leave my sight again."

His hands dance across Bane's jaw. Under his touch Bane always crumbles. Avgust being so glad to see him undoes a tight knot in his chest. He almost doesn't believe him capable of such worry—always so above it all, so in control of everything. But seeing him like this, eyes concerned and cheeks flushed, makes it feel real. Maybe Bane does matter to his prince.

But what if Avgust sees the blood on his shirt, the knife holes torn in the fabric? It's dark, but Bane still worries it will ruin this fragile moment.

He lets his fingers curl into Avgust's hair, brushing it off one shoulder. The dim corridor hides them well, but Bane feels an exposed sense of vulnerability.

"You are the only one there is for me. How could I live without you?" Avgust doesn't look like he meant to say it at all. Bane wants to believe him.

They are standing so close, Avgust's scent fills his lungs, mixed with something else, something more alluring yet Bane doesn't care for it. He grabs at Avgust's clothes and drags him in closer, locking their lips again, deeper than before. Avgust's back hits the wall, and he lets out a small pant. It feels like so long since he's had him like this.

Their mouths swap the iron taste of the red water dried on Bane's lips, somehow making its flavour sweeter when it drips from Avgust's mouth into his. Hunger finally finds him, but it's one that can't be nourished by food. He craves something entirely different.

Between deep breaths and desperate touches, Bane's ears pick up a low throbbing, hammering steadily in his skull.

The sound only gets louder as he breathes in a rich smell that lingers on his tongue, leaving him desperately trying to inhale it deeper.

Bane follows the scent over Avgust's skin, along his jaw, in the crook of his neck where it's most potent. He noses along the skin, listening to the liquid flow just below the surface of the flesh. His mouth waters, and he gulps down the saliva with difficulty, his tongue searching for a different taste. Avgust finds his lips again with an urgency that can only be matched by Bane's own hunger.

Their shared embraces grow more violent. Each pressing of lips dire. Every touch burning. Avgust reaches to untie his own shirt open, exposing hot flesh only for Bane's eager eyes. Bane draws himself back abruptly, the scent in his nose strong and dizzying. But before he can calm his craving, Avgust kisses him again. The taste of him is so sweet it maddens him, soft lips fitting into his like a perfect pair. Bane bites Avgust's tongue in his rush to kiss, to taste, to have. Blood spills between their two mouths and shakes him to his senses. He pushes himself off as a primal want to sink his teeth into flesh and tear it viciously takes over his mind, leaving a confused expression on Avgust's face. Hurt.

Bane can't stand to look at him as he disappoints him yet again, so he storms off before his desire can get in the way of his clear mind. He is unable to explain to Avgust or himself what is happening. The iron taste still lingering in his mouth is a bitter reminder of what he's leaving behind in that dimly lit corridor.

Bane wants nothing more than to go back and find safety in Avgust's embrace again, but something is rising in him. Something that scares him, something he doesn't want anywhere near Avgust—this strange, animalistic urge that makes blood taste lush.

He looks at his hands, skin faintly stained from the Lover's sorrow's crimson waters. There is still dirt under his nails.

XII

A Hollow Shell

"YOU ASKED FOR ME?" AVGUST'S voice bounces off the stone walls of the empty conference room.

His father sits at the head of the conference desk, imposing and tall even in his chair. The rest of the seats are vacant, but the table has papers and maps scattered across it.

"I *asked* you to attend the meeting, how convenient that you show up when it's already over." The king has a stern brow raised ever so slightly. It makes cold sweat break out over Avgust's skin. "Don't think it has escaped my notice that you have been avoiding your duties."

"I have not." He clears his throat as the lie slips out easily. "I have been busy."

"With what exactly? What is occupying your time?"

Avgust finds himself reluctant to answer.

Bane comes to mind, of course. He spends more than half

of his time with him, but even still that isn't enough. There must be something truly wrong with him if the sight of Avgust is enough to make Bane run for a second time. He shatters at the thought that it's not something he can fix. It's not something that will just go away, Bane's disgust.

Avgust fought long and hard to have his father's approval for their birthday getaway, and despite all his pleas, it was Bane that convinced him to agree in the end. For them to go to the countryside after the birthday celebration in a couple of days, alone and unaccompanied, will prove itself more of a curse than a blessing. He can't stand thinking about having Bane trapped in a room with him when he clearly would rather be anywhere else.

"I know where you go at night," the king says.

Avgust stills.

Eden was right, their father knows. The nights he spends with Bane have since ceased, but the suspicion lingers.

The king rises from his seat to slowly pace around, his heavy footsteps even louder in the empty room. He circles behind Avgust menacingly only to end up thoughtfully gazing out the window a few paces to his left.

"I had such high hopes for you when you were born a boy, an heir to the throne." A shiver runs through Avgust at the king's cold tone. "The royal blood flowing through you should mean you are born to rule. Alas, you seem to be the first in our long line of royalty to disprove that."

Avgust never wanted to be a ruler, he wanted nothing more than to escape his fate, but even so he knew he was destined for it. He always thought himself incapable of ruling, but he hoped that maybe he could prove that wrong when push came to shove. Yet as of late, he doesn't know who he is. Unfit to rule, according to his father. Unfit to love, according to Bane.

"I believe it is time for you to become more involved in royal matters," the king says sternly, his hands crossed behind his back as he continues to stare woefully out of the window. "If being king doesn't come naturally to you, you better hope it can be learned. Or you will forever remain nothing but a disappointment."

Avgust says nothing, words heavy at the back of his throat.

"I have half a mind to set you straight by marrying you off. It would force you to spend your time wisely. You are acquainted with Lady Roza, yes?"

"Father, please..." Avgust is not above begging. Lady Roza is a kind-hearted woman, but Avgust would be trapped. She isn't who he wants.

"You must listen to me then. You are past the age of maturity; this is well overdue. What kind of king will you be if you don't even know how to rule a country?" His father's eyes turn to pin him under their iron gaze.

"From now on, you are to attend all meetings regarding the country's future. Whether it concerns strategy, politics or commerce, you are to be present. Am I understood?"

"Wouldn't that get in the way of my religious studies?"

"I'm sure Konstantin will adapt to your other responsibilities."

"But what about my penmanship enrichment with Sofron and—"

"Quiet!" His father's voice rises. "You will attend the

meetings. That is to be your top priority. If any other activity is preventing you from that, I will personally make sure it's terminated. And that includes your religious studies—you have had enough time to get yourself more than acquainted with the scripture. And if you haven't, that can only speak to a fault in your teacher."

Avgust stomps out the need to defend Bane. He holds his tongue again, eyes turned down to the cold stone floor.

"When did I let this get so far out of hand..." the king says under his breath. "So many young men would kill to be in your place, and you are just so ungrateful. I should've known you would turn out like that; you were always so abstracted, always somewhere else. You never showed interest in anything that really matters, not duty, not honour...always consumed by your own vanity, your own amusement. How could I even think you'd be fit to be king when you are so preoccupied with yourself?"

Avgust feels the tears bubbling up, threatening to start falling down his cheeks. They sting at the back of his eyes despite his efforts to keep them at bay.

He is not prepared to take on his duties this soon or this abruptly. The impending weight of the crown feels closer now more than ever, even with his father still alive.

Avgust dreads the future that will come no matter how he tries to escape it.

XIII

Joyless Celebration

THE MAIN HALL IS BUSTLING and lively. Musicians play passionately as the court dances with rehearsed movements. Almost everyone is up on their feet having fun for the health of the prince and princess in celebration of their score. The hall hasn't been this full in a long while, yet Avgust feels alone where he sits at the high table, observing the festivities in his name.

The large summer doors lining the inner wall of the main hall have been opened, letting in the fresh evening air. Guests spilled out into the inner courtyard in conversing groups under the big tree. The small pond has already fallen victim to a spilled glass of mead. Those who preferred dancing over talking remain in the enclosed part of the hall, but everyone gets to enjoy the beautiful view of the yard.

Eden sits at the other end of the table, next to the queen.

Joyless Celebration

She wears a silk, burgundy dress, one with long sleeves that flow past her wrists. Avgust is dressed in a heavily embroidered tunic and a capelet that hangs off one shoulder—wine red to match with his sister.

Bane is here, in a somewhat secluded corner and away from the dancing crowd, his presence almost tangible in the air. Avgust's eyes find him rather quickly, as if a string pulls him in his direction. Bane shifts the second their eyes meet, leaving only the phantom feel of his gaze lingering on his skin. Avgust doesn't take his attention away, he knows Bane can sense his eyes, even while pretending to marvel at the decorations on the walls.

Avgust should talk to him, hear him out, maybe he's got it all wrong. Maybe there's a good explanation as to why he keeps running away. Even if it is as he thought and Bane finds him to be an eyesore, he can pretend it never happened. He can pretend it didn't hurt him. Avgust is willing to act as if they never shared those desperate kisses, if it means Bane will speak to him again. Anything seems more bearable than this silence.

But Bane won't even meet his gaze from across the hall.

Except, Avgust is wrong. Bane's eyes flicker past him before moving away. His attention lands on the whole grand table rather than on Avgust specifically.

Avgust looks to his right, trying to follow what Bane might be concentrating on, and of course he should've known, his father must have called for him. It was silly to assume that Bane would come to the table for him.

"Konstantin," the king greets Bane when he nears, "How do you find the celebration?"

"It's excellent, Your Majesty," he says, polite as ever.

Funny, the king hasn't asked *his* opinion on his birthday celebration. It's no secret that he likes Bane better than his own son; Avgust shouldn't be surprised. Yet there is still a part of him that feels betrayed.

"Have you said your wishes to the guests of honour yet?"

"No, I haven't had the chance." Bane turns to the king's left where Eden is sitting next to the queen and bows to her in respect. "May you be blessed, Your Highness. Congratulations on your score."

Eden only nods politely in thanks. Bane turns to Avgust now, who feels the air get knocked out of his lungs. Their gazes hold each other longer than they ought to, longer than they have looked at each other in the last few days combined.

"Happy birthday, Your Highness." Bane finally speaks, averting his eyes to the floor midway through his wish, like he can't stand to look at him, even now.

"Thank you." Avgust blinks at him but manages to force a polite smile. He doesn't want to make a scene in front of his father.

The nerve...Bane never calls him "*Your Highness*." It feels so distant, detached. Like Bane is nothing more than a servant and Avgust nothing more than his title.

"Prince Avgust, would you mind escorting me to the dance floor?" Lady Roza's voice breaks him out of his thoughts. Lady Roza stands to the side of the high table. The fabric of her dark green velvet dress shimmers under the candlelit hall. She's bold to ask him outright, but he had promised her his first dance.

Her proposition comes in the exact right moment, since he

and Bane are mere acquaintances apparently. Who is Avgust to refuse the lady a dance?

"It would be my pleasure, my lady."

Avgust chances one last look towards Bane and finds him watching as Avgust takes Lady Roza's hand. Cruel satisfaction rises in his chest.

A new song begins and Avgust stands across from Lady Roza in the neat row of men. They step closer when the dance begins, and the couples pair off with the lively rhythm. Bane's heavy gaze is on them, running over Avgust's flesh like a lingering touch. Bane casts his eyes back and forth between Avgust and his father. It's plainly obvious that he is barely paying attention to what the king is saying in favour of observing Avgust instead.

Avgust's eyes narrow in defiance when he looks back, urging Bane to do something about it if he can't stand watching him dance with someone else. Avgust grabs Roza's hand when the dance brings them closer, and in one twirl, Avgust loses sight of Bane. He's no longer standing at the foot of the grand table.

Avgust searches the crowd for him over Lady Roza's shoulder, but he's nowhere in sight.

"We never have so many witnesses, Your Highness," says Lady Roza. "You must excuse my giddiness."

"Nothing I enjoy more than a lady's rosy cheeks. No excuse needed."

"So, tell me, Your Highness, does it make you as shy as it makes me?"

"I fear 'shy' is not a word I'm acquainted with, my lady."

"Of course not," she says with a small smile.

When the music fades into a different song at the end of the dance, Avgust takes them off the dance floor.

"Will you excuse me?" he says.

"Are you alright?" Lady Roza asks.

"Just in need of some air," Avgust assures and takes one of her hands, leaving a brief kiss upon her pale skin. He hopes Bane sees it. "I will be back for another one of our promised dances, my lady."

Her smile is shy but beaming.

When he walks into the inner courtyard people are quick to swarm him with congratulations and compliments for the celebration. Avgust does his best to be courteous, but his eyes roam through the people in the inner yard. If Bane isn't here, then he must have already retired to his room. Avgust can't decide if that would be for better or for worse.

An all too familiar sound grazes his ears—a laugh. Avgust ignores whatever the person talking to him says and turns to search for the sound. He sees that Bane has positioned himself in yet another private corner, next to the columns surrounding the inner courtyard, but now he isn't alone. Avgust recognises the girl next to him as Lady Maya from Eden's court.

Furious jealousy swivels deep in his stomach. She has always had her eye on Bane. Just his luck that she found him alone when Avgust can't bear the humiliation of interrupting them.

She is beautiful, there is no denying that, but visually they stand awkwardly together. At a head shorter, she is far too small not to be dwarfed by Bane's height. It looks silly.

Avgust on the other hand thinks he and Bane have the

Joyless Celebration

perfect difference in height. Not so much that it becomes ridiculous when they stand next to each other, but just enough to notice Bane is taller if you look for it.

She must revel in the fact that Bane *towers* over her. If only she could see how funny they look from afar.

The colours they wear clash harshly. Bane's cotton surcoat is simple but dyed a rich blue that not many could afford. Lady Maya, on the other hand, wears a bright green gown that not only doesn't look good next to Bane's more pleasant palette, but is clearly borrowed from someone with a deeper complexion.

She says something with a polite hand covering her mouth so Avgust can't read her lips, and Bane tips his head back with a strong chortle. He is surprised that she can get a laugh like that out of him. Avgust wonders what she could have possibly said. It can't be that funny. Bane is just being nice. And yet he seems engaged and willingly participating in this conversation; Avgust so desperately wishes he could hear them.

She drops her handkerchief with an exaggerated gasp, and Bane is quick to bend and pick it up. He hands it back to her and she makes sure to let her hand linger on his as she grabs it.

It's obviously an attempt at flirtation, but she doesn't know Bane is oblivious to courting tricks like this one. Avgust would know. He is yet to realise many of the things Avgust does are with very purposeful intent. Like the items Avgust *accidentally* forgets in Bane's room so he would have to seek him to return them. Or the scent he always tries to leave on his sheets, so he stays on Bane's mind even in his dreams.

He had always found it unfortunate, him never noticing,

until now. It suits him just fine for Bane to not realise he is being flirted with. Normally, Avgust would appreciate the art of it, but he can't when the advances of it are aimed towards the one person he could never bear to share.

Bane continues to be too absorbed in the conversation, too happy to be there, almost as if he is enjoying himself in her company. Maybe he is. It's not like Avgust doesn't understand the flattery of having a woman so obviously express her interest in you. Now that he has set Avgust aside, maybe she will actually succeed in securing Bane's affections.

It feels like he has forgotten about Avgust altogether.

Then, just for a split moment, Bane's eyes find his, but he is quick to look away. Like he just wanted to check if Avgust is looking before he continues entertaining Lady Maya.

Avgust never thought him capable of such cruelty. Especially in a moment when they don't know where they stand with each other.

How could he? How could he do this to Avgust and sleep at night? Why would he bask in the attention of someone else when Avgust is all his to have? *How could he?* After discarding Avgust like he never mattered to begin with—twice.

Avgust had spent the entire night—his entire birthday—brooding and moping over someone who barely bothered to congratulate him. And there he is, conversing and, dare Avgust say, courting someone else. Avgust can't hear them, but he can only assume what they are saying to each other is encroaching on romantic. Lady Maya seems far too pleased in Bane's company for it to mean nothing. It lights a fire in Avgust's chest, angry and envious.

Joyless Celebration

Suddenly Avgust knows that he can't pretend it didn't happen, that it doesn't hurt him how he seems to no longer be someone Bane desires. The wound is still fresh and bleeding, and he can't bring himself to apologise for something that isn't his fault, just so they can go back to how things used to be. He isn't the one that should be seeking him out. What Bane did left a lasting mark on his soul and Avgust can no longer think about all they have done in the past without wondering if his affections were unwanted even then. Feeling rejected by the one who has seen the best and worst of you, the most intimate of you, hurts more than any knife ever could.

When Bane makes up his mind, and if what they have means anything to him, Avgust might decide to listen. However, as things stand, he has nothing to say to him. Avgust thinks his intentions are more than clear; Bane is the one who should decide what he wants.

Avgust spots Eden making polite talk with the same lords and ladies that had clung to Avgust before. He decides to save her.

"Ah, Sister! Just who I was looking for." Avgust steps through the circle of people pestering Eden with questions and congratulations. "Will you excuse us, please, the king requests us urgently."

He snags her hand and drags her out of the crowd.

"What does Father want?" she asks as they walk to the other side of the inner courtyard.

"Oh, nothing, I hope," Avgust dismisses with a wave of his hand. "Let's get out of prying eye's way."

They duck behind one of the columns, tucking themselves

in the darkness of one corner.

"Are you enjoying yourself at least, since I'm finding it difficult?" He glares at Lady Maya and Bane's direction.

"As much as I can enjoy myself at an event like this, I suppose."

"What a celebration."

"I remember when we used to enjoy our birthdays more," Eden says. "But it just gets less and less fun as we get older, doesn't it?"

"Life starts to dawn on us."

Eden's mind wanders off somewhere as she stares into nothing with a wistful smile.

"Do you remember our fifteenth birthday feast? When you caught one of the hanging crests on fire, and they had to put it out with mead," Eden says with a small chuckle.

Avgust sighs dramatically, "I tried to blame that on you, but no one believed me."

"I had witnesses! You on the other hand were sneaking off with Bane where no one could see you."

Avgust can't defend himself against that strong point. It had been the night where they shared their second kiss, after an entire year of not talking about their first, which seemed more important than being present at his celebration.

"I did try to clear your name, but Father only got angrier." The laughter leaves her eyes. "Sorry if that affected your punishment."

"It was just the standard disciplining. Nothing you could say to him would have changed his mind, you know how he is."

"Stubborn, like you." Eden shoves his shoulder with her

own.

"Me? You're the one who never admits you're wrong!"

"I'm simply never wrong," she states confidently.

Their laughs die down into a soft silence. Comfortable in the quiet, Avgust speaks. "I truly don't know what I would do without you."

"Oh no, I think you're drunk already," she chuckles, a little bit drunk herself.

"No, I'm serious," Avgust says, a bittersweet feeling swelling in his chest, "If I had been an only child, I'm not sure I would have made it to my twentieth birthday."

"Don't say that." Eden looks him in the eyes, words as serious as they can possibly be. "Besides, I couldn't survive without you either."

They slip out of the celebration and deeper into a hallway that leads away from the inner courtyard. Their steps echo into the empty corridor as they walk away from their own feast.

"I don't know what I will do when they marry me off to some foreign prince in a faraway land. I'll simply have to take you with me." She locks her arm around his elbow, as they climb up the stairs.

"Oh, I'd gladly come with you."

"You'd be needed here…"

Avgust doesn't let his mind linger on that, he won't let it spoil their light conversation.

"Let me dream, Eden."

"Only because it's our birthday."

They reach Eden's room, and she stands at the door. Avgust is not welcome in. He would've gladly spent the rest of the night with his sister, but she clearly has other plans he won't interfere with.

"Well, the night isn't getting any younger and I'm bored out of my mind, so I think I'll be retiring." He fakes a yawn. "You?"

Eden gives him a guilty look and he is proven correct; she does have plans.

"The best of luck to you, noble Sir." Avgust bows, to which Eden scoffs good-naturedly before closing her door with a quiet "goodnight."

He wanders around the corridors a while more, alone with his thoughts yet not letting them bleed into his mind. The muted chatter coming from the wide-open windows manages to keep them tucked away.

Avgust doesn't return to the hall to give Lady Roza that dance he promised.

XIV

Hungry, Depraved Animal

IN THE PAST DAYS, THE sun had become a source of utter discomfort, no matter how much exposure Bane tries to put his body through. He did his best to convince Avgust to leave at night, claiming that it will be too hot to be travelling on horseback during the day.

Avgust seemed very apathetic to his wish, not wanting to lose sleep over travelling at night, so the best Bane could manage to get him to agree to was a few hours before sunrise. He can only hope they reach their destination before noon. The mountain town of Dyvorssel, where they are headed, is not too far from the capital, but he can already sense the change in the air as they go up the hill.

Bane got excused from all of his other duties so he can travel with the prince. He always has to be at Avgust's beck and call. Everything else is insignificant. It's not something he minds usually; he'd choose to bicker with Avgust about the existence of God over swinging a sword any day. Or so he thought.

The warm June air would make for a nice atmosphere, if it weren't for the sun creeping over the horizon and Avgust's obvious displeasure with him. He hasn't spoken a word to him since Bane left him in the corridor. He could barely get him to discuss the details of their travelling arrangements before they left.

He won't pretend Avgust doesn't have the right to be mad, but he also won't pretend it doesn't claw at him. Although, it's for the better. Bane can't trust himself to keep at a distance, so he lets Avgust's reasonable bitterness do it for him. It's unlike Avgust to be this quiet, but it's not unlike him to be this stubborn. He hasn't even looked in his direction the entire journey.

"It seems that we will be arriving soon." Bane tries to ease the tension. "How much further up the mountain do you think?"

Avgust doesn't grace him with a response and instead whips the reins of his horse and leaves Bane a few paces behind him.

It's better this way, he tells himself.

They arrive at a lively inn, held up by wooden beams and walls, just as the sun is starting to get unbearable. Bane is already beginning to feel faint in the sunlight.

He unloads their luggage from the horses, after tying them to the stand in front of the small stable next to the building. Avgust doesn't wait for him, nor does he make an attempt to help him carry the bags. He's already through the door of the inn and likely getting up to no good.

Hungry, Depraved Animal

Once Bane follows through the entrance, all the loud, slurred sounds overwhelm him immediately, but he tries to shake it off. Despite that, it doesn't take long to spot Avgust amidst the boisterous chatter of the small group of people drinking and singing. He is conversing with the innkeeper, a cheerful woman who seems far too willing to pretend she finds him funny.

Bane strides in and rests the two bags on the barstools, settling next to Avgust.

"We would like a room."

"Just one?" The woman raises a playful eyebrow.

"Oh, yes. It's all we can afford; see, we were kicked out like strays from our home with nothing but the shirts on our backs and the contents of our pockets." Avgust spirals out into a theatrical tragedy that couldn't be any less true if he tried. Bane quietly rummages through the heavy coin purse the king kindly provided—trying not to jingle the coins too much and spoil the lie—and digs out a few coins to hand to the woman.

"This is enough for two nights, yes?" Bane barely waits for the woman to nod before he snatches Avgust's elbow and shoves him in front, grabbing the two bags from the stools. They climb the stairs and reach a wooden hallway with a few doors along the walls.

"Why lie?" Bane asks.

"What I do is none of your concern."

Bane ignores the hurtful, snappish tone. He lets them into their room, having taken the key from the innkeeper, and sets their bags on the floor. It's not a spacious room by any means, but the two beds could not be further away from one another.

Which Bane doesn't mind, considering his circumstances; however, he knows that this is something that Avgust *would* usually mind.

"You probably want the beds pushed together?" Bane says with a sigh he didn't intend to let out.

"No, I like them exactly as they are."

"Good."

Avgust pauses and turns to look at him for what seems to be the first time that day. His lips are pressed into a thin line, his green eyes sharp under his furrowed brows. Avgust would hate to know how much he looks like his father when doing so.

"*Good*, is it now?"

"I'm tired," Bane shrugs casually, but his words don't sound as believable as he had hoped they would, "I don't want to be moving heavy furniture."

Avgust's arms cross over his chest.

"Hm, that has never been a problem for you before." His tone is accusatory.

"If you want them moved so bad, then you can do it yourself."

"Well, I don't."

"Then what is this conversation even about?"

Avgust gapes at him, as if he can't believe Bane's audacity. He's not even sure what he's said wrong.

He knows Avgust was trying to pick a fight, but maybe he didn't expect for Bane to actually let him. Or at least that's what his bafflement suggests.

Despite the angry scowl that drags his eyebrows over his eyes and the corners of his mouth into a pout, Avgust looks beautiful. The first rays of sun stream from the window, creating a halo in his golden hair and bouncing off his pale skin, which is pleasantly flushed. His eyes, green and intense, are impossible to look away from. Bane has very little complaints about being stared down when he's under that gaze.

For a moment he looks like he expects Bane to say something but seems to be left disappointed.

"I'm going down to find myself some lunch," Avgust declares, turning away from him, "come with me—or don't." Then, he shuts the door behind himself with a thud that echoes in Bane's skull. A headache is starting to form, he can feel it. He should go after him, but it would be for the better if he doesn't.

Instead, Bane decides to lie down for a while. He hasn't been able to have a full night's sleep since he came back from his grave, nor a proper meal. All food tastes like wax to him now, and he can hardly keep it down for more than an hour.

Bane claims the bed closer to the door, more than happy to avoid the morning sun beams from the window on the other bed. He lies on sheets that feel rough on his skin. Staring at the ceiling he tries to relax, which quickly proves impossible. The moment he clears his mind, it fills again with sounds and smells and images. It's as if he is in the middle of the busy tavern and not alone in a quiet room. Clinking metal cups, loud yelling and the strong, unpleasant scent of sweat and spoilt food is all he senses. Attempting to sleep in these conditions will be difficult, especially with how sleep hasn't been coming to him at all. His dreams have been plagued with soil, a suffocating weight on top of him. It startles him awake most nights.

Despite himself, he lets his eyes close.

***

When his own gasp wakes him, the room is covered in darkness. The bit of sleep he has managed to get did not soothe him. He feels beaten up and even more tired than before, as if he hadn't even fallen asleep in the first place. Bane peels himself off the sheets and decides to go down to the tavern, which sounds like it's in his room anyway.

He hopes some mead can wash away the taste of dirt in his mouth.

Avgust's voice reaches his ears even before he is able to spot him in the busy tavern.

A crowd has flocked around his table, Avgust, of course, the centre of their attention. He has kept everyone more than entertained with his cogitations, which are definitely foolish, but to the drunks around him probably seem revolutionary. Avgust has a natural allure to him. He easily draws people in. And when it's not his cheeky theatrics, it's usually his beauty that lures them. Bane has fallen victim to it himself.

He observes him with interest from a far, unsure what he can expect to come out of his mouth next.

"Let's get another round," he suggests loudly to the table. His cheeks are rosy from the alcohol, but he isn't quite drunk yet. "On me."

The men around him cheer loudly, and some pat Avgust on the back, thankful. Bane finally makes his way to their table.

"So, you finally decided to join me?" He looks up at him with a joyous glint in his eyes, all traces of bitterness gone from his demeanour.

Hungry, Depraved Animal

Bane was wrong; he is drunk, drunk enough to forget he was ever cross with him.

"I fell asleep."

"Come sit." He drags Bane by his hand to the chair next to his, "Maybe you can provide some insight."

Their conversation is about care for stable animals, and Bane ended up not saying a word. He ordered himself a cup of mead and just observed. Despite having zero knowledge on the topic, Avgust's voice is the loudest, which isn't surprising in the slightest. The only people able to butt in the conversation are as drunk as him.

Someone else gets their table a third serving of drinks and their already loud voices become deafening. The barmaid drops a tray full of cups with a thunderous clatter, and the smell of the mead sinking into the wooden floor drags along the inside of his nose. All the sudden loud noises hammer in his head. The smell of everything around him becomes unbearable. Nausea is rising in him; he should get away from the clutter or he fears he might vomit.

"Excuse me." Bane slips out of his seat hurriedly.

"Everything alright?" Avgust grabs his hand, concern slipping through.

"I think I need some air."

Avgust nods and lets him go with a lingering look.

The night air fills his lungs but that doesn't soothe his distress one bit. His throat is dry, even after the cup of mead he just drank. In fact, it might have made it worse, every sip felt like he was gulping sand. No amount of liquid could satisfy his unexplainable thirst.

He stays outside the tavern a little while longer, despite the overwhelming stench of horses and trash. Bane takes in another deep breath, before heading back inside. Still a little shaken, he accidentally bumps into someone.

"Sorry." Bane mumbles as he tries to walk past the man and get to the door.

"You trying to pick a fight, boy?" the man yells. His breath reeks of alcohol.

"I'm just trying to get inside," Bane explains tiredly, but the man purposely blocks his way.

"Like hell you are!"

"I don't want any trouble, please let me pass."

"And if I don't?" The man shoves him with force and ill intent, sending him stumbling a step back in his intoxicated state.

His face comes close to Bane's, a snarl revealing his rotten teeth. His breath burns Bane's nose hairs. Anger bubbles up inside him, his jaw clenches with a dull ache in his teeth.

"Gone all quiet, have you? Yeah, that's what I thought."

That tone is all it takes to tip over Bane's patience, sending him lunging at the man's scrawny frame until he is pinned underneath him on the ground with strength he didn't know he possessed. His teeth tear his flesh open. Blood pours in his mouth instantly, and that rich aroma fills his lungs again, reminding him of the kiss he had shared with Avgust a few nights prior. But now the strong, insatiable hunger seems to be quieting down with every gulp he takes. The heaviness in his throat slowly disappears as if it were never there. The blood feels like medicine calming every one of his aches.

Intoxication rules over all his senses, clouding his mind and making his body move on its own.

Bane startles away. A few moments more and the man would have been dead. He backs off the stranger. It's only now that he realises the severity of his doing.

As the ecstasy fades, guilt instantly replaces it. Avgust's words circle around in his mind, *blood-sucking demon*. Whoever drinks the water becomes like her, a blood-sucking demon. Bane drank from the red waters in his deathly state after he crawled out of the ground. This is the consequence.

The worst part is that he doesn't find what he has just done surprising. Blood seemed to be to his liking, something he had come to expect given his recent brushes with its taste. He wants to feel sick, he *should* be feeling sick. He doesn't.

There is something else he feels, something that he'd rather not, yet it's there. With the immense relief he finds, and the absence of the hunger he has felt for days, Bane is ashamed of how good it felt to rip into a man's throat.

He climbs back up to his feet with a tremble, all due to his psychological state. The man lies still where he leaves him. Left at the mercy of God. Not unlike Bane himself after that night in the forest. Except this time, he is the monster. He wonders if his eyes also glow. Will they haunt that man's dreams like hers haunt his?

Bane stumbles his way through foreign alleys and cobbled streets to clear his mind and stop himself from going back for another taste. The town's houses are small and orderly, compact little homes. Many outsiders are spread throughout the square, street performers and jesters there to entertain. People come down from the peak of the mountain with carts of water barrels filled from the spring. The town is bustling. Bane walks around what is probably the larger half of Dyvorssel, until he finds himself in front of the tavern again.

The door to the inn opens with a creak. The groups of drunks have scattered, leaving a few lonely people drinking in corners. Avgust is in one such shadowed corner. It would have been hard to recognise him were it not for his curls, since his face is hidden in a woman's neck. He whispers something and the woman laughs softly. The pit in Bane's stomach grows cavernous. The anger that has been building for days is finally becoming blinding. His emotions are unstable, and nothing scares him more. He thinks he could kill this woman, seeing Avgust look at her like that, his eyes soft and smile playful.

So, he turns around while he still can. His footsteps going up the stairs are loud enough to be heard, and he hopes Avgust notices. Bane wants him to know he saw.

XV

Tender, Warm Flesh

IN THE MORNING, BANE IS greeted by the sight of the empty bed next to his. It's early. The bar downstairs is still quiet. He sits up and swings his legs over the edge of the bed, hands quickly coming up to his face. His elbows rest on his knees. His fingers dig painfully into the skin under his eyes.

Avgust didn't come back to their room last night, just as Bane expected, but he still finds himself disappointed. Had he hoped they could get back to normal? Maybe. He comes to find he hates the quiet more than he hates the noise.

The door creaks open and two feet lightly pad across the wooden floor. Bane can recognise the sound of those footsteps even in his sleep.

"Oh, you're up," Avgust says like he didn't expect him to be.

"I'm up. Slept well?" Bane's eyes are sharp with barely

contained anger.

"Excellently."

"Is that so…" It's hard to keep the venom out of his tone, "I doubt you slept at all."

"Do you care?"

"I just wonder what *Roza* would say," Bane bites out, "Has it escaped your notice that you're courting her?"

This has nothing to do with Roza. They both know it.

Avgust's eyes are intense as they look into his. He's quiet, like he's waiting for something.

"There's a lot you don't notice," Bane continues, "I let you get away with too much, but I'm getting tired. One day your servant will be brave enough to accept the consequences of denying you."

The power Avgust has, even over Bane's daily activities, was never a problem when it used to mean something. Now Avgust wants his time but wastes it elsewhere.

"What is that supposed to mean?"

"Never mind." He itches to say just what he's thinking, about Avgust treating him like a servant whenever he sees fit and only treating him like a person when he needs something. But it would just make the argument worse, and his patience has worn far too thin.

Bane stands to his feet and paces around their small room.

"Tell me!" Avgust says. It's a demand typical of a princeling.

"What do you want, Avgust?"

As if struck by Bane's question, Avgust cocks his head, a quiet click of his tongue escaping his lips.

"I think it is pretty clear what *I* want, it's you who's

inconclusive." Avgust steps closer, eyes narrowing. "So, you tell me."

The air moves with him and Bane can smell him. His body moves by itself, craving to be closer. Avgust's breath hitches, like he expects Bane to kiss him. He probably wants him to, but Bane is angry. He wants to hit him. He wants to kiss him. He wants to eat him—to sink his teeth into him and finally taste that sweetness he has been craving since that night in the corridor.

He wants it all. He wants too much. So, he steps back and turns to leave.

"Where are you going?" Avgust calls after him. His voice is strained.

"Away," Bane says, but doesn't stop to look at him, "I don't have to stay here just because you want me to."

Bane will walk all the way to the castle if he must.

His feet thud loudly on each step of the staircase down to the bar of the inn. It's empty, like he suspected, save for two figures talking to the barmaid. They catch Bane's eye, and he stops in his tracks. One of them is clearly a knight, but the other man...with the rich fabric of his clothes and the air of importance around him, there's no doubt—he's a royal envoy.

The dryness in his throat is now replaced by a lump.

Do they already know about what he did last night? The man he almost killed...Are they here to punish him for his sins? They must be here to take him and let him rot in a dungeon somewhere for the rest of his life. They must know how good it made him feel, sucking the life out of that man, and that's how they know Bane would deserve his sentence.

Another thought comes to him. Maybe they're here for

Avgust. Has the king found out about the maid he took to bed? If so, his punishment will not be light. Bane almost hopes he is the one to be punished so Avgust can be spared.

"What is the meaning of this?" Bane stutters out.

The envoy holds out a letter.

"This is addressed to you."

A bead of sweat drips down Bane's forehead. His suspicion is confirmed, they are here for him.

He reaches for the scroll, trying to calm his shaking hands. The king's signet seal rests over the edge of the parchment. The thought of him knowing about what he has done strikes a sharp swoop of shame through his stomach. He rips the red wax, unfolds the paper with no precision whatsoever and begins reading impatiently.

Konstantin,

The urgency of this letter leaves me with little time to spare greetings.

In light of recent events, I have been forced to take measures to ensure no child of mine ever strays so far from the path designated for them again. Reconnecting with God and His will before word spreads is of utmost importance.

As such, you are to return to the castle immediately where you and Princess Kaledena will be joined in holy union. The ceremony will commence as soon as possible.

Your safe return will be ensured by the messengers sent to deliver this letter.

King Hares

Part II

XVI

Holy Matrimony

AVGUST WOKE UP THAT MORNING *with a revelation. When he saw Bane peacefully sitting on the stone lining of the pond in the garden, he found the perfect opportunity to act.*

"Bane, there is something we need to discuss."

The young boy looked up from his book, suddenly alert. He stood to his feet, significantly taller than Avgust's juvenile self. This had been right after Bane's rapid growth in height over the summer of his fourteenth year.

"Have I done something?"

"No, no. Not yet." *Avgust dismissed,* "You see, the wedding will host many people, a lot more than we're used to. They'll travel from afar just to come here, and that means a lot of ladies our age will be present."

Bane gulped. Avgust continued.

"It's sure that they will show an interest in being courted, and seeing as you're quite kind on the eyes, your attention will be in high demand."

"It—It will?" Bane's voice cracked. He still hadn't grown into it yet, and it broke on every other word.

"Yes, definitely," Avgust confirmed with a nod, "I came to let you know so you can prepare accordingly. But I'm sure you will do fine. You should have plenty of knowledge on the matter of courting, so you won't need my help."

Avgust turned to leave, of course with no intention of actually doing so, and took one step, two...before Bane called out.

"No, wait!"

Avgust fought off a smile.

"I don't want to court anyone. I wouldn't know what to do!"

"Ah, well I suppose my help might be required after all," Avgust mused aloud, "If you stick to my side, I'll do my best to fend them off of you. But in the case a lady does break through my defences, you must be prepared."

Bane nodded eagerly, relieved at the offered protection from the theoretical ladies.

"Say, Bane, have you ever kissed anyone?"

"No."

"We must change that. How embarrassing would it be for our kingdom to leave a bad impression on a foreign lady. Despicable, really; we wouldn't hear the end of it." Avgust sighed theatrically, "I guess I will have to teach you myself."

"You?" Bane looked at him in shock. "My prince, wouldn't that get me in trouble?"

Avgust shrugged one small shoulder. "It can be our secret."

"Here?" Bane looked around.

There were servants passing through the corridor, far enough away as to not hear them, but close enough to see them if they were to get up to anything.

"No." Avgust shook his head. "Follow me, let's find a more secluded place."

Avgust led the way, Bane following on his heels. It wasn't long before he decided on hiding in one of the servants' stairways on the east wing of the castle. It was rarely in use since it led from the stables to one of the watch towers, and no one had any business being there right now.

Bane sat in front of him, jittery fingers tapping against his lanky legs. His knees were folded awkwardly, far too close to his chest where they sat on one of the steps. Avgust eyed him closely, watching him gulp nervously for the hundredth time since he brought this up. It was quite endearing.

"Pay attention to what I do," Avgust said.

Bane nodded and squeezed his eyes tightly shut.

Avgust suppressed another laugh and leaned in close to his face. The newly arising problem was that no matter how confident he seemed, Avgust also had no idea what he was doing. He puckered his lips and pressed them to Bane's, suddenly nervous himself. It was only a quick peck, but it set Avgust's heart drumming. He leaned back quickly and locked eyes with Bane's wide ones.

"Let's try again."

This time Avgust didn't pucker. He instead pushed his resting lips against Bane's, and they slotted together easily. Avgust pushed closer, but that did next to nothing other than squish their noses uncomfortably. Tilting his head, he settled into a better angle and dared to part his lips. Bane gasped into the kiss, lips parting to match Avgust's.

"My prince..." Bane's breathless voice broke their mouths apart. The dishevelled expression on his face suddenly brought a new meaning to the phrase. It felt possessive, like Avgust was his.

The night of the wedding, not a single lady approached Bane to inquire about his availability. But Avgust had never expected them to.

***

Not forgiving Bane right away for the way he left Avgust to simmer in self-doubt has proven to be the biggest mistake Avgust has ever made in his life. He ruined their last moments together. And for what? By the time they arrived at the inn he wasn't even angry anymore. Just determined to be petty and demand of Bane to beg on his knees for his forgiveness. In the end, it wasn't worth it. Avgust didn't even give him the chance to try, shutting down any attempt at conversation Bane made. Maybe he was going to apologise if Avgust wasn't so ready to pick a fight.

It was so foolish, trying to get a reaction out of him in such a rotten way. He knows Bane saw him talking to the tavern maid, he heard him going up the stairs to their room. He thought he would get what he wanted if he let Bane jump to conclusions on his own, so he spent the night on one of the tavern benches. Tossing and turning all night, Avgust did not get a blink of sleep, but as soon as the first rays of sunlight lit the horizon it was time to reap what he sowed.

Avgust was so sure that it was going to resolve everything if only he could make Bane yell at him. But all it did was make things worse. This only proved that Bane had gotten sick of their skewed version of forgiveness without apology.

Even though Avgust had every right to be mad, that

doesn't matter now, all this stubbornness gained him nothing. Nothing but wasted time. If he knew then what he knows now, he would've just let it go and enjoyed their last day together.

On their way back, Bane hadn't said a single word, still in shock. They both were. Avgust wishes he had said something to him, anything. But he hadn't, he sat there next to him so close, yet so far behind the wall that Avgust alone had built between them. There is no one else to blame but himself.

Large, lavish banners hang from the high ceiling of the grand hall of the castle. Extra tables have been brought out to accommodate all the guests travelling from afar to attend. The entire castle is buzzing with excitement, engrossed in the preparations. All servants are stressing over getting everything set up, making sure each seat has a set of cutlery, a plate and a cup, that the banners hang at just the right angle and height.

It seems everyone is excited to be a guest at the wedding. Everyone except Avgust.

The noise of the preparations has given him a headache and his eyes sting from the night before. Draped limply over a chair in one corner of the main hall, Avgust watches as the decorations get placed to hang from the windows. He hasn't seen his sister yet, since they arrived back at the castle. And he's not sure he wants to. Anger makes him irrational, sadness makes him intolerable, and Avgust has been feeling both at all times since learning the news. He's afraid of what he might say in this state. Still, he'd like to have a word with her. What could she possibly have done to earn such a punishment? Thinking about it, he can probably guess it has to do with her nightly adventures.

Her punishment is one for all three of them, unbeknownst to the king. But even if he knew, it wouldn't change his mind. His decision would please him even more.

Avgust peels himself off the not-so-comfortable chair he had occupied and begins making his way through the corridors. There, too, it's full of busy servants bustling about. So much so it's a challenge trying to shove his way towards the east wing where Eden's room is. Once he makes it up the stairs, the hall is eerily empty. Avgust listens to his footsteps echo in the lonesome corridor as he strides over to Eden's chambers. The knock on the door echoes too, but no one responds.

"Eden?" he calls, expecting her to be hiding from the maids too eager to get her ready. No response. Avgust opens the heavy door, revealing an empty room. She has probably been dragged off to be prepared for the ceremony already, he realises solemnly.

Shutting her door carefully, he decides to wander the halls for a while longer, enjoying the calm emptiness of the second floor. Time escapes him, Avgust doesn't know how long he spends aimlessly walking around.

He suddenly stops. His feet have taken him right to Bane's door. Avgust stares at it, at the dents in the wood, the ridges running up the planks that make up his door. For a moment he considers just walking away, but something in his mind nags at him to speak to Bane. Avgust is not sure what he would say, but his fist is at the door before he can think about it.

It's like the hope he harbours dissipates with each ringing moment of silence. It stretches and stretches until it's obvious no one is going to open the door.

Avgust can't help the ugly sinking feeling in the pit of his stomach. He has never felt more alone. The two people he trusts most are to be married, and nowhere to be found, leaving him behind. Feeling like this—like his gut twists in a knot so tight it starts to eat at itself—might get easier with time. He gets a head start at getting used to it.

Eden's absence is by chance. But Bane's, he can blame himself for. Perhaps he is in his room right now, just unwilling to speak to him. After the way Avgust behaved, he can't be surprised. Avgust pushed him away, and now neither of them can seek comfort in the other.

The dreaded time for the ceremony struck far too quickly. Avgust has made it to the chapel, assuming his designated seat. He sits primly, face blank, feeling empty.

But when Bane makes his quiet entrance, the empty feeling is replaced by that knot in his stomach. Nobody seems to notice his unremarkable arrival, yet he's all Avgust can look at. Seeing him dressed so nicely, with his hair combed through and properly taken care of, Avgust knows feeling like this will never get easier. Bane does his bows to the royal family, not looking Avgust in the eyes. Not looking at him at all. He just takes his place at the altar without acknowledging him, as if they don't even know each other. Avgust tries to not think of it too much, because if he does, he won't be able to swallow back his tears.

The king sits on the throne prepared for him, his wife on his left and his only son on his right. Avgust taps his fingers on the arm of the chair frantically and with close to no rhythm. The door to the chapel remains shut, awaiting the arrival of the bride.

The heavy doors begin to slide open. In walks Eden, clad in a beautiful dress, her veiled head kept down. The pace at which she moves is painfully slow, like she'd rather bolt in the other direction than reach the altar. She probably would, but the guards stationed at the door make it easy to guess why she doesn't. The trim of her dress is edged in grass stains and mud—faint, but definitely there. Upon closer investigation, he sees that the hem is ripped up too. Avgust's brows furrow, his lip caught between his teeth. Then, Eden looks up right at him, her eyes glossy with something between anger and defeat. When she finally sees Bane at the altar, she is downright startled. Did no one tell her who she would be wed to? Avgust wishes now more than ever that he had the chance to speak to her before the ceremony.

It's only then that he notices her hair is not kept in a net. It's cut to one third of the length it once was, and by the rough, uneven cut, he can tell she did it herself.

Her eyes keep flicking up to Avgust's throughout the priest's chants, a desperate pleading look. Bane on the other hand still avoids his gaze like it would kill him instantaneously. Shame is what's keeping his head lowered and eyes trained to the floor, but Avgust can't quite pinpoint *why*. For marrying his sister? Or for what they had done together before he was forced to devote his life to someone else? Either way, the longer Bane avoids him, the more Avgust's guilt consumes him. After all, Avgust was the one who escalated things between them. He was the one to initiate it. Always, from the very beginning. Maybe Bane only accepted his advances out of courtesy, and Avgust was too full of himself to notice. Maybe Avgust's anger with him was a welcomed change. A confirmation that he wouldn't have to deal with Avgust's romantic urges anymore.

When the ceremony is concluded, the guests seep out of the open chapel doors like a herd. Avgust drags behind, waiting until he is alone in the church before following out by his lonesome. He has no intention to excuse himself, sure no one will miss him at the celebration. His father might be the only one to notice his absence, but Avgust can't stay and pretend none of it fazes him, he has to leave.

***

Even in his room, a whole floor above, he can still hear the music and the tumult. It taunts him, a reminder of what he has just lost. Avgust shuts the door tightly and breathes out a heavy sigh. He runs a hand through his hair and ends up gripping the strands in frustration. He goes to his nightstand and reaches for his hairbrush, but something else catches his attention.

A book was left on his bed. One that Avgust recognises immediately, its half-cordate shape, too familiar. It's the bible he gifted Bane a few years back, the one he keeps hidden in his chest. When Avgust had teased him about it, he had claimed it was far too personal to flaunt around.

Picking it up with careful fingers, Avgust caresses the leather cover. He opens it out of nostalgic curiosity, searching for the message he had written in it before he had gifted it. It's there, on the back of the cover, before the first page. The ink's colour has slightly faded with time.

Holy Matrimony

I offer you my sincerest apologies for drowning your other bible in the fountain. It was not a good display of the morals you have been teaching me. Though I still stand by what I said, you should be granted a replacement for my mistake. I leave my heart with you and can only hope you save yours for me.

The heart shape of the book had more significance than Avgust was willing to admit at the time. Right underneath the message, the cover contains something else written in Bane's familiar blocky script.

I have cherished your gift greatly, and it has been my most prized possession. Despite that, I can't keep this now that my circumstances have changed, and I can only hope you continue our studies without me. I pray you can find solace in it as I have for as long as it was mine, but now it's yours to keep again.

Your friend.

A stab to the chest would hurt less than being called his *friend*. He can't believe Bane is capable of such an insult.

It sinks in then, while he holds his own unwanted heart in his hands, that this is forever. Avgust won't wake up tomorrow and have everything be back to the way it used to be.

His grip on the book tightens, knuckles going white with the rage he is trying to keep at bay. Breaths gone heavy, he lets out a yell, the book ripping in his hands. He throws it and it lands on the glass of his mirror leaving a huge crack where it hit the surface. Avgust catches a glimpse of his own reflection, twisted with anger. Anger, at himself and at this hopeless situation. Soon it sizzles out and turns into pitiful sadness. His shaking legs carry him to the mirror where he picks up the book that lies destroyed in the pile of glass. Avgust comes crashing to the floor, choking on his own quiet sobs. The torn book rests in his violent, regretful hands. All he can think about is that stupid message and he can't help rereading the words over and over and over, finding more difficulty in saying them than remembering them.

The inside of the cover, hanging loosely off the spine, is now covered in tear stains, the ink smudged on the words *'It's yours to keep again'*. Bane doesn't want him anymore. And perhaps he never did.

"You poor thing…" Someone speaks, clear yet distorted. "Don't cry. We all ruin things while consumed by anger." The voice sounds feminine, but gruff, low.

Avgust's head snaps around, looking for an intruder only to find himself completely alone.

"Who's there? Who speaks?"

"I mean you no harm." The voice is calm and comforting, soothing to his ears.

"Who are you?" Avgust rasps out, throat raw from crying.

"A friend."

At that, his brows furrow. His heart begins to beat quicker, but his voice comes out strong and sure. "Show yourself."

"Don't you see me? I'm right here" Avgust turns his head around the room again, and notices something shifting in the mirror. A vague silhouette starts to form in the faint light reflected on its surface. Long, dark hair frames a pale face, distorted by the cracks in the glass. Avgust turns around, but there isn't anyone behind him. A shiver runs through him, and he faces the reflection again.

"I see you have torn your book. I can help you fix that."

The book begins to move in his hands, and he watches as the spine stitches itself back together right before his eyes. It seems impossible, yet it just happened.

"I—" Avgust starts to say, but when he looks up, the woman is gone. All he can see now is his own broken face in the glass.

"Wait! Who are you?" he calls out to the mirror, but only his reflection hears it.

XVII

Entrapment

After Eden's many failed attempts at freedom, her nurse's watchful gaze is now accompanied by that of a guard. There is no way out of this room. She is stuck until the decided time for her '*educational activities*' is over. She doesn't even get to choose the activity, and since it is left up to Nurse Vila, Eden is given the choice between embroidering and learning new texts to recite every day. Two things that she would rather not practice at all.

It's all for Eden's sake, they claim, to '*put her back on the right path*'.

'*It's a much more appropriate hobby for a lady than what you have been occupying your time with,*' is what Nurse Vila likes to say.

Ever since they dragged Eden back to the castle, it has become her prison.

She remembers the terror she felt when she realised it was,

Entrapment

in fact, odd to have this many new faces at the tournament. Her last tournament. She mourns the loss of it, in both senses. A win would have been a nice way to retire, but fate had not been very kind to her that day.

All of her father's suspicions about where Avgust's nights were spent, were proven right except it wasn't his son he caught—it was Eden. It's laughable to think Avgust would sneak out to duel for sport, that's why the possibility of the king suspecting it never crossed her mind. Had their father known his own son better, Eden wouldn't be in this situation, caged like a bird.

Left without the chance to sort her dealings with Marten after the guards emerged from the crowd and took her away, she now owes a debt she isn't sure she will ever get to repay.

Her fingers hurt. It's coming along at least, the project she has been working on. It got repetitive after only a few stitches, and she is getting lost in the time wasted on this boring quilt, but there's nothing she can do but obey her orders. She isn't even allowed to join the other ladies. They're keeping her isolated so she'll go mad, she thinks.

Everywhere she goes, she is accompanied. At the same time every morning, she is picked up from her chambers and at night she is led back to her door. In the beginning, she had her hopes for freedom, fantasies of getting away, escaping, but it has been weeks now, and her fighting spirit is starting to fade away.

To make matters worse, Avgust has been distant. Eden can guess why. She hopes he doesn't blame her, but she hasn't spoken to him about it, or at all. A trivial conversation over breakfast or dinner sums up about all the contact they've had lately. Her brother never visits her room anymore. He probably thinks it might get too crowded with the three of them.

By the stories Avgust always tells, one might get the impression that Bane is better company then he is. But he is just...quiet. Bane wakes up at a time unbeknownst to her and spends the day God knows where, doing God knows what. He could be with Avgust but judging by his miserable state, he likely isn't. When Bane and Eden both end up in their chambers at the same time, they don't talk. They have just as much to say to each other as husband and wife as they did when they weren't. Their one thing in common was and remains Avgust.

For one reason alone, all three of them are miserable.

Eden has made good progress today on her tapestry, the greens and blues of the image beginning to melt harmoniously as the project slowly comes together. It's just like she imagined it in her head. The speed at which she has managed to get so much of it done was a surprise. Eden rests the tapestry on the chair next to hers and decides to rest for a bit.

At the end of each day, her hands are tired, and her fingers are full of needle holes. She looks at them; the callouses at the creases of her palms from gripping her sword are fading too quickly for her liking. Rapidly, in fact, disappearing before her eyes. Eden's brows furrow. The more she looks, the stranger it gets. Her hands look wrong, like they're not even attached to her body. The life lines on each hand begin to move like ripples in water, until they slide right off of her flesh.

She wakes up.

It couldn't have been that long since she fell asleep, seeing as Nurse Vila still hasn't noticed she has stopped working. The tapestry lies in her lap like a blanket, rather than on the other chair, and the lines of green she had added are nowhere to be found; instead, the tapestry is left with just the dull blue at the very bottom of the canvas. Still disoriented, Eden's not sure where the needle has disappeared to, but decides to ignore the danger of that as she stands up and folds the tapestry.

"Ready for dinner, dear?" Nurse Vila asks. The guard prepares to escort Eden to the dining hall.

***

The chair at the head of the dinner table stays empty. Her father is on a trip, and his absence looms like a presence of its own. The queen joins them every night as Avgust, Bane and Eden force down their dinner in silence. No one looks at each other, almost like they're each by themselves. Avgust is too busy picking at his plate, Eden tries not to think about how this will be her life until its end, and Bane occasionally replies to Queen Lena politely whenever she tries to break the quiet.

"There was no need to cut all of your hair dear," the queen says, "you had such beautiful hair—it's such a shame." There is no judgement in her words, only her usual sincerity.

Eden cut it in rage, and the desperate need to make herself unfit to wed. They hadn't told her who would be waiting for her at the altar until she had to walk it, and seeing Bane's equally solemn face was both a relief and a torment. It could have been a cruel lord she had never met, which would be an awful fate, but it just had to be the one person Avgust would never forgive her for marrying.

"How have you been adjusting yourselves to your new chambers?" the queen asks.

"The room is wonderful." Bane remains the only other participant in the conversation. "Very spacious."

The queen turns to Eden, the same question extended to her.

The new chambers are uncomfortable. They have to share not only the room, but the bed too. They cannot escape each other like ordinary couples who get to enjoy separate quarters. It has not been stated, but this is part of her punishment, too. She isn't allowed her privacy. Bane is supposed to be her guard when her real one isn't present.

"Yes, I agree."

The queen seems pleased to hear it.

"I'm glad to know that everything is to your liking," she says with a small smile, "you have to be happy and comfortable to successfully conceive."

Eden chokes on her bite. Avgust goes perfectly still next to her. The look on Bane's face is one of absolute mortification. Maybe he doesn't mean to let all of his emotions show this vividly, but it is comforting to know that they are both horrified at the notion.

It shouldn't be surprising, but it's a relief. Not that Bane has tried to make any advances on her, thank God. When they are alone, they just exist in their individual corners of the room, forced into each other's personal space.

Before any of them even try to form a proper response, Avgust gags on his next bite, and begins coughing. He stands up to fill his cup with water from the pitcher on the table.

Composing himself, he steps away from the dinner and bows just slightly.

"The choking stunted my appetite, if I may be excused." It's not a question. "Enjoy the rest of your evening."

If it was anyone but the queen, they would've seen through to the real reason Avgust wants to leave so abruptly. Fortunately for him, the queen has kept her childish innocence well into adulthood. Eden doesn't think Avgust cares if the queen believes it, but it's better if she never catches on.

Eden intends to follow Avgust, even knowing he might not like to see her right now. But just as she's almost up on her feet, the queen speaks.

"Kaledena, tell me about—"

Eden watches the door shut behind Avgust's retreating form, and she turns her attention to her stepmother. In a perfect world, she could afford to ignore her without fearing it might affect her punishment. But in a perfect world she would not be in this situation at all. She sits back down and listens.

Keeping her answers brief, she is able to free herself of the conversation soon enough. Bane had already excused himself a bit ago, leaving Eden to fend for herself. When she exits the dining hall, her guard is waiting just outside.

"Before I return to my chambers, I would like to see my brother."

The guard doesn't protest against her wishes and silently trails after her as she strides up to the second floor, heading directly to Avgust's quarters. Once at his door, she raises her fist to knock, but the sound of hushed voices stops her in her tracks.

She tries to listen, but all she can make out are faint murmurs and broken words. One of the voices is definitely Avgust, the other is too quiet to hear, but Eden can only assume it must be Bane. She had hoped this would be her golden opportunity to finally speak to Avgust, but at least she's glad to know the two of them have made up.

This also means she gets the room to herself tonight.

Guard in tow, she returns to her quarters and keeps the door open no more than a crack as she slips through, lest the guard see she's alone.

Only she isn't.

"What are you doing here?" Eden asks sharply.

"This is...my room?" Bane says, the book in his lap forgotten in favour of staring at her in confusion.

"Why aren't you with Avgust?"

"Am I supposed to be?"

"Did you not go speak with him?"

"We haven't talked since this morning when he asked me to pass the bread."

Bane, no matter how hard he's trying to pretend he no longer cares for Avgust, seems to be keeping a detailed log on every interaction they have.

"I see."

Who was Avgust talking to, then? Whose voice had she heard? Is it possible he has found other company for his nights? When she tries to recall the sound of the voice her memory is distant and foggy, like she hadn't heard it at all.

XVIII

Wheat, Mud and Bile

AS QUIETLY AS HE CAN, Bane closes the creaky door to his old room. He hasn't dared return since the wedding, afraid of what he'll find, afraid of what he'll find himself missing.

The room is dark. Dust flies in the faint beams of evening sunlight from the crack in the curtains. Bane decides to keep them closed, not only to keep the sun away, but he feels embarrassed to be here, seeking what he has been craving.

It's like time has stopped moving in this room, it's exactly as he left it. Even the air might be the same, still. He almost believes that he could open the chest and find the holy book Avgust gave him, as if he hadn't given it back.

Bane goes to the bed and tosses the covers off, praying the maids haven't bothered to change the sheets after he was moved to the marital chambers.

The air shifts with the top cover flying through the room, and Bane can tell they haven't been touched. Anticipation builds in his chest—excitement.

A soft honey smell embraces him, warm and familiar and everything he has been missing.

Dipping under his weight, the bed welcomes him back. He buries his face in the sheets, chasing after the last traces of Avgust's scent left in the fabric. He wishes to pretend it is Avgust himself he is holding onto instead, but he can't. The rough cotton can't pass for his soft skin, no matter how much Bane wants it to.

So much time has passed since Avgust last stepped foot in here, it's a miracle that there is anything left of him at all. The scent is so faint, he fears it might be his imagination playing tricks on him. Even so he will take what he can get.

With one last deep inhale of the sweet scent into his hungry lungs, Bane forces himself away. If he stays a moment longer, he won't be able to leave. He moves away from the bed and immediately misses the comfort of Avgust, even if he is not really there. Like usual, he has left something of himself behind, this time to haunt Bane.

Even when they fought for longer, he still had reminders of him all around. Avgust made sure of it. Now he is left with nothing. Bane still sees him at meals, but he doesn't get to be as close as he longs to be. He had grown used to their messy relationship, both the tender and the hostile parts. Before, Avgust paying attention to others wasn't something to cry over when Bane knew he would be his alone later. It still bothered him even then. But seeing Avgust now only serves to remind that he can never have him again. It doesn't look like it took long for Avgust to forget him. Now his sole attention has been claimed by Lady Roza, and Bane is helpless against it.

He always thought that when Avgust inevitably marries, they would still find a way to be together.

Bane never thought that he would be the one to end up married. He didn't plan to ever marry. Even now, maybe they could've found a way to be together anyway, if it wasn't for everything else. If Avgust didn't hate him. If Bane wasn't a monster.

Bane can't help but blame himself for wasting the very little time they had together. For leaving him hurt and disappointed so many times, even if he had to for Avgust's own good.

Bane should've dropped to his knees and begged Avgust to forgive him the instant he wronged him. He should've fought his newly rising hunger harder, so they could spend their final moments together. But that's a mistake of the past Bane can't go back and fix.

He forces himself to leave his old room—the only room in which he can pretend Avgust is still his—and takes down the corridor.

Entering the dining hall has only gotten harder since the wedding. Bane is hungrier than ever. Coming from the empty corridor into a room with people is a struggle when all he can focus on is their beating hearts.

He takes his seat, facing Avgust and Eden. The queen sits at one end of the table, the other still missing the king.

Bane begins to slowly fill his plate with food. The few things he chooses will still be too much, he knows. They will taste the same—like wet flour and mud. But he still picks a variety: chicken, bread, potatoes.

"I haven't seen the court in so long," Eden laments.

Bane takes a tiny bite and tries not to gag. It's disgusting but he is *starving*. He keeps eating, although he knows it won't satiate his hunger.

"Your punishment is very cruel, dear," the queen says with a gentle caress on Eden's shoulder. "Maybe the King can be persuaded to change his mind?"

"If anyone can get him to agree, it's you," Eden says, but there's not much hope in her voice.

The heavy doors to the dining room open and in walks a messenger. He stands next to the queen's chair and leans close to whisper something confidential for her ears alone, but Bane hears it too.

"Your Majesty, the king has returned. He has been injured. Your presence is requested in his chambers."

She jumps to her feet and follows the man out of the room in a hurry, her skirts flying behind her.

Bane is left alone to the company of Avgust and Eden to eat in silence. He chews slowly and forces the bite down his throat. Everything around him irritates him—this entire situation irritates him. The cutlery hitting the plates, the light of the candles flickering in his peripheral vision. But most of all, the fact that Avgust is sitting right across him, so close and yet so out of reach.

Eden sighs, "I wish I could check on the court. Avgust, have you seen them lately?"

Bane pauses, considers not saying anything, but does

anyway.

"Surely he does, he has gotten *very* close with Lady Roza." Bane's eyes are scorching as he holds Avgust's gaze. "Isn't that right?"

Avgust swallows down his bite and smiles overly politely. "Of course. We spend a lot of time together, especially now that I have no other social engagements."

After the king cut their religious studies, Avgust has not been around much at all. He seems to be actively avoiding him. Rather, they're avoiding each other.

"I didn't know you kept such close watch of me." Avgust's smile is annoying and all too bright. "One would think your wife should be keeping you too busy."

"We keep busy." As soon as he says the words, there's an aggressive kick to his shin under the table. Judging by the displeased look on her face, it was Eden.

Bane is entirely aware of the implications of what he said and fights off a grin when he hears Avgust's heart stutter. It's beating fast now, and Bane can almost imagine the blood rushing under his skin. There is no way he can finish his meal now that his focus has shifted onto blood.

The hungrier he gets, the less in control of his emotions he is. It's difficult to rein in his temper, especially around Avgust, who smells *so* delicious. Bane could devour him in one go, between kisses and bites, and drain him like the sweet thing he is. It takes a lot out of him not to give into that fantasy. If he killed Avgust, Bane would have nothing to live for. No matter how tempting it might be.

"Is that so?" Avgust shifts in his chair, the expression on

his face one of disguised revulsion. One brow lifts slightly over his sharp eyes. "Well, good thing you have former experience to lie on. Although I'm not sure if it would be of help in your current arrangement."

"Is it possible to not talk about this at the dining table?" Eden says, but it's in vain. Bane can see the determined look on Avgust's face. Whatever comes out of his mouth next will be beyond inappropriate.

"Of course, apologies," Bane offers hoping that they will fall into silence again. He isn't so lucky.

"Let's change the topic then," Avgust begins, "For example, do you think God forgets about the sins of his children as easily as they do?" His harsh eyes stare down Bane. A question designed to wound him.

Does Avgust really think Bane could ever forget what they were? As with many things Avgust says or does, Bane can't be sure. Even after everything that happened, he never wished he could forget what they had. The memory of Avgust is what he goes to sleep thinking about, and what he wakes up with. And he never believed himself forgiven by God, or even by himself. Maybe this is why Avgust said it, because he knows it's not true.

"Is giving into temptation absolved by simply pretending it never happened?" Avgust continues.

"Avgust." Eden warns, but Bane doubts she understands what this is even about.

"I'm curious. And considering that our religious studies were put to an abrupt end, I thought I could ask you now."

"I can advise you to take your questions to the priest." Bane rises to his feet, feigning calmness. His dinner remains unfinished.

Avgust is the one person who can hurt him the most, solely because he knows him so well. He never pulls his punches. When Avgust strikes it's always vicious, he could always dig deeper, go lower. It's like he can read Bane's mind and pull out what is most sensitive.

He knows Bane can't forget him. He *has* to know that. And Bane is hardly successful in escaping his perverse desires, not even now that he is married to a woman as he ought to be. It may even be worse now that he has to acknowledge he harbours no such feelings towards his wife, and probably never will.

The argument is over. Avgust crossed a line, and he knows it. Bane hopes he is satisfied with himself.

"If you would excuse me."

A silence falls around the table, as the tap of Bane's shoes against the floor announces his exit.

XIX

The Woman in The Mirror

THE SUMMER WEATHER IS NICE and warm today, with rays of sunshine streaking through the panes of the castle windows.

Avgust sits cross legged on the floor of his room, the mirror right in front of him. His eyes are puffy from crying, but Eulalia's presence soothes him from within the looking glass.

He has gotten used to the distortion in her voice, yet he can't pretend he doesn't notice the ever so slight differences in her appearance every time she shows herself in his mirror. Today, her hair is a midnight blue, not the usual jet black. Her eyes change between different shades of brown, from chestnut to hazel. Of course, all of this can be justified by the lighting or reflection, but a faint scarring forms on the side of her face that deepens with every visit she pays him. Avgust can never bring himself to ask about it, afraid he might offend her when she has shown him nothing but kindness.

Since the wedding, he has found himself in a worse state than ever before. Eulalia has been his one escape from reality. Bane hasn't spoken to him unless it's to start a fight, and Avgust isn't blameless either. It's so unfair that this is what their tender love has turned into. Eden has no real fault in this either, but she still drives a wedge between them.

"I used to fear this," he says. "When we were younger, we used to play together, all three of us. Bane and Eden used to get along well. They're still getting along it seems…"

He shivers at the thought that the same gentle touches he had grown used to may not have been solely for him. Now that it has been so explicitly confirmed, he can't deny the reality. Bane is somebody else's now—no longer Avgust's to keep.

"You've given him something more special. She can't take that away."

"It doesn't matter what I've given him."

"Love always matters, dear. It's not something easily forgotten," Eulalia says calmly. She never lets him doubt for long. "Whether he deserves it is another question."

Avgust's heart throbs painfully. Of course Bane deserves love. Avgust's love. Maybe Eden's too, and Avgust needs to learn to live with that.

"If he doesn't know the value of what he has lost, then maybe he never should have had it at all," Eulalia says.

Avgust hates the thought of that. No matter what they are like now, nothing can erase what they had.

"You are better off without the burden of such love."

Eulalia is right. Bane has been nothing but hostile and

unpleasant recently. But again, Avgust hasn't been friendly either. He still can't find it in himself to put the blame for everything on Bane. But he is slowly beginning to dwell on the little things Bane did to hurt him. They leave him angry, but fury is far better than anguish.

"It's perfectly fine to be angry," Eulalia states, as if having read his mind. Somehow, she always knows exactly what to say. She understands him like no one else. "You mustn't keep it in, it will kill you to harbour such strong feelings without expressing them."

"What do you suggest?"

"Unleash them," she encourages, "let the pain they've caused you become their pain, too. It's unfair to be the only one suffering."

Avgust lets her words settle, really considering them. The part of him that says this would be wrong echoes quieter and quieter until he can't hear it at all. Why shouldn't he let himself relish in others' pain? Isn't that the least he deserves after everything Bane put him through?

Eulalia would never mislead him. She has his best interest in mind. Always. Like any true friend would.

XX

The Dream

BIRDS CHIRP A DISTANT SONG, the blue sky a lively painting with white clouds and a bright sun. Endless green surrounds them, trees upon trees as far as your sight can reach and beyond. A gentle warm breeze sways its way between them, rustling the field. Avgust plays with a blade of grass in his hands while Bane lies half asleep on his chest, lazily combing through Avgust's curls. The way it is supposed to be, bodies intertwined in an embrace with no one around to see or judge. Bane lifts his head and their eyes lock, exchanging so many unspoken things. Grass, held between Avgust's fingers, touches the side of Bane's face, which rips a melodic laugh out of him. His smile seemingly brightens with the shine of the sun. They beam together. Avgust laughs with him.

Bane's lips are soft under his, willing and just right. They slot into the kiss like two lost pieces of the same whole. Avgust feels his chest expand with relief, like he can finally breathe after too long without air.

Suddenly it all dissolves into nothing. Greenery and warmth sink away as lifelessness and coldness replace them. Humidity makes it difficult to breathe, and so does the awful stench of rot and stale water. Avgust's legs are deep into a pond, up to the knee, he realises. Everything is swallowed into a black void so vast and empty, Avgust can't tell where it ends or begins.

There is something in the distance. On the edge of the water, something almost human. It's too far away for Avgust to even try to make out a face. It's hunched almost in half, covered in shadow. Dark fabric, a cloak it seems, fallen over the middle of its back hides the rest of its body. The skeleton-like frame turns Avgust's way with what looks like immense difficulty. It nearly flinches, caught off guard. He swears he can hear the cracking of bones as it readjusts itself to stand tall.

Before it gets the chance to close its robe fully, Avgust catches a glimpse of its body, wrapped in worn stained bandages that are barely holding together.

The creature stalks closer and crosses the distance with speed that doesn't quite match its slow, languid steps. Yet the waters stay undisrupted, the fabric of its cloak floating behind it. The knee-deep water almost bends to its will, letting it cross effortlessly, but a pool of green mire rots around it with each step closer. The water hugs it, keeping its now almost fully exposed lower half out of sight. The closer it gets, the stronger the rancid stench becomes.

The remains of what was once a hand moves the cloak back

The Dream

over its shoulders, covering where its bones were protruding out. The hand reaches forth. No meat is left beneath the skin, it clings directly to the bare bones underneath, and where there is no bone to hang on to, it's torn, leaving cavities all over its palm.

Avgust averts his gaze from it as it reaches to caress his face. Its fingers meet the soft flesh of his cheek, so rough they scratch his skin. The hand slides down his face, curving over his jaw and down his neck, slowly. Almost gently. Thin, bony fingers wrap around his throat with sudden force that makes Avgust choke. He clutches the thin forearm of the creature, threatening to snap it in half, but its strength persists, beyond human. His lungs feel like they will burst inside his ribcage with the lack of air, and Avgust finds himself missing the stench of the stale water. Pressure builds inside his ribcage, and it grows more painful with each slow, dragging moment.

He wakes up. Breath returns to his lungs slowly, but the burn stays even outside the nightmare. His own face stares at him from the broken mirror propped at the foot of the bed.

"What's wrong my dear?" Eulalia speaks with a soft cadence.

Avgust still only sees himself in the looking glass, but he knows she's there.

"Nothing. Just a bad dream."

She falls quiet for a moment.

"What kind of dream?"

It's strange like this. She almost doesn't feel real when Avgust can't see her.

"Let me see you, please."

His face disappears from the reflection, and she takes his place. The sight of her is very welcome, Avgust has gotten used to her presence. Her hair is slightly shorter tonight, but he can't spot any other obvious distortions on her.

"What kind of dream, Avgust?" Her voice is calm, but it's not its usual calmness. It sounds odd.

"It felt so real. I don't know what to make of it…" Avgust still can't catch his breath. The phantom feel of hands around his throat lingers.

"Good thing it was just a dream," Eulalia says, a smile lighting her face, "and you have a friend to comfort you."

Avgust nods. "Thank you." He is glad to have her. She's right, it was just a dream.

Dreams can't harm you.

XXI

Shedding Velvet

WHAT KIND OF MAN HAS the overwhelming desire to suck the life out of other beings? A man? A demon is what he is, what he has turned into. He can hardly recognise himself lately.

The bliss he felt after nearly killing that man from the tavern was only momentary. His aches returned a few days after he got back, and there is no sign of them going away any time soon.

After his troop was deemed unnecessary because of the sudden lack in numbers, he was left with the choice to either join another or retire. Bane took the question to the king with the intent to never go back to being a serving knight. Surprisingly, the king agreed with his decision not to transfer to another troop. '*You are needed here now more than ever*', the king had told him.

The welcome but sudden change left his days empty of any activities that could possibly distract him. Now, hunger consumes his mind—barely controllable hunger that gets worse around Avgust. Seeing him from across the table every day is torment. Oh, how he must hate him; Bane sees it in his eyes. But he can't reconcile with him, he can't be left alone with him, it's too risky. Yet Bane always leaves the table moments after Avgust, in hopes that there will be some trace of him left in the air. The smell of honey has entirely faded from his sheets now; that was all of Avgust that he would allow himself to have, a lingering fading scent. Giving Avgust's heart back to him was the hardest thing he had ever done, but it was necessary. Avgust is better off hurt than dead.

The story Avgust told him had left its permanent mark. Bane can't help it; his mind keeps bringing him back to it again and again and again. *A monster feeding off the blood of the living.* Isn't that exactly what he is now? But admitting that would also mean admitting what he swore wasn't true. The night in the forest, the night he felt death, yet he rose to life again. He couldn't pretend it didn't happen. He can't deny the obvious.

There is a pattern to this suffering. All these omens happening right after he lets himself act on his lustful desires is no coincidence. It's a sign. In which other way is he meant to read this if not as direct punishment? One as great as his vice.

To deny his love for Avgust now that he has been so harshly punished for it would be a pointless lie in retaliation. As if any punishment could ever render his love untrue.

He had always hoped that strong faith could outweigh his sins, yet he still had to witness himself turning into a monster.

No crueller punishment when all you want is to be good.

All his senses have heightened only to extend his torture. Every person that passes by, every living being, he can feel their blood pumping, can hear it as it rushes through their veins. And now that he is forced into this union, into sharing a room, sharing a bed, it's all he can think about.

He falls asleep usually out of pure exhaustion just from the effort of trying to ignore the sounds around him. Now he is used to the constant headache from the ever-present cacophony in his head. Even at night when the castle finally quiets down, he is left with Eden's heart pounding in his ears, making it impossible for him to even try to distract himself. It's too close: too close to ignore, too close to not inspire thoughts of the blood pumping through her body.

Sleep does not provide him relief for long. Even in dreaming, terrors plague his mind. Every time he closes his eyes he is back in the dirt, the immense weight of it crushing him, suffocating him. No matter how much time passes, it doesn't go away. He still feels the burning in his lungs and the taste of the soil.

Most nights he is completely restless; on the rare occasion in which he is lucky enough to have a dreamless sleep, it's cut short. When the first blazing rays of the sun hit his face, Bane immediately wakes up. Without a single sound, he sneaks out in search of refuge, for himself and for the safety of the people around him, which he can only find underground. He spends his days in hiding lately. The fear of hurting someone again consumes his every waking moment.

The underground cellars of the castle are often empty and

most importantly dark. It's where he has chosen to hide away until the sun falls. No one ever passes through here, meaning there are no temptations that could break his composure. The walls are cold and damp down here, with small windows that barely let in the sun. Despite the low light, he can still see fine down the wide corridor that houses empty crates and barrels.

The cellars are used as storage, but there are two holding cells that have always remained empty, as far as Bane knows. Apart from the door with the spiral staircase he comes down through, there is another door secured with a lock. He assumes the dungeons extend past it, or it perhaps contains other stored items. Bane can't be sure.

For the most part, he keeps to the guard area in front of the holding cells, having found himself an old creaky chair he probably shouldn't trust to hold his weight. He leaves a few things that he has prepared on the table next to it.

Leg bouncing up and down, he tries to sit still and not pay attention to the wood creaking under him. But even when he is perfectly still, there are falling water droplets that echo through the empty cells. He can't decide if listening to the sporadic drops would calm him down or drive him mad.

Bane is more irritable during the day. His senses easily overwhelm him, and his sanity hangs on a thread that wears thinner by the minute.

Before he accepts the nature of what he has become as permanent, he wants to at least try one last thing. He did some reading to acquaint himself with the methods of bloodletting. Bane forcefully took blood out of another, so maybe if he takes some out of himself it would improve his condition. At first, he thought that he would eventually puke it out, like everything else he had consumed recently, yet he never did. He decided that he should make a willing sacrifice of it then.

He couldn't acquire the proper tools, but he will have to make do with what he has. Even if that means using a dagger, a dirty piece of cloth and a cracked pot to perform this treatment. Reluctantly, he rolls his sleeve up.

Having targeted a vein that goes up his forearm, he wraps the piece of cloth around his arm, tightening it with his teeth. Then, when it swells, he picks up the dagger from the table and punctures the skin, expecting blood to pour out.

He presses the pot towards the cut he made, trying to force it out. A few moments pass before he is sure something has gone wrong—there is still no blood coming out at all. The edges of his cut seemed to have dried. Running his fingers through it, he realises that the wound has already closed itself. Bane takes the dagger again and makes a deeper cut, this time on his palm. He squeezes his hand into a fist, pushing his fingers inside the cut to keep it open. When he releases his fist, there is not a single drop of blood left on his fingernails.

He stares at it in disbelief, as the cut shuts itself right before his eyes. An image flashes in his mind, a memory from that night in the forest. The night he was turned into a monster. His attempt to remedy himself only confirmed his most dire theories about his condition. But he can't be surprised by something he already knew was true.

Despite being sure of his monstrous nature now, he is left with more questions than answers. Bane sinks into his chair, unsure how his body is able to function at all. There are no books on vampires, only the villagers' folklore, which is already proven wrong; he doesn't die in the sun. When Avgust told him that vampires fear the sun, Bane didn't imagine it meant they were just extremely bothered by it.

Bane wishes he could ask him more. Avgust probably has a collection of other stories he's itching to tell him most theatrically. Half of them would probably be useless and overdramatised, but Bane would still love to listen. Maybe Avgust would like to tell him as they hold each other at night, like they used to do. Bane would fall asleep half-way through the tale and its story would still be of no use, but maybe the comfort would be enough. The hunger would be gone, Bane would be able to hold his rationale, and he wouldn't be a threat. In another life, he could allow himself to love Avgust like he yearns to.

His thoughts are interrupted when a door shuts somewhere in the distance, and then a pair of footsteps begin descending down the stairs. Panic strikes him, both for the safety of the newcomers and because he isn't sure he is allowed to be down here at all. He's on his feet within seconds. Bane lodges himself in a nook between the wall and a stack of barrels, crouching behind a crate that hides him from the view of the door.

"This one's heavier than the two yesterday."

"Both combined, if ya' ask me."

Their voices get louder before the door to the stairs creaks open and two guards walk in. The stench of fresh decay fills his lungs. Through the crack in the wood of the crate Bane hides behind, he sees they are carrying a corpse wrapped in linen cloth.

"Third one this week. They are dropping like flies."

"Quiet you idiot, the king doesn't want the people to know the plague has reached the castle."

"Don't speak of it then!"

They pass right by Bane's hiding spot and stop to readjust the body that hangs off of their shoulders. Bane's breath catches in his throat, nervous sweat running down the side of his face. The men stay in place for what seems like too long, and Bane begins to feel trapped in the tiny confinement he had shoved himself in. There is the sudden taste of dirt in his mouth that he tries to swallow away, but it persists. He can feel it scratching the inside of his lungs again, as if it had never left. His desperate need to cough it out would compromise his hiding spot, so he bites his tongue in hopes the sudden pain will distract him. It doesn't.

Soon he finds himself short of breath. He reaches to find the cross that hangs over his collar, finger running the pendant along the chain back and forth in a repetitive motion.

The guards finally move past him.

Keys jingle and the locked door opens to reveal what Bane can only assume is the outer courtyard.

"It's a good thing to keep it quiet. It would only cause a ruckus."

"The maid who found him better not speak of it, then."

The voices fade and the door shuts behind the two men. Bane dislodges himself from behind the barrels and falls down on his knees. Still desperate to ease his burning lungs, he coughs. There is nothing to come out of them, yet the feeling stays. The sound of his own heart drumming in his ears and the breath he can finally release from his throat do nothing to soothe his overwhelmed mind. He looks to the small window at the top of the wall, the sun is still beaming out, but he cannot stand to stay in the dark, suffocating cellars.

Bane bolts out through the same door the men used. Despite being blinded by the bright light outside, his eyes roam around in search of a place to hide. Before his mind can even catch onto it, his feet take him towards the woods. The wind rushes past him as he runs, enjoying the breeze on his skin. When he is deep enough, he stops under a tree to collect himself.

The shadows of the trees provide a bit of relief to his aching head. His senses have calmed now, and his mind feels clearer with every breath of fresh air. He never thought to seek refuge in the forest from the sun, he never thought he would feel fine under the shade. It's secluded enough; no one usually strays this far from the road. Bane can easily spend the time until sundown here, shielded by the trees, away from people. It's quiet too, unlike the busy castle. Ease finally floods over him. He breathes in, breathes out, relieved.

The wind carries to him a faint but all too familiar scent. Slightly different, not as sweet, but still intoxicating. Bane's ears pick up a rustle somewhere in the near distance and his head snaps in its direction. It sounds like an animal, a large one. It moves slowly, perhaps wounded. Bane inches closer, cautious not to make noise and startle it, but it feels like he is moving way too fast. When he spots it, it spots him too, large antlers all bloodied, shedding velvet. The bright red antlers compliment the animal's white fur, making it stand out against the deep-green surroundings even more. What a magnificent creature.

Moving lumberly, large dark eyes look into Bane's, as the elk's heart threatens to burst out of its chest. A beat passes, and before the creature can start to run, Bane has already tackled it to the ground, teeth sinking into the tender flesh of its muscular neck. Its blood fills his mouth instantly, and he eagerly gulps the life pouring in. He remembers the taste of the man's blood and the vitality it brought him. Bane sinks his teeth deeper. He remembers the taste of Avgust's blood, spilling into his mouth, as sweet as the kiss they were sharing. The last kiss they ever shared. He breaks away from the elk's neck.

It's already dead.

Bane is standing over the body of the beast, its lifeless eyes staring back at him. He can't stand to look at it, yet he keeps looking. What does he do with it now? He can't just leave it like that, to rot, murdered for nothing.

XXII

Earth to Earth

ALL THESE PEOPLE DYING IN the same exact way is no coincidence. *'In their sleep'* is what the humans are likely thinking, and they wouldn't be too far from the truth. However, being drained of all the life you have to offer isn't exactly the same as peacefully dying in your sleep. Ursedius is feeding on them. Her brother is somewhere around, seeing as the bodies he drains are like a trail leading to him. He has grown weak, and his energy needs replenishment.

When fate last brought them together, centuries ago, Ursedius and Lemana's encounter did not end well. She is not surprised that he isn't eager to reunite. But the form he chose to present as, a wolf. A sick, dying one at that, puzzles her. Why take this shape? Why not present as himself? He was always vain; he wouldn't want to walk around like this. Not if he has the choice. Maybe he doesn't possess the strength to keep himself in a better host.

Lemana can't be sure, but there must be something wrong with his own body if he chooses to not use it. Maybe that's the purpose of the drained bodies, to serve as vessels—temporary, as their deaths might suggest. But he is likely looking for a more permanent candidate. The reason why is unclear, but it wouldn't surprise Lemana if the superficial wound she gave him the last time they met is the reason he has forsaken his own body all together.

Lemana hasn't gotten much further in her quest to retrieve what lies at the bottom of the Lover's Sorrow. She can only hope it has nothing to do with her brother's search for a vessel—that would only complicate things. Lemana knows she's slowly running out of time to figure out a way into the lake. How many more bodies would her brother need to drain before he regains his full power?

They used to always sense each other, always drawn together by the sting of their magic. But they have grown too far apart, beyond repair. His energy is weak, so weak that when Lemana catches a sting of it now, she almost can't believe it. It's so meek and faint she nearly misses it.

The energy leads her to the hill of the castle, outside the walls. She can sense him there, under the dirt. Not very deep in, his energy pulses to the surface with ease. Lemana knows that whatever is under there has been left for her to find.

With nothing but her bare hands, she begins to shed away the layers of soil. Finally, she strikes something solid and it's not at all what she expected. In the ground lies a man. Dead for at least a few days, yet in unnaturally pristine condition for having been buried. She studies his restful face, still feeling the energy pulse within him, and then life reigns over his features again. The corpse's eyes open and he sits up. It's not a heartbeat that pumps him awake; it's energy. Bones crack as his neck cranes to look into her eyes, soulless and empty. His mouth opens and a voice speaks from within his chest—Ursedius's voice, merged with that of the dead man.

"The water only recognises *me*, even when I'm not whole. Your search must conclude, look no further."

The body stills, before it falls limp again, back in its shallow grave. The once plump, fresh corpse begins to spoil rapidly. Deflating and hollowing out as the skin turns green then red, before thinning out and disappearing entirely. Moss peeks out from around the ribs, the spine fully wrapped in it, already claimed by earth. Skull and bones turn to dust from which clovers grow. Soon the remains barely resemble what they once were. It has served its purpose; this vessel may rest now.

Gaze focused on what remains of the body, Lemana stares in disbelief. Bringing her all the way out here where she can be seen is one thing, but all of that just to tell her to give up is audacious.

She gets back on her feet, fists clenching, white-knuckled. Exhaling in annoyance, she kicks a pile of dug-out dirt back into the grave. They haven't spoken in over seven centuries and *this* is the first she hears of him? Her chest fills with spiteful anger. If he's the only one who can go into the lake and come out, so be it. She will find him and drag him to the water herself if she has to.

Lemana doesn't know what possesses her, but she takes her

brother's eye out of her small bag. She looks at it with all her built-up rage, yet still cannot help the feeling of comfort that it brings her as it sits gently in the palm of her hand. Decades of conflicting emotions swirl within her.

"How dare you?" she asks the eye. "How dare you send me messages telling me to give up, how dare you speak to me at all after what you did?"

Huffs of frustration leave her lips as she tries to calm herself and not hurl the eye as far as she can throw it. The feeling subsides slowly, the more she forces herself to breathe. The eye in her hand helps to calm her, despite herself.

Something moves in her peripheral vision and her time to be angry is cut short; now she's on edge. A person approaches her, and Lemana feels her chest heave out in relief at the familiar face.

"Oh, it's you." Lemana breathes out.

The woman from the tavern approaches, cautiously looking around.

"Who were you speaking to?" Eden asks.

Her hair is chopped short, and she tucks a strand behind her ear when she notices Lemana looking. She thinks this hair suits her better, despite the uneven cut of it.

"I was thinking out loud is all," Lemana dismisses quickly. "No one around here to speak to."

"You said you have no interest in the castle," Eden says under a furrowed brow, one eye squinted in distrust.

Lemana eyes her cautiously but says nothing. Eden, studying her up and down, ends up fixated on the ground. For a moment, Lemana's heart skips at the thought of her noticing the grassy carcass dug into the shallow hole in the earth.

"What are you doing here?" she speaks again, and Lemana tries to figure out if it's an accusation, if she has seen the dead man.

"I was looking for someone."

"Someone from the castle?"

"Something like that," Lemana says. If you could count a reanimated corpse with a message as *someone*.

"Someone I would know?"

"Would you know *anyone* from the castle?" Lemana raises a brow, sceptical yet intrigued.

"I live here." Eden's whole demeanour changes, as if she just let a secret slip. She clears her throat nervously.

"Oh, really?"

Of course, the golden mane would be connected to the castle, why else would Ursedius bring Lemana here? She tries to hide the sudden pleased gleam in her eyes. An opportunity is presenting itself, and she must find a way to benefit from such a happy coincidence.

If, according to the vision, Ursedius is interested in the golden mane for some unknown reason, then Lemana must dangle her in front of him like meat to a wolf. She should shape her into a vessel too irresistible to pass on, vulnerable and ready to be claimed. Eden's wary nature wouldn't make her an easy target, but Lemana is up for a challenge if it means stopping her brother. Ursedius has chosen her, so his target is already set on her back. It wouldn't be too hard to infiltrate her mind, lower her defences to set the trap and wait for Ursedius to do the rest. He won't be able to resist.

Lemana's been quiet for far too long, she can feel it in Eden's steady, analytical gaze. She doesn't know she just gave Lemana the solution to all her problems.

"How does a member of the court find herself alone out here? Don't you have guards?"

"What do you think? They would never let me out here willingly."

"Never alone, yet it must get so lonely living in such a big castle. If you ever find yourself in need of company…" Lemana says, taking a step closer to Eden who lets her.

She shakes her head. "That can't happen. I'm not even supposed to be here now."

"Oh, poor thing; that's just cruel. Why wouldn't they let you roam free? What's the worst that could happen?" Lemana's voice is slow and sultry, the same one she uses to make the men she hunts bend to her will before she even needs to force them to obey. Eden, however, seems to grow more reserved at her words. Lemana tries a change of tone.

"They are wise to be suspicious of you, seeing as you've sneaked out already." Lemana blinks slowly up at her, using every trick she knows as a means to disarm Eden. This might be the first human who hasn't been quick to fall for her charm.

"I should be going back to my chambers, before they notice I'm gone," Eden says. "So this is goodbye."

"Wait!" Lemana grabs her wrist when Eden turns to leave, her fingers lingering a bit longer than they should, until she has Eden's full attention. Lemana doesn't think she can do this with charm alone. She tugs at Eden's mind ever so slightly, just to get her in a more agreeable mood.

"I was wondering if you could do something for me."

"What is it you want?" Eden's tone is cautious, but not as suspicious as before.

"I want you to let me in. Can you do that?" Lemana blinks innocently.

"'In' as in *inside?* Inside the castle?"

"Yes, inside."

Lemana doesn't elaborate. Eden doesn't need to know what permission she's being asked to grant. After all, Lemana can't get in her head without consent, but she can without her knowledge.

"I suppose I can," she says almost immediately, with Lemana's gentle, disarming nudge at her mind. "Well, one way past the inner wall is here." Eden motions to the side entrance they're standing in front of. "And there's also the stables, but you would have to bribe the stable boy and he might not even be alone." Eden thinks for a bit before continuing, "Of course, the main entrance is an option, but the guards won't let you through. As for the castle itself, given you can't enter through the central door either, I think the windows are your best bet. That's how I come and go, now that I'm not allowed to leave, but it's more convenient for going out then in." Grimacing with a shrug, Eden says, "There's also the sewage, but I definitely discourage you from going through there."

When Eden's instructions come to an end, she looks at Lemana in confusion, like she hadn't realised she was saying any of it until she was done.

"And I have your permission to go inside?"

Eden says confidently, "What damage could you do?"

XXIII

Intrusion

MUCH LIKE HERSELF, EDEN'S FINGERS had numbed. They couldn't stand a chance against the constant poking of the needle. Her days of reciting and embroidering are threading like beads, one after the other, with so little difference between them that they have started to blur into one. The one time she broke out of the routine was yesterday when she saw Lemana lurking around the castle from her bedroom window. Eden still isn't sure she doesn't pose a threat. Apart from that, quiet days with Nurse Vila turn into silent nights with Bane. Over and over and over again. She can't see the end of it.

"Oh, child, don't look so glum."

Eden can't find it in herself to lift her eyes and meet Nurse Vila's. She doesn't feel like it matters anyway.

"What do you say we rejoin the court today?"

"I'm not allowed." Eden's voice comes out monotone. She doesn't even want to let herself entertain the idea that it could be possible.

"I can't stand to look at you so lifeless. You could use some company." The nurse smiles warmly. "I'm sure the ladies would love to have you back. Now more than ever."

"Wouldn't Father mind?"

"I'm sure he would appreciate more feminine influence on you anyhow." The nurse rises to her feet and urges Eden to do the same. "Come on now, let's go."

It's only when Eden is standing in front of the door to the great chamber that she realises that she really is going to rejoin the ladies. She thought that inevitably something would interfere, something would stop her from getting this little bit of freedom, but now she stands moments away from it.

The door opens tortuously slow and with an agonising creak. All conversation halts. Three heads lift to look at her. The silence after her arrival is so loud, one could hear a pin drop, and something tells her the ladies aren't exactly *thrilled* about her presence. Of course, it might also be the surprise of seeing her again so unexpectedly. But if she is to trust Nurse Vila's words, Eden must look dreadful, which on its own is something to earn a welcome like this one.

"Good morning, Your Highness." Georgiana dares to speak first, meeting Eden's eyes. The rest of the ladies give her a polite nod in greeting, which Eden returns. Another silence stretches while she takes her place in the empty chair reserved for her.

"How have you been?" Lady Roza asks from the chair

next to her.

"The same."

Truthfully, she hasn't been the same since she was caught. Lonely and locked away like a prisoner in your own home affects one's mind. But she can't tell them any of that.

One chair stands empty in the corner of the great hall. Only Lady Roza, Lady Georgiana and Lady Irena are present today.

"Where's Lady Maya?"

The silence becomes louder. The other ladies look at each other with confusion and sadness.

"Did nobody tell you?"

Eden's heart sinks before she even hears the news.

"Lady Maya passed away in her sleep two nights ago."

Shocked, Eden doesn't react. Sorrow overwhelms her. Why had no one told her? Are they really so adamant about her isolation that she isn't allowed to know of her friend's *death*? Her father has always been cold, but she never knew he was so unfeeling.

Nurse Vila leaves the room with an empathetic smile on her face. She wants them to have a moment between themselves.

"We missed you terribly!" Lady Roza jumps to her feet and goes to wrap Eden in a sudden hug. Eden can't quite tell if it's simple politeness, or it's prompted by their shared grief. Nevertheless, it feels nice to be embraced.

"Is it true? What they say about you being caught participating in duels?" she is quick to ask, clearly not wanting to linger on the topic of death.

Despite what her father might want, Eden is not ashamed.

She had been better than most men she fought despite her womanly stature, which speaks to her skill—skill she acquired over time, after losing more tournaments than she can count.

"It's true." Eden's eyes dart to Georgiana in search of judgement. She finds none.

"You fought as a knight?" Roza asks.

"A knight without title, yes."

Three pairs of wide eyes look at her with bewildered curiosity.

"So, you duelled against real knights?" Georgiana asks calmly, but there's a smidge of excitement in her wide brown eyes.

"Sometimes; mostly retired soldiers and...such." Eden almost lets herself be excited, she hasn't really spoken to anyone in so long. But some of the looks her story gains her are disheartening. Better stop before she is met with more aversion to what she wants to say.

"I can't imagine why you would want to; those swords are far heavier than they ought to be," Lady Irena says finally. She hasn't said a word since Eden has entered the room. "And I could never stand to get so muddy."

Eden's lip quirks up. "My boots are still caked in mud that I cannot scrub out." She can't help but think fondly of any reminders left from her days as a *knight*.

"We didn't want to believe the gossip, but it seemed too much like something you would do." Georgiana shakes her head, smiling.

A laugh tears itself out of Eden's chest, hearty and genuine. She hasn't laughed in a while.

"Eden, I must say." Lady Roza stretches out a hand to her knee to get her attention. "Your wedding dress was truly beautiful. I've never seen one of such detail and craft." Eden politely accepts her compliment with a nod. She can't recall a single thing about said dress, except how extremely confining it was.

"What does your husband have to say about you fighting?"

"He, uh..." Eden scrambles to find a believable lie. Her and Bane rarely speak, let alone on topics that matter. "He hasn't said anything about it."

"That's good." Lady Roza sighs with a tiny smile. "I imagine most men wouldn't be too pleased with a woman fighting. But it doesn't seem in Konstantin's nature to be a harsh husband."

"I suppose not," Eden says dumbly.

"So, how are you settling as a wife now?" Lady Irena looks up from her embroidery loop. "I imagine it's a welcome change."

"Let us hope all of us can be happily married soon, too," Roza says, they all hum in agreement. Yet Eden cannot bring herself to wish such a fate upon her friends.

"Lady Roza's courting attempts have found the most success of us all; I suppose she ought to be the first to get wed," Irena says, and Eden swears she can sense judgement in her words.

"Courting? Who?" Eden asks. She might have missed more than she thought during her absence from the court.

"Oh please Eden, don't pretend you don't know." Her cheeks rouge with bashfulness. "You just want to make me say it." Lady Roza finally notices the confusion on Eden's face and clears her throat. "Well, with the prince of course. Avgust."

Lady Roza is of noble and pristine lineage, all things that Eden's father values, and it's not beneath him to arrange a loveless union for his children as she has come to find. If Roza is lucky enough and her intentions reach the king's ears, she might get the wedding she dreams of.

"Perhaps I should call on him today." Lady Roza's suggestion is met with nods and hums of approval.

"I think he ought to be the one calling on *you*," Irena rebukes.

"If I stand around waiting, Lady Irena, this marriage will never happen."

They continue to bicker, but Eden has no interest in keeping up with it. She marvels at Georgiana's embroidery. One might think that her and Eden's shared disinterest in the craft would leave her with skills no better than Eden's, and yet while Eden's hoop is a mess, Georgiana's is nearly perfect.

"Let's ask Princess Eden her opinion." Roza's voice startles her.

"I'm sorry?" Eden has lost the thread of their conversation.

"If I should call on the prince or wait for him to call on me. He is your brother after all, you must know what would make a better impression."

"Well, if he would like you calling on him, I cannot know. It's not something that we have discussed, but from what I've seen, my brother is very *obvious* and bold in showing his affections." She clears her throat, she's painting them a clearer picture than she wished to. "When he has someone he is interested in, he isn't shy to let them know."

"I was the first and only to dance with him on his birthday," Lady Roza whispers under her breath, her eyes lighting up. This isn't what Eden had alluded to, but she understands the confusion. Roza hasn't seen the real extent of Avgust's advances; she doesn't know how he speaks of Bane. Of course, she would think that saving a dance is some grand gesture of affection.

"But he has never declared interest in anyone before? When have you seen him do so to know this about him?" Of course, Georgiana is the one to notice Eden's slip up. "You must know something that we don't."

"He is interested in someone?" Lady Roza's eyes widen. "Someone sitting in this room perhaps?"

"Oh, I can't spill his secrets so carelessly." Eden is quick to deny but Lady Roza has already decided the answer anyway.

Silence falls after that, everyone occupied with their work. Eden holds her embroidery hoop in one hand and threads the needle through the fabric with a fine motion. Fingers quick and skilled.

"You've improved your craft in your time away." Lady Georgiana speaks next to her, voice close, but echoing.

She lifts her head and is greeted by the apathetic faces of her court. Only there's four of them. Lemana sits politely in one chair, an embroidery hoop lying untouched in her lap as her sharp eyes study Eden intently. She's wearing a white undergarment like a dress, like she always does.

"How are you here?" Eden hears herself ask. None of the other ladies seem to notice the newcomer or hear her speak at all.

"Isn't it obvious?" Lemana shrugs, then brings her attention to the embroidery, picking it up in one hand and the needle in the other. Eden watches as she begins to poke around the threads already made, seemingly without rhyme or reason. It's like she's trying to move some around and remove others completely. Eden thinks that the resistance of the threads will make her realise that this is wrong, but Lemana precedes unfazed. Thread after thread breaks under her needle, as if torn with a blade, others lie loosened in large loops that stick out in chaos.

'*This isn't how you do it*', Eden thinks, but it must've slipped out of her lips because Lemana lifts her head to look at her.

"I beg your pardon?"

"The embroidery." She points to the ring in Lemana's hands that looks entirely ruined, colourful threats hanging detached and tangled. There used to be a finished picture on the piece of cloth before Lemana got to it. Now what's left of it resembles truly nothing—a mess if anything.

"There isn't only one way to do it." Lemana cocks her head. "Don't worry about it, I know what I'm doing."

Lemana stabs her needle one last time into the messy tangle of thread.

XXIV

Ashes to Ashes

UPON OPENING HER EYES, EDEN realises she isn't with the court anymore. She was just talking to Lemana, yet somehow, she is back in her room. Come to think of it, she doesn't remember how she ended up in bed. Half of last night is missing when she tries to retrace her steps, and despite supposedly sleeping through it, Eden has never felt more exhausted in her life.

As she gets ready for the day the only thought left in her head is of Lemana. Like a residual mirage of the dream, like she's still in her mind somehow. They didn't even finish talking, according to Eden's memory. There's an itch to go out and find her, but Eden's presence is expected in the library for her daily chores. She will be assigned a new book of verses today, which is something she isn't looking forward to, but is preferable to reciting them over and over again until her throat is dry.

Nurse Vila welcomes her in with a warm smile which Eden struggles to return.

Memorising verses never fails to make her doze off, even on the uncomfortable wooden chair she usually occupies. Eden tries her best to stay awake or at least to pretend that she is, gripping the book and keeping her head from tilting too low.

Despite her efforts, Eden's eyes flutter closed, and she drops the book. The loud thud wakes her back up.

"Are you alright dear?" The nurse asks, alert from the sudden sound of the book hitting the stone floor. Eden sees an opportunity.

"Oh, my head is spinning. I slept poorly last night; I think it would be wise to go lie down." She places a hand on her forehead and leans over the arm rest of the chair. "Only if you wouldn't mind halting our lesson."

"Well, yes of course, go!" The nurse ushers her out of the room. "I'll fetch the medic."

"No!" Eden says quickly, "I wouldn't want anyone fussing over me, it might just make the headache worse."

When she goes out of the room her stationed guard meets her to be escorted to her quarters. Eden stumbles as she walks, requiring the occasional assistance of the guard to keep her balance.

"Make sure to not let in any visitors, please," she says as she retreats into her room, and as soon as the door shuts, she drops the act. Quick in shedding off her slipper shoes, Eden slips into the familiar well-worn pair of boots, still covered in mud from her last fight. She grabs her heavy cloak out of the dresser and drapes it over her shoulders.

The window, although not her preferred means of exit, has become the only one. Eden sits on the windowsill before swinging a leg over the ledge and grabs onto it as she begins descending down the wall. The uneven stones that make up the castle provide great ridges for her to grip, making her forearms burn. When her feet meet the ground, the first thing she does is make sure no one saw her. She bolts to the side entrance into the outer-wall yard. A hood covers her head as she makes her way through the crowd of people, passing all the servants going in and out.

She is headed to Starosel, her debt to Marten keeps her up at night. Her confinement has kept her from doing right by him for far too long. Eden knows the walk is long, but it goes by rather quickly. When she makes it to the edge of the treeline, it's like no time has passed at all. She appreciates every minute she gets to spend outside the castle now, but the songs of the birds start to sound strange and distorted. Maybe she should have stayed home.

Eden finds herself all alone. There's something in her gut that tells her she shouldn't be here.

She blinks awake slowly. It's night and she's still in her room. Bane isn't here yet.

***

Avgust didn't show up at dinner tonight, she worries something might have happened. Eden finally brings up the courage to go visit him again. Ear to the door, she listens for any voices on the other side and only after she hears nothing does she dare knock. She's nervous he might not even answer, but the door swings open not long after.

"Eden!" Avgust greets her warmly with a smile. "Please, do come in."

She pretends it doesn't surprise her and takes a cautious step into his room. It looks just like it did the last time she was here—neat and clean.

"How have you been? I haven't seen you in a while," Avgust asks casually.

Eden sighs. "They're making me learn verses and recite them. When I'm not forced to embroider, that is."

"Really! And you're not enjoying it?" he asks earnestly, "It sounds like fun."

"Of course you think so." Eden goes to sit on the bed.

"If it's any consolation, all they make me do is listen about politics. But you probably find that as a better alternative to your chores."

"Anything is better." Eden pauses, her fingers smoothing over the crinkled bed cover just to have something to do with her hands.

"May I be frank?" Avgust asks suddenly. "You haven't come in so long I thought you might be angry with me."

"Angry with *you*?" Eden blinks rapidly. "You have way more reason to be angry with *me*, if anything."

"Me?"

"You know...in light of recent events." Her eyes are back on the bed, following the motion of her hand that's still fixing the wrinkles of the bedding.

"No, of course not." For a split second, something flashes

in his eyes, like a dull sadness he doesn't allow himself to feel, but he looks away and it's gone. "I'm way past all of that; I could never hold a grudge against you."

"I'm glad to hear," she says, "but if you need to talk about anything, even if it's to badmouth me, I'll listen."

Avgust smiles softly. "Thank you."

The room shifts slightly and the space morphs like a memory. Avgust sits still, smiling, but not saying anything. He looks at Eden like he's seeing past her.

"Who is that?" Another voice breaks the silence. Eden turns to find Lemana standing behind her, and confusion swirls within Eden's mind. When she turns back to Avgust, he is gone, the whole room is. It's like she is floating in empty space.

"My brother," Eden answers before she can ask any questions about Lemana's presence.

"I see. I too had a brother, long ago." Her solemn look tells Eden enough to know not to ask. "Tell me more."

"I don't know what I would do without him. I feel like he is the only person in the world that truly wants to listen to me and now that we don't talk much..." she chokes on her own words, "it feels like I'm missing a part of myself."

"And..."

The words come spilling out of her mouth like flowing water, like she has no control over what comes out.

"I love him, of course but he isn't without his faults. Everything is handed to him, his life has been sorted out for him from the moment he was born, and yet he still doesn't want anything of what he is given. Not to mention how impatient he is, how incredibly vain, and how he always believes in the worst possible outcome before he even stops to think." Eden clamps her mouth shut. She does think all of this, deep down, but she would never say it out loud, let alone to someone she has spoken to only a handful of times. Eden regrets having said any of this, she isn't even sure why she is spilling Avgust's worst qualities so carelessly.

Lemana says nothing, like she knows Eden will continue talking even without wanting to.

"He thinks I took his friend away from him, in a way he can never have for himself. He probably hates me for it. I think he is distant now because he blames me. I would blame myself too in his place. I blame myself now."

"Interesting." Lemana makes a remark under her breath, she seems more annoyed than anything by what she has heard. Eden falls quiet for a moment, desperately praying that this is all she has to say. But she knows it isn't, and Lemana knows it too.

"Is that everything?" Lemana prompts Eden to speak. It's in such a way that feels like she is the one who decides if Eden will or not.

"He has been strange recently; he doesn't speak to anyone anymore, only to himself it seems. I worry about him, but there isn't much I can do when I'm locked away for most of the day."

"He speaks to himself?" Lemana seems amused, like that's the first useful thing Eden has said so far.

"Yes, I've heard him. I haven't told anyone, of course. I am afraid they might see him unfit to rule if word gets out. He is not really favoured as it is, imagine if they found this out, too. I'm trying to protect him, but he is starting to scare me."

Lemana nods, as if she already knew all of this. As if Eden is simply confirming something.

"Good." Lemana barely lifts up a hand to stop the next thing Eden might blurt out. She falls quiet finally. "That's enough, you can rest now."

Eden snaps up in her bed. She takes in the surroundings, unsure if they're even real. She's in her room, and it's dark. She pinches her wrist. One single candle faintly lights up the corner of the room behind Bane's head. He is reading some book or writing in it, Eden can't quite tell. Despite the candle right next to him, it's too measly to provide any actual light. It's a miracle he is able to see anything at all.

"Are you alright? You are sweating," he asks, looking at her with concern. She didn't even notice he had turned to her.

"Yes I am," she reassures, more for herself than anything, "I just had a really vivid dream...that's all."

"I could tell; you were talking." He turns back to his book and traces the page with a finger.

Eden feels a bead of sweat trickle down the side of her face.

"What was I saying?" she asks cautiously.

"I don't know, mostly nonsense from what I could make out."

It calms her, though not by much. She swallows thickly, her throat dry and scratchy.

"Why are you still awake?" Eden asks as she sits further back on the bed, leaning on the wall.

Bane looks at her strangely, "It's barely past sundown. You are the one that excused yourself from dinner and went to bed early."

"Didn't I go speak with Avgust?"

"How could I know?" Bane snaps, his approachable demeanour gone in seconds, "I have no interest in what he does with his time."

Eden doesn't respond, but she itches to point out how blatant of a lie that is. She turns on her side, away from the light, and closes her eyes again. Just as she's about to fall asleep, sharp light hits her face, peeking through her shut eyelids. Averting her head away, she realises she isn't lying on the soft bedding or even lying at all. Eden opens her eyes to be greeted by the morning sun shining on her face. Her feet are bare on the still-wet, dewy grass of the inner court's yard. Thankfully it's just past sunrise, most of the castle has not yet awakened, and the handful of people that happen to pass nearby don't try to engage with her, only throwing confused looks her way in passing. If they did try to speak to her, she wouldn't know what to tell them, she has as much idea why she is here as they do.

Walking in her sleep has never been a problem before, as far as she is aware. She has to admit it scares her, feeling so unaware of what has happened or how she got out here. Nobody stopped her, which is somehow worse. The stone of the castle floors is cold as she starts to head back to her chambers.

Eden takes a step forward to be met with the smell of polished wood. Her eyes can't focus on the object in front of her, she is standing too close. Backing away she realises where she is—this is Avgust's door. She looks around, there is no one else in the corridor with her. The sun is setting outside the window already, yet she has no recollection of the day passing nor if it's still the same day. If she were to ask, most would look at her as if she had lost her mind. And maybe she has. But maybe Avgust wouldn't. She decides to knock on his door, but there is no answer, which has become quite common these days. The door creaks open under her fist when she tries knocking again.

Cautiously stepping in, she finds no sign of her brother. Everything is the same as the last time she was here, except the mirror now stands almost flush with the frame of the bed. Half of it rests against the bed frame and the rest cracked. She catches a glimpse of herself—half her chopped hair falls out of her snood, her dress is not put on properly and she seems to have put on only one of her shoes. The cracks in the mirror aren't the biggest issue in her appearance.

She shuffles out of the room, turning towards her chambers, but in the blink of an eye she is already in the dining hall, fully dressed and having already finished her food, yet she doesn't remember getting there. She pinches herself under the table, and the expected but still sudden pain causes her to close her eyes.

Upon opening them again, she isn't in the hall anymore. She finds herself back in the corridor of the west wing, not too far away from Avgust's door again. The chill night air from the wide-open windows brushes her skin under the thin fabric of her nightdress. Every shadow in the ill-lit, endless corridor seems unnatural and animated. Pinching her arm does nothing to confirm or deny if she is asleep or not. Nothing around her can help her make out the truth.

Fear settles in the pit of her stomach. She isn't even sure if she is awake at all. The moon is still high in the night sky and almost all candles are out, and an idea comes to mind. Eden dislodges one candle out of its metal holder on the wall and scratches her initial into the wax with a fingernail. She puts it back in place and hopes next time she finds herself unable to differentiate sleep from reality, she can use it as a marker. Her bare feet pad softly through the empty corridors that feel even larger in the dead of night as she makes her way back to her bedroom.

Next time she awakes, she's in the middle of the hallway just past the kitchens. She is dressed properly this time, but she's left just as disoriented as all the times before. Her memory lapses don't give any clues as to what she is doing there, or if it's even real. The unfamiliar giant painting on the wall suggests it's probably a dream, but the more she looks at it the more she starts to doubt that it hadn't always been there. She remembers the clue she had left for herself, and she's suddenly running towards the other side of the castle and up the stairs until she reaches Avgust's door. When grabbing the candle out of the holster, she is almost entirely convinced that the mark won't be there. Yet it is. Her scratched initials stare back at her from where she etched them into the wax. She lets out a sigh of relief.

"What are you doing?" a familiar voice asks.

When she turns, Lemana is there, just a few paces behind. Eden looks down to her hands where Lemana's eyes are focused. She's still holding the candle.

"I had to see something," she mumbles, before putting the candle back in its place.

"Is everything as it should be?"

Eden ignores her question to ask a more relevant one, "How did you manage to get in here?"

"Through the kitchens." Lemana tilts her head, then whispers, "Like you taught me."

"I did, didn't I...?" It's not like she doesn't remember, but Eden isn't sure if it happened at all. "Why are you here?"

Eden has stopped questioning how exactly Lemana makes it into the castle, but she cannot understand why she comes so often.

"I needed to check on you."

"Check on me?" Eden asks, "Why, is there something I should worry about?"

"No." She shrugs it off casually. Lemana feels a lot more animated than she is usually. Eden starts to doubt the security that the candle has provided her. "Not yet."

Eden's brows scrunch. Before she can begin to worry about whatever that means, she hears steps in the distance. Guards? Or worse—her father. Not only is she not where she is supposed to be, but she's with someone who isn't supposed to be in the castle. Her mind starts working, looking for a way out. They are at a dead end, and the only possible escape is through the window or to barge into Avgust's room. Eden chooses the latter. She tries to turn the handle, but the door is locked. Panic quickly overtakes her as she desperately looks around, as if a way to escape would appear out of thin air. Then she sees it, a space between the walls, just around the corner further down the corridor. Without hesitation, she grabs Lemana's hand and leads the two of them into the cavity.

As Eden is trying to hold her breath, Lemana bursts into laughter at seemingly nothing.

"Why are you laughing?" Eden whisper-yells. Her nerves

spike, as she hopes the guards don't hear. "Shh!"

Trying to get out words, Lemana fails as her laugh persists.

"Why does the royal castle have holes in its walls?" she finally manages to say but still can't contain her giggles.

"What?" Eden's face scrunches in confusion. "Be quiet, they will find us!" Eden's hand flies up over Lemana's mouth before she can even think about it. "Would you stop?"

Their eyes lock and Eden's heart thrums one heavy beat. She releases her, and Lemana actually falls silent.

"Apologies," she says seriously, her usual demeanour returning.

"Do you not understand the severity of all this? You can't be here," Eden scolds, "And me, I shouldn't be here either!"

Lemana nods. "Oh, I completely understand."

Eden can tell she tries to remain serious, but she still finds it amusing. It's sort of surreal, seeing her laugh. Eden can't recall even seeing her smile.

Footsteps approach their hiding place, louder and louder the closer they get. Eden holds her breath before her eyes snap open and she finds herself in bed.

***

Eden sets off on her way to settle some matters she's been putting aside. The guards think she's sick again, and nurse Vila has been getting increasingly worried about her health with the amount of times Eden has feigned sickness, but that's a problem she will worry about later. After escaping through the window, Eden chooses not to take the village road and instead decides to pass through the woods, in hopes to avoid anyone from the castle who might recognise her.

"Where are you going?" Lemana pops up as if summoned, her long hair a mess, almost like she had run here.

Eden doesn't even pretend to be surprised by her arrival and instead shrugs.

"To the village, attending to some matters."

"I'll come with you," Lemana rushes to say, but she seems taken aback, "I need to speak with you."

"Oh? Go ahead."

"No, not here."

They're not in the village yet, but close enough for Eden to understand why Lemana would prefer to wait until they're alone. It takes them just a few more minutes of walking to reach the outskirts of Starosel. Even from here, you can hear life bustling. Eden hasn't had the chance to visit during the day and it's a pleasant surprise how different it is.

There was always a cozy feeling in the evenings when the houses still had a light or two on, while the shops were still closing. However, when night settled the streets were almost eerily empty, except for those gathered around the rink.

Daytime is like another realm. Eden has only seen this many people at once at court balls or special gatherings, but this seems to be just a normal day for the villagers.

Lemana looks wary being around this big of a crowd, but Eden makes sure to stick by her as they go towards the village centre. They reach the market, where merchants shout loudly about the low prices on their produce and advertise their services. Wooden tables displaying all kinds of goods run so far along the street Eden can't see where they end. Some are covered by a tent, while others are out in the sun. Shoppers move along the street, packed tightly against each other. Eden takes Lemana's hand and pushes through the people.

"Where are we going?" Lemana asks, and Eden isn't exactly sure. She knows Marten works at the market, but she doesn't even know what he sells. They traverse past so many interesting stands. Eden even catches Lemana looking curiously at the goods they sell more than once. Finally, an auburn head pokes out through the crowd. Eden starts shoving her way through with more determination, until they're standing face to face with Marten.

"G'day, what can I help you with?" he asks cheerfully, motioning towards the trinkets displayed on his table. Eden drops Lemana's hand and leans over to speak directly to Marten.

"I was sent by the Lord of Steel to repay a debt that he owes you." She clears her throat. "I'm his cousin."

Marten's face lights up. Relief washes over him.

"I really thought I'd never hear that name again! I honestly thought he was dead."

"No, no he is in perfect health. Just…busy." Eden can feel Lemana's eyes poking holes at the side of her face, but she does her best to ignore her and keep up the lie.

"Here." Eden hands him the sack of coins she had prepared. "Before anyone gets the chance to rob me."

"Wow!" He inspects the coin bag, opens it to peer inside and turns to look at Eden like she's grown a second head. "How much exactly did your cousin say he owes me?"

"He said he owes you quite a lot. Said you've done a lot for him. And for being his friend and all."

"I see. So, folks were right, he is some rich lord. I know this much money couldn't possibly have come from those tournaments."

"Tournaments?" Eden feigns innocent cluelessness, blinking dumbly.

Marten looks at the two of them like he just got a brilliant idea.

"Say, are you from around here?"

"No, we are from...the north. Very north, it's our first time here. We've never even stepped foot in this village before," Eden lies.

"Well in that case..." A large smile stretches across his face. "Would you two care for a tour around our sights?"

"Ah, well, we are in a bit of a rush."

"It will be only the real gems of Starosel. And for really cheap, I promise!"

Eden finds herself more than undeniably curious.

"Alright then."

"You won't regret it!" he assures them as he starts collecting his merchandise from the stand, carefully placing it in his large bag, "Oh, I'm Marten by the way." He stretches out a hand to them and Eden takes it.

"Eden," she says. It's not known as the name of the princess, so she doesn't fear getting recognised. "This is my friend, Lemana." Lemana shakes his hand, as if not entirely sure why it was offered in the first place.

Their tour begins and they make their way through large

streets and tight alleys. They have almost reached the outskirts of the village, and they still have not gotten to their first destination.

"Are we close?" Eden finds herself asking impatiently.

"Oh, yes," Marten says, "nearly there!"

"Where are we going?"

"Our first stop is a marvel of architecture." He waves his hands in the air. "The peak of human mind and imagination."

Soon they stop in front of an old wooden shack that barely holds itself together. It's a miracle that the people coming in and out are not disrupting the structure of it or worried it might collapse on their heads. Marten lifts the fabric draped over the entrance and gestures for them to follow him in.

Spacious tables covered with all kinds of trinkets—mostly junk—span the shop. Many shiny things are put on display, some metal, some wooden, some crystal. There aren't any two items that are the same, each one special in its own way.

To Eden's surprise, Lemana seems bewitched by the different trinkets, her eyes wide and glistening with interest. A particular item holds her attention, an amulet of some sort. A small crystal rests in the centre of a silver ornament that tightly hugs it. The rays of light that manage to peek through the windows of the shop, reflecting on the gem, are probably what drew Lemana in to begin with. The whole craftsmanship of the amulet is truly impressive, almost unbelievable to think someone made this with their two hands. Yet Eden can't help but be more captivated by Lemana's child-like interest in the trinket. Looking at her now, she seems more human somehow.

When she realises that she is being watched Lemana stiffens

again, pretending she was never intrigued in the first place, like it is beneath her, and continues browsing further into the shop away from Eden.

"Nicu, what do you have for me today?" Marten asks, his cheerful smile even wider. A tall woman, large in stature, sits behind the counter. Her hair is chopped short, much like Eden's, only neater and more intentional. Her face is serious, but not unkind.

"Depends, are you going to pay me?" the burly woman says, her voice rough. She has a deep scar across her lip.

"You are in luck today." Marten brings out his money pouch and holds it high for the woman to see. The coins jingle inside as it droops heavily.

"Impossible. That's a rarer sight than a pig with wings," the woman says monotonously, yet with amusement. "In that case, I saved this just for you, I thought you'd appreciate it."

She places a small circular item on the table, a rusted copper colour. Marten picks it up carefully. The top opens like a lid—it's a compass. He turns it in his hands, not taking his eyes off it, looking more and more intrigued.

"It's broken," Eden can't help but point out.

"I was counting on that." Marten seems to perk up even more at that. "I pick up junk and fix it up. That's what I sell at my market stand. How much?"

"Seven silver coins."

"Come on, Nicu, I do wish to have some money left by the end of the day."

"For you, I can do five."

"That's what I like to hear!"

He takes the compass and wraps it carefully in an old piece of cloth before putting it in his bag. The woman, Nicu, also hands him a bunch of rusty nails and tacks all curved and bent like they were used before. Marten happily stores them away.

"Thank you, Nicu, see you next week!"

They make their way to the door and take a small street to the right of the building, where other small shops are squished next to each other.

"Your friend seems...quiet," Marten says carefully, but Eden can tell that isn't quite the word he was looking for. "Where did you guys meet?"

"A tavern," Lemana says before Eden can sprout out a lie.

"A tavern? You two don't seem like the type."

"Eden is the type; I was simply passing by."

"Why didn't you say sooner." Marten perks up, turning to Eden. "I know just the place to end our tour, but before that we have one more stop to visit."

As they walk down the streets Eden can't help but stare at all the people around, everyone focused on their own thing, doing their tasks. It all seems so mundane and ordinary, but very peaceful and fulfilling. There is purpose in the simple lives they lead.

The smell of raw meat and blood hits her nose as they reach the butchery, their second stop. It is soon after that Eden realises that this isn't a tour at all, and Marten is just taking them along for the tasks he has for the day. She finds she doesn't mind. It feels like an authentic peek into the daily lives of normal people who get to do normal things.

A girl their age steps out the butchery holding a bucket of

blood with both hands. She doesn't seem to struggle, but she almost spills it when Marten rushes to take it out of her hands.

"Allow me," he says chivalrously, and she gives up the bucket into his hands. Upon realising who she gave it to, a particular light reaches her eyes.

"I would have let it spill on you, if I had known it was you, Marten."

He doesn't really react apart from a gentle shove at her with his elbow.

"Where do you need to put this?"

"Out back behind the shop."

Marten takes a tiny alley between the buildings and leaves the three of them alone to go dispose of the blood.

"Must take a strong stomach to deal with this much blood and meat all day," Eden says playfully. The girl turns away from where she had been watching Marten retreat into the alley.

When she faces them, the first thing Eden notices are her dark, thick eyebrows that overpower every other feature on her face. Her blond hair, which reminds her of Avgust's in colour except longer and straighter, is kept back by a kerchief. She is tall–visibly taller than Marten, but not that much taller than Eden.

"You don't know the half of it." Her deep brown eyes are as warm and inviting as her smile. "Friends of Marten's?"

"Something like that," Eden says.

"I've never seen you two around before." The girl leans against the stone wall of the butcher shop, arms over her chest. "I'm Evelie."

"We're just visiting for the day."

"Oh, where are you staying? The Forest-Edge Inn or with that vile woman from the other side of town?"

Eden freezes and can't come up with what to say. She doesn't think picking one of these options will lead her very far if Evelie knows the people she's about to lie about. Then, Lemana speaks for what feels like the first time in a long while.

"We're staying with her cousin."

Eden keeps forgetting she has to play the role of her own cousin. Acting isn't a talent of hers, despite the double life she used to lead.

"Oh, how wonderful—"

"Is your father here?"

Before she can ask any more incriminating questions, Marten is back with an empty bucket. Evelie turns his way as soon as she hears his voice, eyes immediately softening.

"You are not going to go asking again this soon," she scolds, "he might actually start chasing you around with the cleaver this time."

"No, I've decided that I'm going to have to steal you actually, if he keeps denying me," Marten says as he slides closer to her, "when the right time comes."

"As if he'd let you."

"He won't even know what hit him."

The two smile at each other in that sickly sweet way only couples do.

"If not to ask for my hand, what do you need him for then?"

Marten's face brightens even more. "To pay him up."

"I can't believe that." She places a hand to his forehead.

"Are you quite well, do you have a fever?"

"I'm serious!" he says through a chuckle, shoving her hand away.

"Father!" Evelie calls out and soon a large man with a wild, blond beard, sticks his head out through the window of the butchery. His smile immediately fades as his eyes land on Marten.

"What is he doing here again?" the man grumbles and goes back in. "I'm not giving him more free meat, if that's what he came for!" he shouts out from inside, before he makes his way outside through the front of the shop. "No matter how much my daughter pleads on your behalf."

"No, that's not why I'm here this time." Marten holds out a hand in defence.

The man's eyes look like they're about to bulge out of his head when Marten holds out the coin bag, digging in it to pay what he owes.

"I fear I might be dreaming." He looks so pleased he might actually let Marten marry his daughter in that one split second.

"This should be all." Marten shrugs, handing him a handful of coins. "I'll see you soon."

The setting sun begins to paint the sky as they near their final destination. Eden feels the now emptying streets become more and more familiar. They make a turn and suddenly she knows exactly where they are going.

They pass by the rink, long abandoned and empty.

"This is where your cousin used to fight." Marten points out to Eden, "He was unbeatable!"

Eden knows that not to be true but pretends to be

impressed.

"You said you've never seen him fight, right?"

"Never," Eden says.

"You've missed out. He was a sight." He wears a longing, wistful smile.

They stay at the rink a little while longer as Marten seems to be reminiscing. Soon they head to the tavern. The familiar smell of mead and old wood welcomes them right in. They sit at a table inside, one that she knows all too well. The same one where she would usually sit and treat everyone with the money she won. It brings a bitter sort of nostalgia to be sitting here again without everyone else.

Marten orders drinks for them and doesn't seem to notice Lemana only pretending to be taking sips out of hers.

"I'm sorry for the question but," Eden starts, "today it seemed that you usually don't have much money. Why treat us, why spend it all in one night?"

"What's the point of having money if you're not going to use it?"

Eden supposes he has a point.

Their conversation flows easily, with mostly Marten talking, Eden responding occasionally and Lemana simply observing.

"Looking at you in this light, you really remind me of him," Marten says, "He would always sit there you know, in that chair."

Eden's heart drops to her stomach. "Oh." She hadn't even realised she sat in her usual chair. Force of habit, she supposes.

"Have you met him?" Marten turns to Lemana and

excitedly asks, "The Lord of Steel?"

"Only briefly," she says, almost nonchalantly, but there's a mischievous glint in her eyes when she looks to Eden.

"Don't you think they look alike?" He points to Eden, and she resists the urge to smack his finger away.

"One might think they are twins." Lemana's response takes her aback. She didn't expect her to jest so. Eden strikes a warning look her way, but Lemana pretends not to notice.

"That's how family works," Eden says, trying to save her skin from the building suspicion growing on Marten's face. She looks down to the table, her fingers toying with the empty cup in front of her.

"Why don't you get another round of drinks, *Stranger*?"

"Only if it's my treat," Eden responds, rising from her chair, then freezes. It's not an unusual thing to call a stranger, but it's the way he says it with purpose that makes her fearful.

Marten's face lights up at her reaction. "I knew it! I knew it"

"Can you be quiet? I shouldn't be here at all!" Eden shushes him, panicked.

"Yes, yes sorry."

She sighs heavily, "What gave me away?"

"You and '*your cousin*' happen to have the exact same eyes." Marten smiles at her. "Shape, colour and all. You're the same height too. I just had a hunch."

He continues, "You know they shut down the rink after they took you."

"They did?" Eden hadn't known that.

"It wouldn't be the same without you anyway. It's for the

best." He shakes his head. "What even happened?"

"They wouldn't allow a woman to compete." A princess much less. "So they locked me away."

"They knew you'd try to escape."

Eden grins. "How do you think I'm here?"

Their evening ends with even more pleasant conversation, the strange tension now completely dissolved with her identity no longer a secret. Marten took the news better than Eden thought possible. They share goodbyes, and she makes him a promise to visit again as soon as she's able to sneak away.

Now she and Lemana walk back towards the castle, taking the forest road.

"Oh, I almost forgot, I got something for you." Eden takes out the amulet that Lemana seemed to like back at the shop. "I saw that you were looking at it."

Lemana doesn't answer as it dangles off of Eden's hand, chain wrapped around her fingers.

"You shouldn't have," Lemana says.

"It's nothing, really."

"Thank you." There's something off in her voice, almost like guilt. "I'll keep it."

Eden observes her as she stashes it away in her pouch. A silence stretches between them.

"What did you want to speak to me about?" Eden asks.

Lemana's eyes are back on her, steady and piercing.

"I won't be back for some time."

Eden is surprised to find herself dejected. She hasn't noticed when exactly she began to care whether Lemana shows up or not, but she has grown quite used to her presence.

"For how long?"

"I can't know. Worry not, I will find you again when the time comes," she assures, but Eden can't help the feeling of disappointment.

"Why do you have to leave?"

Before Eden gets an answer, Lemana has already disappeared into the depths of the forest.

XXV

The Rose and the Thorns

BANE ARRIVES AT THE CONFERENCE room. He was about to head out to the forest and spend his day reading, but alas he was summoned. The king's request isn't one that he can ignore.

The door is shut, and voices can be heard from the other side. The king yells loudly, and Bane immediately knows he's speaking to Avgust. That's confirmed when it finally crashes open. Avgust rushes out, but stops in his tracks, straightening up when he sees him. His entire body goes tense. One of his cheeks is an angry red and it's clear he has been hit. It makes Bane's stomach churn.

When the king used to hit him when they were children, Avgust would do nothing but cry for days. He has always hated people knowing he craves his father's love and cares about his opinion, but he used to allow Bane to see it all. Now he turns away, hiding the side of his face.

On instinct, Bane wants to embrace him and let him cry it out. Their eyes meet for a split moment, before Bane looks away instead.

The king comes to stand behind Avgust and only then notices Bane's arrival.

"Konstantin. Just who I need. Come in, both of you." He turns and walks back into the room. A bothersome limp has been present in his step ever since he fell off his horse when he returned from his trip.

Bane pushes past Avgust and doesn't wait to see if he is coming. The door slams shut after them, the sound echoing through the large hall.

The king addresses him directly. "You are to accompany the prince to a meeting with Lady Roza. They need a chaperone."

Bane isn't sure what to say. Clawing his eyes out would be preferable to witnessing another meeting between Avgust and Roza. Avgust looks similarly exasperated. Yet neither of them dares to defy the king.

"She should already be waiting for you out by the gardens." The king turns with a wistful look towards the window. "Go."

Avgust must have angered him badly to earn himself such an arrangement, but Bane doubts he minds. Roza is who he wants after all, and now that he gets to agonise Bane too, he must be overjoyed.

It's an unfortunately bright day today, even though it's already afternoon. Lady Roza waits for them outside, by the entrance of the fortress.

"Good day, my lady." Avgust kisses her hands in greeting.

"You look radiant today."

Oh, how he must be all over her when they are alone. Just like he used to be all over Bane. It's for the better, maybe, that Bane is here to make sure it doesn't get out of hand. It is why he's here today after all, even if he'd rather spend his day slamming his head into the wall.

"Konstantin will be joining us today, the king insisted," Avgust explains.

Lady Roza giggles, "I see, so our courtship has his blessing?"

This is the last nail in the coffin of Avgust and Bane's relationship. It's dead and buried now, or it will be once Avgust and Roza are married.

Avgust offers his arm to her, and she happily takes it. Bane falls into step behind them, keeping enough distance so he won't have to hear them talk. But his enhanced hearing proves to be a nuisance in that regard.

"I must say, I have never seen a dress suit a lady this beautifully," Avgust says, tone loud and obnoxious. It's obvious he wants Bane to hear their conversation.

Lady Roza gasps lightly. "You are such a flatterer," she says, blush taking over her cheeks.

Avgust leans in close to whisper to her, brushing her braided hair out of the way. It might appear like an innocent gesture, but once Avgust's gaze finds Bane's over her shoulder, it couldn't be denied that it is, by design, to torment him.

Bane cannot take his eyes off them, though they burn with the image on display. Avgust doesn't seem to even say anything in her ear; Bane would have heard it. The urge to leap over and strangle them both one by one is strong. Roza would be first because Bane would enjoy killing her less. She doesn't know how carefully planned this torture is. She is just a pawn in this game. Avgust, on the other hand, knows exactly what he's doing.

"You must excuse my boldness; I am not used to us having an audience," Avgust says, tone still.

"Your Highness! Don't go feeding people's imagination by saying things like that."

"Oh, Konstantin knows how to keep a secret." Avgust catches his eye. "Isn't that right?"

"Of course, Your Highness," Bane deadpans, "I bow at your command, after all."

Their gazes cling onto each other, pure fire raging between them. It's Avgust who turns around and keeps walking, and Bane counts it as a win.

They walk to the entrance of the labyrinth. Two stone benches sit symmetrically on either side of it. The tall bushes cast shade onto this part of the yard, and it's a relief from the sun. Bane still walks behind the other two, clutching the cover of his book with force anytime Avgust's face finds itself close to Roza's.

"We would like to take a stroll further into the labyrinth. You may stay here," Avgust commands. Bane doesn't point out how that's explicitly against the king's orders.

"As His Highness wishes," Bane says bitterly.

Avgust's jaw twitches at the name. Fighting a smile, Bane finds himself a seat on one of the benches by the entrance of the labyrinth.

Intertwining their arms, Avgust takes the lady further into the green bushes. They stand too close. Bane feels exactly how Avgust intends. If he doesn't end up killing him, Bane might go over and steal him back. It's not like Avgust deserves it, but Bane wants it too much. He wants him back—he *needs* Avgust to be his again. The looming threat of his marriage to Lady Roza makes him even more desperate for it.

But instead, he takes a deep breath and opens up his book. He forces himself to read, but the words don't mean anything as his mind busies itself thinking about what might be happening in the labyrinth.

He doesn't want to think about it, is scared to, because his imagination is far too vivid. They're all alone in there, secluded and private. He is supposed to chaperone but couldn't bring himself to disobey Avgust's orders. Not because they override the king's, but because Bane doesn't particularly mind staying away from them. So, he stays seated and seething.

Even through the distance and the walls of leaves, Bane can still hear them. Whether that's a blessing or a curse is yet to be determined.

"Are you certain we can just leave Konstantin? Can we be left alone so casually? Isn't that defying the king's wishes?"

Bane likes to know they're still talking. Falling silent is when it would become a problem.

"Clearly he doesn't care about his duties enough if he lets us go so easily."

"Maybe we should go back," Lady Roza voices her concern, *"I don't want us to get him into trouble."*

Avgust seems to think about it, pausing.

The Rose and the Thorns

"*If that's what my lady wishes...*" he says.

Hearing this confirms what he already knew: Roza isn't a bad person. It's not her fault that she might end up getting exactly who Bane wants. Avgust is the one at fault for flaunting her around just to evoke a reaction out of Bane.

The two of them make it out of the labyrinth not long after that. It's worse but it's also better; Bane prefers to have eyes on them. He pretends to still be reading.

"Konstantin, if I may ask," Roza speaks, "how is the princess doing? There are rumours that she is ill."

"Oh, let's not bother him, he seems to be enjoying his book," Avgust tells her.

He and Roza sit on the opposite bench, close together. The small distance between the two of them doesn't last long before he moves closer to her, he is not ever hiding the fact that everything he does is to irritate Bane. But Bane is determined to not show any sign that would let Avgust know he is succeeding.

"My intention isn't to bother him, at all. The ladies and I are really worried about her and who better to ask than her husband?"

Avgust frowns at the word *"husband"* so subtly, one might have easily missed it. Bane didn't. *Good.*

"The princess is alright, she just needs rest," Bane says. "The medic and Nurse Vila take good care of her."

"I'm glad to hear that. Please give her my best wishes." Her eyes grow sad as she speaks. Her concern may be caused by Lady Maya's recent passing.

"I will." Bane nods before bringing his attention back to his book.

They don't try to include him in conversation again, which Bane is grateful for. He doesn't want to discuss any of the trivial matters he hears them speak about. Their conversation sounds boring enough as it is, no need for his input. Bane can feel Avgust's eyes on him occasionally, but he never looks back.

When it's time to part ways, all three stand from the stone benches at the entrance of the labyrinth and take towards the fortress of the castle. Bane drags behind. Avgust and Roza stop ahead of him to exchange their goodbyes. This time they aren't walking too far ahead, and Bane can hear them perfectly well, even in their quiet voices. He can't help but feel it's deliberate.

"I had a wonderful time today; you truly are exceptional company," Avgust says charmingly.

"You think so highly of everyone." Lady Roza looks at her feet. "How can I know you don't call everyone you converse with 'exceptional company'?"

"Oh, but my lady." Avgust pauses and finds Bane's eyes. "You are the only one for me."

That stops Bane in his tracks.

How can Avgust be so cruel? To speak the same words to her after he had spoken them to him? And how could Bane be so naive to believe that they held any significance. That they were special, dedicated only to him.

Foolish to think that anything Avgust ever gave him was truly his.

XXVI

The Sorrow of the Lovers

MARRIAGE HAS BECOME A REAL threat now. Lady Roza is as nice as they come, only Avgust cannot be trapped in a marriage he doesn't want. But what can he do?

He needs advice; he needs someone to understand, someone who knows how this feels. Eden may be the only such person.

If they were able to exchange calm words, Bane might have come to mind too. But he is not too sure Bane hates his marriage as much as Avgust had hoped he would. It almost feels like a betrayal, him being happy with someone else.

Although Avgust's experience with romance has been expansive, he was only ever happy with Bane. For Avgust, everyone else's attention came easy, but Bane's had to be earned.

Avgust shakes away the thought, and hurries to Eden's quarters. He has to ask her; she is the only married person who he can talk to. Really, he doesn't want to know anything about their marriage, but...

His hand hesitates before knocking, praying to God, if there is one, that Bane will not have returned yet. He looked in need of a walk to clear his head. Avgust would be lying if he said that wasn't the desired effect he was aiming for by flirting so explicitly with Lady Roza, but he is surprised it had worked this well. Maybe too well. Bane isn't usually one for emotional outbursts, but walking off alone is as good as one.

The door opens, with a disgruntled Eden on the other side. Her hair, still short and uneven, is messy, like she may have been lying down before he came.

"Sister!" Avgust pushes his way into the room, making himself comfortable on the bed. He wonders if this is the side Bane sleeps on. "I need your help."

Eden barely looks at him as she sits on the other side of the bed, looking down at her lap. He takes it as an invitation to keep talking.

"Father intends to marry me."

Her head snaps up, "To Konstantin?"

Avgust's brows furrow.

"No, he is married to you." And it would be a crime punishable by death for two men to marry.

"Right. I remember now," she says.

"You forgot?"

She's acting strange.

"Never mind that, I don't know how to change Father's

The Sorrow of the Lovers

mind," Avgust dismisses.

"You can't. You have to be grateful that he isn't doing worse."

She's right, and that sends a wave of fear through him. In the need to fidget, Avgust stands and paces around the room. He stops at the desk in front of the window and takes a look at the scattered papers. Some of them are written in Bane's script, careful blocky letters, and Avgust itches to see what he has been writing recently. As much as he may want to infringe upon his privacy, something else catches his eye.

At the edge of the desk is another pile of papers, covered in scribbles and nonsensical words. He catches a few words, like *'wax'*, *'sleep'* and *'disappear'*, that were written like normal. It looks like Eden's handwriting. Avgust wonders what it means.

He may want to ask, but something tells him not to.

"I think it's time to go. I feel the medic coming."

"Feel?"

"Yes." She doesn't elaborate and pushes him towards the door. Once on the other side of it, Avgust is left to stare down the empty corridor. He has no choice but to leave, he supposes, but this conversation didn't solve a thing.

Avgust hurries back to his quarters. His most-reliable friend awaits him patiently, ready to distract him from the dread he feels swelling in him.

The mirror is blank until he speaks her name, and Eulalia doesn't need to be called twice. Her usually dark eyes shimmer with white reflections today.

"What ails you, Avgust?" she asks with a kind, motherly tone. She is the only one who cares to ask these days.

"Is it so obvious that something's wrong?" He sighs as he tosses himself on the bed. He had moved the mirror right in front of it, all by himself and with great effort. Eulalia had said that she wouldn't have him sit on the cold stone floor for hours while they talk.

"There's always something that troubles you, friend, but you know I'm always here to listen."

"It's my father."

Her face softens with empathy. "Again? Oh, my dear boy."

"I wish he would just let me be. He didn't particularly care what I was doing before! He pretended to, but he would simply assign someone else to care about me in his stead." Now that Bane has other duties, he no longer bothers with Avgust's well-being. No one is there to fill that role now—only the woman in the mirror.

"Tell me, Avgust. What has he done?"

Avgust hugs himself into a little ball, sitting at the edge of his bed, knees to his chest.

"He wants me to marry." Avgust's eyes find the floor. "I tried to protest, but...he hit me."

"Oh, poor dear. How could he do that to you?" Her voice soothes him almost instantly, consoling him just by the simple fact that she cares.

"He talks to me like a child. He has no respect for me, yet he wants me to obey everything he says." Avgust groans in frustration. "'*You haven't concerned yourself with the issues we're facing in the castle, the plague that has found its way here,*' he says. As if I don't know people blame *me* for it!"

"That must be so difficult for you, dear," Eulalia consoles.

The Sorrow of the Lovers

"I wish he would just go on another trip and never come back!" Avgust could scream.

"Would that please you?"

"Very much!"

Anger responds for him, thinking about how his life might just fall back into place if his father wasn't here to demand things of him. But then if he's gone, the crown falls on Avgust's head and so do all of the duties he wants no part of.

His father is at the centre of all his problems, really. He is the one who married Bane and Eden. He is the one who wants Avgust to fill the role of king. He's the one who wants *him* married. Everything would be better if he wasn't here.

Avgust calms down, rationality returning to his head in pieces, and looks back at his friend. The cracks he had made in the mirror still distort her face, but she doesn't seem bothered by it. Avgust wishes he could see her without them.

"Have you always been trapped in the mirror?"

She hums in amusement. "I'm not trapped."

"Then why don't you ever come out?"

"It's more complicated than you think," she says, her face revealing no emotion.

"We can talk face to face. Like friends do." Avgust hugs himself tighter, cushioned by the bed.

She smiles. "We are friends, Avgust."

"Why me, then? Why my mirror?"

"I *was* once you, Avgust, betrayed by those closest to me. This is why I came to you. I felt your pain and hoped you'd understand mine too."

Avgust doesn't consider himself betrayed, but he does feel

left behind. Maybe that's betrayal in itself.

"The story you told me?"

"Yes."

"So, what did you do? When your lover left you for another?" Avgust swallows thickly. Maybe they are alike.

"I'm not proud of what I did. I punished them."

She doesn't say anything else. Quietness falls around them, making room for unpleasant thoughts to spring out.

"Did you have anyone to confide in back then, like how I have you?" Avgust asks.

"No. When I was just a child, I was taken into a family, but they never saw me as one of their own. I never belonged. I was different. Only their daughter accepted me as I was, and I loved her dearly. We grew close, closer than we should have, some might say, and we soon spent every waking hour together, but..."

Avgust wants to pretend he doesn't see himself in that, he wants to pretend a certain name doesn't appear in his mind when he hears *'closer than we should'*, but he can't. The name persists and the gaping hole in his chest splits open anew.

"I had other friends too, many, yet she was still my favourite. Until one day, I met a boy, not much older than myself. We had so much in common, and I had never felt so seen. Affection blossomed before I could realise, and I inevitably fell in love. I introduced him to my friend, and they got along like two lost mosaic pieces. I couldn't be happier that the ones I thought most precious to me could love each other like I did. But unbeknownst to me, they had been meeting in secret when the moon was out, and their friendship bloomed into something else entirely. And suddenly…I was left behind. The forgotten catalyst. The one thing that connected them." Her face twists with sadness, but her eyes remain empty. "Much like yourself."

The church bells ring in Avgust's head, chanting the haunting memory of the one day he wants to forget. He understands her pain in a way he wishes he didn't.

"The one friend I would confide in, Avgust, is the very same one who took my lover from me."

XXVII

As a Deer Pants for Flowing Streams

BREAKFAST HAS ONLY GOTTEN WORSE to endure as the days pass. The queen has been away to tend to the king after his recent injury. With her absence from the table, there is no one to try to keep a conversation going, and Bane, Avgust and Eden are left in complete silence.

Bane seems to be the only one to even occasionally look up from his food or acknowledge that there are other people at the table with him. At least today he doesn't also have to actively pretend that he is eating like usual, neither Eden nor Avgust notice or care.

They each are way too focused on their own food. While Eden seems hypnotised by the porridge in front of her, Avgust seems to be amused by his. Bane doesn't dare to even look his way, but he hears him as he tries to hide his chuckles. What's so funny? Bane cannot fathom, nor does he intend to find out.

As a Deer Pants for Flowing Streams

By the end of the week this new routine has started to become unbearable. He has started missing the empty conversations with Queen Lena. Keeping food down for more than half an hour has become impossible now, the taste of it has slowly started to morph away from unpleasant and has started to taste so foul even the smell makes him gag. But he'd prefer it over having to sit in this draining silence with these two.

Thinking about the gross flavour of the food reminds Bane of what he has developed a taste for instead. After his encounter with the elk, he has acquainted himself with the barrel of animal remnants the castle butcher gathers, which happens to contain mostly blood. The strong smell lured him in, still shaken from the elk's blood, still so sensitive to any smell of it. His feet led him there in the dark as he was making his way back to the castle. There was no one around to see; there was no harm in having a taste. So, he dipped a finger in the barrel. This time the taste was revolting, gagging even, yet he craved it still. He went for it again, again and again. Gulping handful after handful. Blood dripped down his elbows, until there was nothing left of it.

Even though his body was buzzing, it was the worst he ever felt. He was disgusted with himself afterwards; no amount of water could wash away his shame. The shame of taking a life, the shame of knowing how good the foul liquid from the barrel made him feel.

The silence lets his mind wander wherever it pleases. Bane can't stand it anymore.

"Is there something wrong with the porridge?" Bane asks, taking a pretend spoonful of his own. Eden has her eyes fixed on her bowl and doesn't acknowledge him whatsoever. "Eden?"

Her head snaps up, as if she was asleep until now, her eyes red and eyelids drooping. "Oh, I'm sorry, what did you say?"

"I asked if there is something wrong with your food?"

"No, not at all, it's great, very, *very* delicious." Her hands move under the table, in a jittery motion that Bane can't interpret.

"Well, you haven't tasted it yet so I—"

"I have!" she cuts him off. "I've already finished..." Eden looks down to her full bowl. She freezes in place for a moment, almost as if she didn't expect it to be.

"Eden, are you feeling alright?" Bane's brows furrow with concern.

"Yes, of course, I'm fine."

"You worry me."

Avgust laughs, and then his hand slams against his mouth, muffling his amusement. Bane's head turns to him.

"Is there something funny?" He doesn't state it, but it feels like Avgust finds the idea of Bane caring for Eden laughable. As if he thinks Bane's absence of desire towards her means he must also not possess compassion. Does Avgust suspect his lie? That Bane and Eden carry out their marital duties? What a cruel way to show them Avgust has figured out the truth—by laughing. Just because Bane never wanted her, never thought of her even once in that way, despite their sleeping arrangements, does not mean that he wants her to be unwell.

"No." Avgust shakes his head, gaze still locked on his porridge. "No, of course not."

Despite what he's saying, his giggles bubble out again, quieter and mean.

"You should maybe stop laughing then."

A loud clank brings his attention back to Eden, her spoon sinking uselessly in her untouched bowl.

"Eden, maybe you should go lie down."

She is quick to excuse herself at his suggestion, bolting out the door like she would rather be anywhere else.

The meal ends abruptly with Avgust leaving after her without an excuse of his own. Bane, left alone, drops the pretence of eating and leaves after a minute or two to let them get far from the dining hall. He chooses to take a different route today on his way out to the woods, having decided to use them as a permanent refuge now. It's a better option than the damp dungeon, so the inconvenience of getting to the forest is negligible. Now he can move incredibly fast, he recently discovered. It drains him but between the exhaustion from starvation and the never-ending hammering pain in his skull, the refuge of the forest is worth it. He would also rather happen upon an animal than a human. The thought of taking an animal's life used to be unthinkable and now it has turned into the lesser evil. Bane can hardly recognise what his mind has turned into.

He would have taken the outer hallway and enjoyed the view of the inner courtyard, but the sun is far too high already, and the thought alone makes his head spin. Instead, Bane takes the corridor that leads through the knights' quarters. He tries to pass it quickly before he even gets the chance to peek inside, but the door to the armoury is ever so slightly ajar. His curiosity gets the better of him and he pushes the door open.

Instantly, he's met with Avgust's armour, perched upon

its usual stand. Or he supposes it's more accurately Eden's. He remembers that night when he and Avgust encountered her, a helmet idly hidden behind her, but Bane cannot remember a thought or care ever crossing his mind about where she was headed. His mind was occupied with other things, consumed by his heart's desires, blinded by Avgust's shine.

The more time he has to think about it, the more evident his real punishment becomes. His bloodlust is a vice meant to assure that he becomes truly irredeemable. He was standing too close to the sun, and now he is cursed into the shade, forever denied its warmth.

Bane runs a hand over the chainmail, which now stays abandoned in its dirty state, likely to never be worn again. At least by Eden. It's a custom-made suit; Avgust will probably be forced to wear it at some point or another, whether he wants to or not.

"I wonder how you even survived all these years being as unobservant as you are."

Bane startles out of his thoughts, whipping around to find Aleksander on the bench seat along the wall. "I could have easily slit your throat, and you wouldn't have even noticed."

He sits slumped, elbows resting on his knees. His hair, greasy and unkept, hangs in front of his eyes. Yet still, Bane feels the venom in his gaze.

"Aleksander," Bane acknowledges him, not quite as a greeting. "What are you doing here?"

"I'm here to collect Stefan, Christian and Mihai's belongings to send back to their families." His tone is glum. "They sent me to the other troop when you returned…and of course the one time I find myself back here, I happen upon you."

Aleksander falls quiet as a mouse. Despite the familiar hostility that was always reserved for Bane, he doesn't seem quite himself.

"I used to be the head of the troop; everyone bowed to me and followed my lead like I knew better than any of them." There is a particular light on his face for a moment before it dims out as quickly as it came. His face now scrunches in disgust. "And now I'm no better than you were when you first came here…" His voice grows softer, in angry acceptance. *Defeat.* "But look at you now. I'll never understand how you did it. You are not exceptional in any way, you're not even mediocre, and yet here you are. Married to a princess. The king's favourite, always the king's favourite. If he could only see you for what you really are, he would strip you of all your privileges and titles and give them to someone more deserving."

Bane can't even say anything in his defence. He isn't quite sure how he did it either. He never understood why the king favoured him, and sometimes, recently more than before, he wished he wasn't favoured.

"My demotion, Christian, Stefan and Mihai's death—it's all your fault. Everything is your fault. And the worst part is I know you don't feel responsible. But again, why would you?"

Bane stays rooted in place. He can't deny it. He doesn't feel responsible for their deaths. It was their punishment. Despite not actually knowing what really happened to the three of them, he knows they were the ones who buried him under the dirt. Their faces flash before him, eyes blank and empty.

Bane feels guilt for a lot of things, but this isn't one of them. The guilt he feels is not for their fate, but for the satisfaction he felt when he heard the news.

Leaving the knights to be a husband to the princess is what caused the dismissal of the troop—what made Aleksander into someone less than he once was. Maybe Bane finds some sort of satisfaction in that too. He doesn't like that it's there, but it is, settling in his chest. Victory, but at what cost. Bane truly can't recognise himself anymore.

He doesn't respond before he turns out the door, walking fast through the halls, back on his way to the forest. He hadn't realised how used to his own company he has become, but he so desperately wants to be alone.

Bright light seeps through the windows lining the corridor and pierces Bane's eyes like needles. His head is lowered, and his hurried steps deliver him straight into another person. He stumbles back and loses his balance, toppling down to the stone floor.

At the end of an outstretched hand, he meets green eyes that look at him with concern. Bane doesn't deserve neither the worry nor the kindness of Avgust's helpful hand. He gets up to his feet by himself and ignores the painful pang in his chest at the hurt in Avgust's eyes.

"You should stay away from me." Bane's voice comes out raspy, harsher than necessary.

Avgust huffs, offended. "You really can't stand me, can you?"

"No!" Bane says before he can even think. "Things are just different now..."

"*Things are different.*" Avgust repeats under his breath.

"They are. It's better if you stay away."

Avgust's expression sours with every word.

"So, what, I'm not allowed to see my *brother-in-law*? Why not?" Avgust's voice drips with venom. "Is it our past you wish to hide from?"

"I'm not hiding from anything."

"Only from yourself."

"Why is it that you're so concerned with me when you have women to court? They aren't keeping you entertained enough, I suppose?"

"I can have more than one person that concerns me."

"I've noticed."

Avgust falls quiet, jaw slack in shock.

Bane speaks again. "It's surprising you're so stuck on our past when even then you had other conquests."

"It's more surprising how quickly you've been able to forget it." Avgust comes so close to his face, Bane feels his breath tickle his skin. "Your wife must be a good enough replacement then?"

His scent settles in the air around them, alluring and maddening.

"Replacement? Are you mad? Is that what you think of her?" As if Avgust could ever be replaced. Even his twin cannot compare. Bane inhales the sweet smell, greedily holding it in his lungs.

"Or maybe I was only holding space until you found yourself a woman. You must be happy now that you are back on the right path."

"You have no idea..." Bane's words trail off. They are standing so close.

Their eyes haven't parted for even a second. Before he can stop it, Bane's hand claws at Avgust's shirt, dragging him even closer. He breathes him in again, and Avgust's eyes fall on his lips. The rapid rise and fall of his chest is hypnotic, but his hammering heartbeat is even more so.

Bane pushes him before his composure breaks, and Avgust steps back. It takes him a moment to catch his breath, and the sharpness in his eyes is quick to return.

"Don't pretend you are something you are not," Avgust says. His rage reverberates through him. "You can't hide what you are, and you can't pray away what you've done."

His words strike him in more ways than he intended. And still he is baffled by how low Avgust would go just to insult him. Maybe *this* is what he deserves.

He needs him to stay away, and if that means he must make Avgust grow to hate him, then so be it. If that hatred will keep him away, Bane will learn to swallow down the weeping of his heart.

XXVIII

So Pants my Soul for You

THE CELEBRATION FOR THE PRINCE *and Princess's fifteenth birthday was taking place that night, and the grand hall had never looked so bright. Off the walls hung bright decorative banners, adorned with the crest of the kingdom. The tables were organised with shiny plates and cutlery, awaiting the lavish meals being prepared. The heavy velvet curtains, draped from ceiling to floor, were drawn away from the high windows to let in the beautiful light of the moon, which mingled with the yellows of the lanterns in the hall.*

Despite the large number of guests, Bane found him easily in the crowd. Avgust was entertaining a group of ladies with his usual theatrics, and they seemed hooked on his every word. Ever since they were little, he loved being the centre of attention.

Avgust was never shy in keeping his opinions on the ladies of the court to himself, how beautiful they were, how the dresses they wore complimented certain features of theirs, and yet Bane still wondered if any of them actually had his attention. Let alone if something ever happened between Avgust and a lady. He never dared to ask, out of a sense of modesty that Avgust clearly didn't seem to possess, and because he wasn't sure he wanted to know. If he were ever given the opportunity, Avgust would recall his romantic endeavours in great flowery detail, storyteller that he is. He always seemed to know everything, at least when it came to that sort of thing.

Bane was sure that Avgust was more than familiar with matters of the heart, but he never wanted to be explicitly proven right. Yet now he found himself wondering if he was to Avgust what Avgust was to him—a first and only experience—or if Avgust had felt another's lips after Bane's. Was the kiss they shared something that Avgust would even be able to recall, or had it completely faded from his mind?

Bane wished it would leave his mind too and yet he was unable to shake it off. It was the last thing he should be thinking about, but he couldn't stop.

It came back to him suddenly, a lightning bolt in a blue sky. At first, he tried to fight it and dismiss it, but it was to no avail. The memory of their kiss followed him in his dreams, and the longing for more plagued his every waking moment. Bane couldn't take it any longer.

He tried to find solace in prayer, in the holy books, but nothing would bring him relief or consolation. That had to be the greatest test of his faith, and he knew it was a losing battle.

Bane had to dispose of any trace of Avgust in his life if he hoped to be rid of the thoughts that haunted him; but how was he to do so when their lives were so intertwined? Bane was his preacher, serving him in any way he could, and Avgust was Bane's closest and dearest friend. Maybe his only friend. He couldn't just lock him away in some dark, distant corner of his mind. Someone like Avgust cannot possibly be cast aside.

Maybe a man stronger in his faith would've been able to do what needed to be done, but Bane had come to find he was no such man. He hoped giving into his desire this one time would purge the thought, the need for more, entirely out of his head.

Making his way through the crowd, Bane perched himself next to Avgust and the herd of ladies.

"Ah, Konstantin," Avgust called out, but it sounded unnatural. It wasn't the name he called him when they were alone. "I was starting to worry you would miss the celebration."

Bane was not in a state fit for idle chatter. He needed to get this off his chest, lest he went mad.

"Avgust, may I speak with you?"

"Well yes, I have been waiting to receive your congratulations all evening."

"But the prince was just about to tell us one of his stories," one of the ladies protested, and the rest made their agreement known.

"I'll be back before you know it, my fair ladies. Fear not, my absence will only make my return sweeter." Avgust delivered his usual antics with a hand over his chest. This was yet another thing that could push Bane over the brink of insanity, because he could never know how genuine it was when Avgust was this charming with him. After all, he treated everyone that way, like they were important, like they meant something to him.

Bane could not stand to hear another word of it, so he dragged Avgust off to one side of the hall, along one wall where the closest person was several steps away. Despite the distance, he still couldn't help but look over his shoulder to make sure that no one was suspicious of a mere servant dragging the prince around as if he had any right to do so.

"What is it?" Avgust asked as though he already knew exactly what was on Bane's mind, like he was waiting for the words to spill out of Bane's mouth, yet he wouldn't dare speak them himself.

"I know I shouldn't be mentioning it, especially not here. It definitely isn't the time nor place. I should probably wait for the celebration to conclude, but my mind knows no rest."

"No, no go on, but I've had a glass or two already, so just speak clearly. Better to get it off your chest if it would stop you from enjoying the feast, whatever it is."

"I wanted to bring up something that happened some time ago..."

Avgust probably has forgotten about it by now. It has been well over a year since. It probably wasn't as important to him as it had become to Bane. Maybe he should leave it as it is, as a thing of the past. This sinful craving would eventually fade. He hasn't done or said anything that he might regret or be punished for yet.

"Bane, are you feeling alright?" Avgust began to lift a hand to his forehead, but Bane caught it by the wrist and kept it there.

"Avgust..." Bane's gaze quickly swept over the room a second time. When he found Avgust's face again there was panic in his eyes. Doubt spread in the green of them like a forest fire swallowing everything in its way. Bane couldn't stand the sight of it.

What came over him, he didn't know; it was a sudden surge of bravery that set him moving. He pushed Avgust back, until they were hidden behind the thick red drapes that lined the windows of the great hall. It was just them in the quiet dark with their small breaths that filled the space. Bane could make out the faint outline of Avgust, his wide eyes and mouth hanging open. It sent a thrill through him.

It took very little contemplating before Bane was pressing his lips to Avgust's, hidden in the uncertain safety of the dark. He wasted no time to return the kiss and dragged him closer by the neck, as if Bane might escape, as if he would ever want to.

The kiss was familiar, yet it couldn't be more different than their last. More mature, hungrier, and more practised on Avgust's part. Bane followed along eagerly, letting him set the tone.

His suspicions about Avgust's experience were confirmed, but Bane couldn't bring himself to care, now that he got to have him.

Avgust's mouth drowned out the involuntary pant that Bane let out. He could taste the alcohol that lingered on his breath, but it wasn't what intoxicated him, it was Avgust himself.

Lost in the kiss, he was sure he could stay there forever, behind the curtain in the great hall as everyone else celebrated Avgust's birthday, while Bane was the only one that actually had his attention. It was that very thought that forced him to remember where he was and how much they shouldn't be doing this, not then, not there. Bane pulled away, breathless. Which flame was he nourishing, that of his love, or that of the eternal fire it dooms him to? That deep craving that had him kissing Avgust in the first place had only grown stronger, insatiable, with no sign of it ever going away.

✲✲✲

The almost-empty, small satchel bag lies limply on Bane's bed. All he has in there is a simple sheathed dagger. There is not much else he needs. He looks at the Holy Bible on the desk, forgotten there weeks ago, and contemplates taking it with him. It has failed to protect him in the past, so he doesn't feel the strong conviction to bring it with him wherever he goes like he used to. It stays just where it is.

Bane, having waited the day out, is headed to Starosel on a personal mission to search for the woman that did this to him. The one that was able to speak in his head, the one that cursed him into the shadows. He is determined to find her and take home some answers. The dagger is with him just in case he finds himself unable to fight her, power against power. She knows how to use hers, Bane doesn't.

A knock on the door startles him. He hasn't had visitors to this room, and Eden never knocks. The room is just as much hers as it is his. Half the reason he decided it was safe to venture into the village by himself was because he didn't think he would be missed.

Bane opens the door to find a small boy watching him with wide eyes.

"The king has requested your presence in the throne hall."

"Oh."

Bane hasn't been summoned in a long time; recently, he'd only gone on his own to check on the king's health. He had assumed what the king had been saving him for was marriage to the princess, and once that duty was fulfilled, he had forgotten all about him. Bane is both glad this isn't the case and worried what else he might be needed for.

He sends the messenger boy on his way and takes off down the corridor.

The heavy doors of the throne hall close behind him as Bane arrives.

"Konstantin," the king says in greeting, "I have summoned you here today on a more personal matter."

"It would be my honour to help, Your Majesty."

So Pants my Soul for You

It's clear the king's injury is still bothering him by the way he sits with his hip strangely contorted. Unfortunately, Bane suspects that it will continue to bother him until the end of his days.

"It's regarding Avgust and his unpreparedness to rule. My time as king is undecided, and he has been of age for a couple of years now, it is expected of him to be ready. No matter what I do, he never listens, so I think my methods haven't been radical enough."

"Your Majesty, I'm sure that when the time comes, life will have prepared him." Bane can't help but plead for Avgust.

"I have decided it is time he marries. Eden's marriage to you has been nothing but successful in setting her on a path more suited for a lady. I believe a companion he trusts would ease the prince into the role of king."

Bane holds his tongue.

"If he is aware of your help on the matter, it would help smoothen the news. You are his closest friend, after all."

It's hard for Bane to keep calm. There was a time in which that was true, but friendship between them has been long forgotten, for reasons set in the two furthest extremes. Now they are neither close nor friends. Something tells him if Avgust were to know Bane had anything to do with this decision, he would fight it more.

"The ladies of the court seem like the most sensible option. He already knows them, so trust would come easily after that. He seems to have his eyes set on Lady Roza already."

A lump lodges itself inside Bane's throat at the thought. It feels wrong to conspire with the king about which lady Avgust will be forced to marry. Bane is being made complicit in the sentencing of his own lover to a marriage with another. Avgust is the last person he would ever wish such a fate upon. And the king choosing the one woman Bane cannot stand to see with Avgust as his future wife is like a knife to the chest. It's a bitter reminder that Bane's heart still beats for Avgust.

Avgust's insincerity when it comes to romance is not uncommon, but he does willingly spend time with Lady Roza. He may harbour real feelings for her, there's no way of knowing. Her feelings would be harder to deny, she has never been shy about making them known. It has always maddened Bane.

"What is your opinion on the matter?"

Bane's opinion is not the fairest one, which is something he can admit. This would be the outcome he hates most—Avgust married to Lady Roza of all people on this Earth. Bane supposes Avgust must have felt similarly when Bane was forced to marry his sister. But Eden was hardly even a friend, while Roza is the reason Bane has never been confident enough to stake his claim on Avgust, since they never seemed to be alone in their relationship.

"I will be frank, Your Majesty. Lady Roza is a well-respected lady of the court, no doubt, but I don't think she is of the right status to be a fair match for the prince. I don't believe she would have enough insight to understand royal matters. You need someone who can guide Avgust into being a competent ruler, and she would simply fall short."

It's hypocritical of Bane to be making these sorts of comments on other people's ranks, considering his own status and how many times he has found himself in Avgust's bed.

"I see. What do you suggest?"

"I think that you shouldn't be restricted to only the ladies of the court," Bane says, before he has the proper time to think it over. "If you don't mind me sharing my thoughts, Your Majesty. Perhaps you should expand the width of the search for a suitable match. Marriage can be a great opportunity to straighten the relations with one of our neighbours. And who could be a more competent royal guide than someone already of royal blood?"

No matter the state of their relationship, Bane can't let this happen. It's inevitable that Avgust will have to marry soon, the king seems set on that, but the least Bane can do for him is delay it. A wider search would win him at least a month's time but it can also lead to nowhere, which would set the king back to considering the ladies of the court. Even if Avgust ends up married to Lady Roza, at least Bane will have more time to stomach the idea—if he is ever able to.

He continues, "Your marriage is one such as that, Your Majesty. Wouldn't you say there is no better way to achieve true allyship between nations?"

"You are right, I will see what I can do to arrange a political union. I trust your judgement, son." The king nods, pleased with Bane's suggestion. "You are free to go. I will summon you soon to further discuss this matter."

Bane leaves the hall with a quick stride, lest his mask of pretence falls, and the king can see how greatly this conversation has upset him. He isn't sure if he is more upset at the circumstances or his own pettiness.

Bane reaches the stables and doesn't hesitate before he mounts his horse and whips the reins with urgency.

***

By the time Bane makes it to Starosel, night has almost fallen.

The yellow lights in the windows of the houses are just beginning to light up the streets. Bane thinks the woman he is looking for might venture into the village to feed. He just needs to wait her out. If she is still even here, she could've easily already left this place.

Voices carry over between the song of the crickets as he jumps off his horse.

"Beware the demons of the night!" His ears catch a distant yell. Bane ties up his horse's reins to a fence near the water trough of a cattle pen, then makes his way to the source of the voice.

People have gathered in a sparse circle, whispering between themselves as one man, perched atop a wooden crate, speaks loudly. The villagers barely pay Bane any mind when he slots into the crowd.

It was the yelling that caught his attention but the severed head the man waves around is what kept it. He holds it in the air by the hair as it dangles gruesomely. It has been dead at least a few weeks and has started decaying a long time ago. The stench coats the inside of Bane's nose.

"Give this a rest!" one woman from the crowd shouts, "How many times are you going to bring this thing to the square?"

"As many times as is necessary for you to believe. The nights are not safe!"

The man, quite old for someone so passionate, has a thick white beard peppered with a few darker strands. His eyes are set in determination, but there is horror underneath. Despite having killed one of these creatures of the night, he still seems terrified of them.

"Look for yourselves, look inside its mouth, see its beastly teeth!" He pushes the head into the faces of the crowd, and Bane almost gags when the smell of death gets stronger. The severed head belonged to a woman with long white hair, a sunken face and an empty gaze.

"Put that rotting thing away!" another man yells.

"They are growing in number. They will call out to each other until they outnumber us. There is more of this coven somewhere nearby, because new ones keep showing up to our village! They have a way of finding each other," the old man explains, bringing the severed head to rest by his side, still hanging by its hair. "It's that cursed lake, I tell you! It calls to them. You will see soon enough, although it might be too late."

When the already negligible crowd gets fed up with the man's antics enough to leave, Bane dares to step up closer.

"Excuse me?"

The golden cross Bane wears drips over his fingers. He wraps the chain around them, toying with it.

The man lifts his head, greeting Bane with wary eyes.

"Can you tell me more about these creatures?"

"Boy." The man's distrust at the unfamiliar face is instantly replaced by his need to talk. "Come, come. The sun is going down, it's dangerous out in the open."

They swerve towards the north side of the village, slowing when they pass a stone building with a wooden sign hanging above its door. '*The Forest-Edge Inn,*' it reads, and Bane's hand meets the doorhandle just as the man calls out to him again.

"Further down this road, my boy. Follow me."

They walk to the edge of the village, and Bane starts to grow anxious. He is alone with a man who has killed a night beast, it might only be a matter of time until he discovers Bane's own beastly nature—unless he already has.

His heart slows its beat at the sight of the small cottage that starts to take shape in the distance. There is something standing tall in the front yard. Bane can't quite figure out what it is. The closer they get, the clearer it becomes. Pierced on a wooden pole, almost as tall as him, is the head of the fire dancer. She who gave him death.

"Don't be frightened, it can't hurt you now."

Her lifeless eyes are not as bright as he remembers them. They don't burn with their golden fire anymore, their light now dimmed to a dull yellow.

Bane should be glad that the creature that took his humanity has found its end, but he isn't. He is met with more sorrow than anything. Looking at her horrifyingly still face, he can't help but feel regret. Yes, she is the one that turned him into a monster, yet he feels sorry for what had happened to her. Despite not knowing her, it feels like a connection has been severed, one that hangs limply from him and no longer leads to her.

She said that she would return to him. Maybe she would have if this man didn't get to her first. Maybe she would have taught him how to embrace the beastly nature she bestowed upon him. Bane would feel less alone. He will never know now.

There is a certain sense of closure in knowing what happened to her, despite her tragic fate. It's something that he can only dream of having regarding his homeland, his parents. It's good to know he wasn't forgotten or abandoned again, although it doesn't change the fact that he was again robbed of a mentor. Of a mother.

"Come, boy," the man says, "Let's get inside."

Bane hides his anger well when he follows him into the cottage. Its wooden walls are old and creaky, the atmosphere is suffocating. A strong smell of incense hangs in the air, and it doesn't bring Bane the comfort that it used to.

The man sits Bane at a small table with just two chairs, one worn and chipped, the other almost pristinely new. He leaves him in the main room, before entering into a doorway just off to the side.

"You've killed two of them? These...beasts?" Bane says, finding himself struggling with the last word. He can think it as much as he likes, but saying it is like admitting something about himself. The man comes back with two cups and a kettle.

"They find me. I'm easy prey, alone in a house more in the woods than in the village."

The man shrugs and serves them each a cup of herbal tea. Bane takes a polite sip, knowing he will retch it back out later, before speaking again.

"How do you bring yourself to kill them, knowing they

were human once?"

"I don't find it matters much. When one turns into a beast, there is no coming back from that. The human part of them is lost forever."

Bane knows he can't fully return to being a human, but he isn't solely a beast now either. He might find himself thinking or acting differently in some respects, but he doesn't feel like the human side of him has been rooted out completely.

"They choose to take in the beast by drinking the cursed water. There is no one to blame but themselves."

Bane would have never chosen this. It's impossible to see a world in which anyone would choose this life.

"When did you kill the one in the yard?" He gulps around another tasteless sip of the tea, just to have something to do.

"Long ago. Must have been weeks at this point."

Bane wonders, had he started realising things sooner, if he would have been able to save her. He should've come sooner, if only he could've accepted his condition faster.

"I see you have your reservations. Don't feel bad for the beast," the man says, "empathy is a human emotion that they don't possess, don't waste yours on them."

From Bane's own empathy alone, the man's claim is proven false. Anger may have ruled his actions in the beginning of his transformation, but he finds himself to be much kinder when he isn't hungry. And kindness, like empathy, is something a beast wouldn't be capable of.

"Is it necessary to cut their head off? It seems excessively brutal," Bane asks.

"There is no other way, boy! Leave their head on their

body and they will rise again and return the favour. Or worse, turn you into a beast like them," the man's gravelly voice speaks with certainty. "And it won't feel bad when it's done with you."

Despite the man's conviction, Bane knows some of what he's saying to be untrue. But Bane has no real idea of his new potential, his new abilities. Can he really find others like him, be drawn to them like the man says? Can he live past death again? He supposes when he was stabbed and buried, he should've died.

"*Brutal*," the man repeats under his breath, "How can I be brutal to a creature that only knows brutality?"

Bane doesn't think he could ever harm another creature in such a cruel way. What he is and what he has already done has been out of necessity. Is it really so monstrous to exist? Does he deserve to be slain on sight for what he is? Could the fire dancer have been incapable of any empathy like this man says, if she was kind to him even when she turned him?

"If you ask me, I'm doing a righteous thing, purifying the land of those beasts. No one appreciates me for it, but they'll see."

To be chased and hunted like pests for their nature is not humane either. Bane feels stronger kinship to the woman that took his life, than to this man who fails to see his deed as cruel.

A long time ago, Bane made a selfish choice, hoping he could be forgiven with enough repentance. Loving Avgust was always his first sin. The only one that Bane could never bring himself to regret.

His very nature, the one of a beast, the one he never would have chosen for himself, is his second sin. Can he be blamed for what happened to him? Is it fair to be blamed when there is no way to turn away from what he has become?

Does it even matter if he is forgiven anymore? Is forgiveness what he should ask for when it is God who made him so? Fighting against what you are is like swimming against the current of nature—a foolish fruitless endeavour.

Everything the man said has left a bad taste in his mouth. Most of all his insistence that this is right. That this is a good thing. How can killing in such a brutal way be moral? Bane might've turned into a monster, but his soul isn't that of one. At least not the monster the man claims he must be. Bane could kill him effortlessly if he so chooses, but he wouldn't. That's the difference between a beast and a man.

XXIX

The Wounded Hare

THE MEDIC'S FLEAM PIERCES THE skin of Eden's forearm. Blood draws, dripping down her arm and landing in the dish placed underneath. She sits in a wooden chair, the backrest digging into her back uncomfortably as one elbow rests on the armrest.

"This isn't really necessary." Eden sighs, irritated by the slow pace of the procedure.

"You've been unwell for far too long," Nurse Vila scolds, a worried twitch in her brow, "I won't have it any longer."

"I've been feeling better lately." She hasn't. In fact, she has only started feeling worse. It's less noticeable, both because it seems to be all in her head, and because she let the habit of sneaking out die. There is no reason to now and excusing herself to *"rest"* has become pointless.

"Take it as a preventive measure then."

"Fine." She rests her head on her free arm, as her blood continues to drop into the bowl. "How much more time is this going to take?"

"Not much longer." The medic serves her a stern eye from underneath his brows.

She huffs, but she is in no rush really. Eden realised how good of a distraction Lemana had been these past weeks only when she stopped coming. She was the only thing that provided her a break from the uniformity of her routine, even when she briefly began losing her mind.

Lately she has become so easily irritable and impatient, probably caused by her lack of sleep. She barely gets a wink at night, and nights turn into days impossibly fast before she even gets the chance to sleep. The moment her eyes close when the moon comes out, she can already feel the sun trying to peek through her eyelids.

"I'll come check on you in a bit," the medic informs. Then he and the nurse leave her in the room—alone—with only the vexing sound of the drops of blood hitting the metal dish. Her chair isn't even turned to the window. Not that she has much interest in it. It only reminds her of the freedom she can't have. Her only view is that of the door, which is too far away for her to even try to make out the patterns in the wood to pass the time. There are only so many times she can note how brown the wood is in her mind before she starts to lose it.

How much longer will she have to endure this?

The sound of the drops falling one by one is maddening, yet as she listens to each one, counting their spaced-out splatters in the slowly filling bowl, she begins to find herself dozing off. She doesn't fight it much. Quite the opposite, she welcomes it.

"Come to me," a faint voice whispers in her ear, far away, yet Eden feels breath brushing against the skin of her neck.

"Meet me in the woods tomorrow," the voice echoes in her head, like the sound bounces off the sides of her skull. She turns to find the source of it, but nobody is there.

"You know where I'll be." The more it speaks, the more familiar it starts to sound. "Meet me there."

Lemana.

The door swings open, startling her out of it, and Bane casually enters the room. When he realises that he's not alone, he quickly stiffens.

"Were you asleep?" he asks, still standing by the door, not looking at Eden. His eyes are pinned on the wall behind her.

"I believe so."

"What happened to your arm?" Bane points at where it rests over the arm of the chair yet avoids looking at her. Maybe he hasn't got a strong enough stomach to handle the sight of blood. Every day Eden realises how little she knows about the man she shares a bed with.

"I had blood let out." It's only now that Eden notices that her arm is bandaged, the dish is gone and it's already dark out. "Did I miss dinner?"

"Yes." He lifts a hand to his face as if to scratch his chin, but it's obvious he is covering his nose. He finally dares to move across the room. "Are you feeling better now?"

Eden nods. For once it's not a lie. Although her improvement has nothing to do with the bloodletting. Lemana came to her; Eden knows it wasn't just a dream. It was a message. For the first time in days, she has something to look forward to the next day.

As soon as dawn breaks, she is up. After putting on her dress and sliding on her old boots carefully and quietly, so as not to wake Bane, she rushes out. The corridors are empty—not a soul to see her. She makes her exit quicker and easier than she anticipated, but she isn't complaining.

When she gets to the forest, the mist hasn't even had the chance to lift yet. There is still a chill from the night in the air, the sun has barely lit the sky. She leans on one of the trees and begins waiting.

"You received my message."

Eden hears her before she sees her.

"Lemana?" She looks around to find her.

"I wasn't planning on seeking you out so soon but..." Lemana appears next to her, as if out of nowhere. "Something dreadful is ahead, I won't be able to prevent it alone." There is tension in her brows, all her features move so expressively, so oddly human. It's unlike her.

"What do you mean?"

"There is no time. Will you help me?"

Eden nods.

"I knew I could count on you." Lemana conjures a glass blade out of thin air. Eden's eyes widen, but she doesn't question it. "Keep this and keep it close."

Lemana gives it to Eden, who wraps her fingers around it. Lemana's dark, calm eyes meet hers, as if reassuring her. Eden tightens her grip on the blade. She expects the blade to melt

The Wounded Hare

in her hand like ice, or trickle down between her fingers, but it stays sharp.

"How do I know when to use it?"

"You will know." Lemana doesn't let Eden's eyes wander away from hers. It's something in her voice, something that makes Eden unable to look away. "Now let's practice."

"Practice how?" Eden blinks.

"Be quiet, you will scare it away."

Suddenly they aren't under the tree anymore, they are crouched down behind a bush, Lemana right next to her. They are preying on an unsuspecting hare. Its coat is oddly put together as if combed. It's mousy brown, standing out against the greenery, and it's not hard to keep an eye on it.

"You want me to kill it?"

"You must be ready when he comes. You can't know what form he will present himself as, you must be cautious of everything." She looks over to the hare. "Especially the seemingly harmless."

Eden is still hesitant. She looks at the hare again, it is innocently standing between two tall trees; it poses no harm to anyone. One ear twitches, and it turns to look their way, its eyes are a warm brown and void of any fear.

"Go straight for the heart," Lemana says against the shell of her ear. "It will suffer less."

Eden takes a deep breath then steps out of their hideout. The hare doesn't even flinch, it gives her an idle look, then turns away. She inches closer, now exposing the knife in her hand, yet still the animal doesn't move. The only difference now is that it looks riddled with confusion, dawning on its animalistic features in a rather human-like way. Not fear—puzzlement.

It tugs on her heart, but Eden swings the blade and misses. The hare finally makes an attempt to get away but fails. It begins crawling in the opposite direction. Its leg is wounded, she notices. On her second try, she is more precise, but not quite enough. She manages to slice its throat before it could slip out of her vice grip.

Blood splashes all over her hands and clothes. It sticks to her face and neck, and she can feel it in her mouth, its taste sickening as it melts on her tongue. The animal tosses and wriggles on the ground, choking with every breath it tries to take.

"Put him out of his misery." Lemana appears behind her, her breath a whisper against her ear again, placing a hand on her shoulder. Eden lifts the blade one last time to strike it right through the chest. It stops moving. It's dead.

Eden pulls the weapon out. The rabbit is gone and so is the forest. She kneels on the floor of the throne hall, under her blood-red hands lies her father's lifeless body. As his glassy eyes look at her, she stands frozen over him. His robes are stained red, a pool of scarlet right over his heart. Eden jumps back and off him, slipping in the puddle of blood around her father's body.

The blade dissolves into water in her hands. It trickles down, washing away some of the blood on her hand, but it doesn't wash the culpability away. She is unable to look at the body again. Yet it's like her gaze never left it. The image is permanently engraved in her mind. The still eyes, never to close on their own again. The blood forever losing its warmth, cooling down on the stone.

Eden must get away from it, even if she is unable to shake away the sight from her mind, she needs to physically be away from it. She pushes open the heavy doors, leaving sticky footsteps on her trail as she gets out of the hall.

Two guards lie peacefully dead right where their post should be outside the door. No sign of a weapon used on them—she chooses to believe their deaths weren't her doing. She takes the shoes off her feet, and heads somewhere she knows she won't be a danger, as her own father's blood dries on her hands.

XXX

Long Live the King

THE ENTIRE ROYAL COUNCIL HAS been summoned for an emergency meeting. All council members talk over each other, their words not quite reaching Avgust's ears. The voices all merge together into an incomprehensible mess. He can make out the occasional phrase or word at times, but their meaning escapes him.

There is no place for polite speech right now—the king is dead.

No one tries to talk to him. Avgust doesn't know what he is expected to tell them anyway. Does he interfere and demand order? Would they even listen to him if he tries to? Does he have the power to command them yet?

A man, skinny but loud-mouthed, manages to get through Avgust's complete dissociation.

"This is an insult to the monarchy!" he screams, "To the

entire kingdom!"

Avgust has seen him before, but he has no idea who he is or what his role is supposed to be.

"...in broad daylight..." the head priest mumbles to himself, signing the cross.

"It could be the disease that killed him. The guards found at the scene seem to have contracted it."

"No disease slaughters you like a pig. Whoever did it must have had someone assisting from the inside," another council member suggests.

The captain of the guard opposes, "My men were always loyal to their king. Don't you even dare question their allegiance!"

An argument ensues and Avgust sinks back into his thoughts. He worries his lip bloody, knowing he is no longer next in line for the throne. The crown is soon to fall heavy on his head. He is the ruler now. It's just a matter of days before they coronate him.

He should be angry that someone has killed the king, he should be as agitated as everyone on the court is, he should be devastated that his father is dead. Yet he feels nothing. There is a cavity where his emotions used to be, and it gapes wider the more he lets the thought of his father's death settle.

It is an outrage—murder right inside the castle walls—but he doesn't feel it. He is to be crowned, people will demand decisions and answers from him, but how is he supposed to oblige when his mind is elsewhere? Avgust will be expected to marry even sooner than he thought.

His eyes find Eden's empty chair.

She wasn't in her chambers when they went to collect her, she had locked herself in the tower the night before. Workers that tried to get to their shifts this morning, only to find the entire staircase locked, reported to the queen instead. Avgust overheard. He can't know if Eden has found out about their father and if that's the reason why she has locked herself away. But it wouldn't surprise him if it wasn't, given her state lately. Maybe she doesn't yet know, and maybe it is for the better. Eden may not be in her right mind to handle the news. She is in enough distress as it is.

"Avgust." He feels a hand on his shoulder. The queen's kind eyes greet him. "Go to your chambers," she tells him.

"But I have to be here," he protests, but it's too obvious he would much rather be anywhere else.

"There will be time for you to be the ruler after your coronation, until then take your time to mourn."

"And when is that? The coronation?"

She looks at him confused, as if that's something he should've known already, as if it was mentioned way too many times for him to even need to ask.

"The day after tomorrow. Now go and rest."

He doesn't resist any more, he wants to leave. Avgust only nods to her then turns away from the shouting and yelling still happening in the hall. He moves across the room, no one questioning or even noticing his exit. The door closes behind him, but the loud voices inside don't get any quieter, only fading when he starts walking. Avgust makes his way through the corridors where everything seems slow and ordinary. People pass him, some give him concerned or empathetic looks, some don't look at him at all.

"It must run in the family." Avgust stops in his tracks. "They are both unstable, one is violent, and one is out of her mind." The voice is distant, coming from around the corner of the corridor.

"It's all coming from the mother; our king was always devoted and faithful." The conversation echoes closer, he stays in place, hidden behind the corner.

"I heard the princess was yelling at the poor people who were just trying to get to their working posts."

"What did you expect?" A huff. "She has been going around the corridors aimlessly for weeks now, it was only a matter of time before she became hysterical too."

"Hard times are upon us. There is only decline ahead of us with a future ruler like that."

Fortunately, they continue ahead, paying no mind to Avgust who is slumped against the wall, as if he's invisible. He doesn't have it in him to scold them, to listen to their excuses for the way they spoke. They are right to think so. Avgust can't judge them when he thinks the same about himself too.

He is more concerned about what they said about Eden. How could he have not noticed the extent of her condition? Guilt flares up in his chest. He has been so consumed by his self-pity that he has become unaware of everything around him. Avgust shouldn't have shut her out like that. The marriage wasn't her fault to begin with.

Avgust finally continues walking, the immense weight of his ill-conceived decisions dragging behind him with every step he takes.

"Your Highness?" A voice startles him, and Lady Roza appears out of nowhere, a little out of breath as if she was trying to catch up to him. If so, Avgust hadn't noticed. "I went to your chambers, but they said you weren't there. I tried to go to Eden's first, but I wasn't allowed in. Have you managed to see her yet?"

"No, I haven't, there was a meeting about—" He cleans his throat. "There still *is* a meeting about..." His words trail off. He can't bring himself to say it, not out loud. Hearing it makes it final, hearing it from his own lips would make it real.

"Such a horrible tragedy I can't begin to imagine how you feel."

Lady Roza continues to say kind words of condolences and empathy, but they quickly begin to blur. His head is pulled under water, the depth of it blocking out every sound.

"Avgust?" He finds her hand on his shoulder, her eyes so full of concern that Avgust feels as if he would crumble under them. "Are you alright? Truly?"

Then he does crumble. He lets himself be held in the middle of the corridor. And he cries. He cries as if he were all alone.

Roza rests his head on her shoulder, where Avgust tries to hide his cries. Her hands sooth over his hair, like a mother would.

Loud sobs bounce off the walls, and as they reach his own ears, Avgust's sorrow is swallowed by his embarrassment. He tears himself away from Roza's embrace and runs down the hallway, as fast as his legs can take him. Tears stream down his face in anger, in grief, in humiliation.

Finally in his room, where he can hide himself away, Avgust doesn't feel the comfort he was hoping to find there. The shame of breaking down in front of Lady Roza still lingers in him. Dragging his feet as he walks in, he sighs and sits on the bed, looking at nothing in particular.

"Avgust, I'm glad to see you," Eulalia speaks from the mirror. He hadn't even meant to summon her. "How are you today?"

"My father was murdered." His tone is solemn, yet his words put a small smile on her face, almost undetectable.

"And? Are you satisfied?"

"Why would that satisfy me?" Avgust's brows furrow.

"Isn't that exactly what you wanted? Your father out of the way?"

"Not like this." He gets up and starts pacing around the room. "I just wanted him to let me be, for things to be the way they used to. Now they can never be."

"I'm sorry to hear you feel that way, but you can't deny that it's what you wanted. You told me so yourself."

Avgust stops. A grave realisation finds him. "Are you the one responsible for this?"

There is a beat of silence. A beat in which he hopes he is wrong, that he hadn't unintentionally wished for his father's death.

"Well, friends are supposed to help each other. Isn't that right?" Her voice is so calm, it's maddening.

"I never asked for that!" Avgust rebukes, livid. It's the first emotion he lets himself feel without shame. "I never asked you to do that!"

She tilts her head innocently. "Do you really not recall? I just did as you *wished*."

"I didn't mean it." Avgust's voice breaks a little. He had meant it. But he never really wanted it. Guilt settles into the pit of his stomach, churning thickly until it threatens to pour out of his mouth.

"Don't lie to yourself," she scolds, her face now stern, far from its usual inviting demeanour. "Or to me."

"You don't know anything!"

"You are being ungrateful, Avgust." Her voice is cold, a mother disappointed in her child's behaviour. "If you refuse to thank me, at least accept that it was your wish I granted. I did it for you."

Avgust stands up abruptly and grabs the mirror, pushing it to the wall where it used to be long ago. He rips the covers off his bed and throws them over the mirror, covering Eulalia's traitorous visage. His breathing is heavy. Avgust feels as if he is about to cry again, a sob swelling in his chest, but he has no tears left in him.

A series of knocks on the door startles him. A sequence he thought he'd never hear again. Avgust scurries to the door and swings it open, flushed red from the movement.

"What are you doing here?" he asks, still out of breath.

After the last time they saw each other, he didn't dare imagine him coming to him again, for any reason.

"I come to give you my condolences." Bane's eyes are deep pools of sincere sympathy. Avgust can't bring himself to look away.

"Thank you, that's very thoughtful of you." It's all Avgust

can say. He sounds too polite, too detached as if he doesn't really mean his words, but he does. Bane has always been able to put aside his own feelings for the sake of others. Even if he may hate Avgust now, he still came.

"How are you holding up?"

"I'm not entirely sure yet. It's like my mind won't believe it unless I constantly remind myself it really happened."

Bane's feet shuffle on the floor, switching the weight from one leg to the other.

"And you?" Avgust asks, realising Bane is likely affected by all of this too, maybe even more than Avgust. "He was more a father to you than he ever was to me."

"I..." Bane clears his throat. "I'm handling it as best as I can."

They stay silent for a while, eyes stuck on each other, exchanging words unspoken. Words locked away forever, that will probably never be said out loud. What Avgust said to him the last time they ran into each other echoes in his mind. He is sure that Bane hasn't forgotten it either. But here he is, standing in front of him as if it didn't matter.

Avgust doesn't have a chance to linger in the moment—Eden passes behind Bane, running like a wild horse, acknowledging no one and nothing in her way.

"Eden?" Avgust calls out to her, moving past Bane to have a better look as she grows smaller in the distance of the hallway. "Eden, where are you going?" he shouts after her.

Concern flames up in his mind. Before he can think, Avgust rushes after her as a pair of footsteps fall in line with his. Bane is quick to catch up with Avgust's hurried pace.

"Eden, wait!" he shouts again, to no avail. She doesn't stop even when she pushes right through a group of maids.

Not a single person they pass seems to take notice of the scene rushing past them. Even the women Eden pushes out of the way don't react as they continue as normal. It's like time had stopped. Eden leads them down the corridors, through the door and out to the inner yard. Sun beams hit Avgust's face once they are out of the castle and in the inner yard. Her running pace has only become faster and faster the further out they go. Avgust starts to find it hard to keep up, but he tries his best to not lose sight of her. Eden trips on her dress, but it doesn't even slow her down.

"Where are you going!" Avgust tries to shout after her again, slowly starting to fall behind, even though he tries to push past the burn in his chest from running.

Eden enters the labyrinth.

They follow after her.

XXXI

The Labyrinth

LEGIBLE, STRONG ENERGY BEATS FROM just beyond the castle walls, like a heart. Lemana can feel its location with precision, something her brother made sure was impossible until now. What has changed, if the familiar dull pulses of his energy are now suddenly stronger than they ever were, coming from a place she can finally pinpoint?

Lemana's first thought is to check on Eden. Making her dreams speed by when night comes was Lemana's way of keeping her mind unguarded and open. Now, however, her mind is locked and no matter how many times she tries, Lemana can't infiltrate it. Someone else is already in there.

On her feet before she can even think about it, Lemana bolts through the forest, rushing past the trees like a river stream. Entering Eden's mind that very first time was a shot in the dark. There was no promise that Ursedius would take the bait; there was no sure way to know that breaking the girl's mind wouldn't be for nothing. It has come into fruition, the risk of invading her thoughts, turning her into prey that's all his to take. This is Lemana's chance to catch Ursedius. For the first time since she has arrived in this foreign land, following in his tracks, she knows exactly where he is—whose head he is in.

He has entered her trap and it's only a matter of time before she finds him.

When Lemana comes face to face with the castle walls, she remembers she should be able to just walk through, but the front gate is closed, and several men guard the entrance. Something has happened indeed. She will need to use one of her tricks in that case, if there's no other way for her to penetrate through.

When she approaches the gate, the guards stand in her way, instructed to keep everyone out. The men's bodies lock up, just as she commands their minds to do, and they have no choice but to let her pass through.

The castle is nothing like the bustling, crowded place Eden's dreams had made it out to be. The outer courtyard is almost entirely empty, and those few that are outside look hollowed out of any emotion. It may be from whatever event devastated the occupants of the court that made them purge the castle of outsiders, but their fragile human minds have bent under the strong pulse of Ursedius's power. He is near.

Lemana remembers the way to the kitchens and enters through the little side door, just like Eden had shown her. There isn't anyone around to stop her, even while the kitchens seem to be full of unsuspecting servants, oblivious to the energy bursting out from right under their noses. No one tries to stand in her way when Lemana makes it out the other side of the kitchens and into the courtyard within the inner wall.

It draws her closer, pulling her in stronger the further she goes into the castle yard. It's coming from the labyrinth. Right in its heart lies the source of the energy.

Through thorns and vines, Lemana cautiously enters. It swallows her further into the pathway surrounded by nothing but walls of leaves. The entrance behind her weaves itself shut, and Lemana tries to remain calm. He knows she's here.

She treads carefully, but every turn she takes leads to a dead end, until she passes through what looks like a room carved out of the foliage, entirely unlike something that would belong there. It's dimly lit, and she feels like she is farther away from the centre than she should be this far into the labyrinth. The path that led her here no longer exists when she turns back; it has become one with the wall. There is no way out of the square, of this room-like trap. The sky above taunts her as the only way to freedom.

"Lemana, we've been waiting for you," a voice calls to her, gently, softly. Familiar. She turns around in the spacious room with caution, which might soon turn into fear.

A table awaits, lavished generously with food. She isn't alone.

"Come have a seat," her brother says. His face is youthful, cheeks rounded, and his eyes are still a pair. He sits on one side of the table and next to him is someone Lemana didn't think she could ever hope to see again. Julietta, the last human who ever showed Lemana kindness, whom she last saw alive centuries ago. Lemana stays put right where she is. Everything is wrong and impossible, yet the feeling of home settles in her chest.

"You wouldn't want your food to get cold," Ursedius prompts again, and her feet move before she can command them not to. There is only one other seat with a plate and cutlery, where she finds a chair drawn back and waiting. Lemana sits while eyes follow her every move.

"A nice reunion, isn't it? Just like old times." Ursedius smiles and it almost looks genuine, except for the strange tilt to his mouth, as if looking at a reflection instead of him, flesh and bone. Julietta sits silently, her mouth shut in a tight smile that, for the first time in her life, Lemana doesn't find comforting.

The table, occupied by three, hosts another presence somewhere just out of sight. Lemana feels it like eyes on the back of her neck when she looks to the dark corner. At the head of the table, there is no one, but the darkness stares back at her.

When she looks back to her brother, he no longer resembles the version of himself that she spent her youth with. Instead, blood covers the left side of his face, a gaping hole where his eye used to be. It's an image that flashes for a fraction of a second before he is back to how he was before, normal and unscathed. Lemana looks away, scourged by the memory.

"Is something wrong?" he asks. His voice is strange, like the first wave of sound before it begins to echo.

She shakes her head.

"Then eat." He gestures to the food on the table. "Don't you like what I've prepared for you?"

The dishes laid before her all smell of childhood. They remind her of innocence long lost, and family she no longer has. It's an indulgence when she brings the fork to her lips, tasting memories she wants to relive again. The flavour is savoury and luscious, the bite warm on her tongue.

Lemana never realised she closed her eyes at the pleasure of the taste, but when they snap open, alert, Julietta lies on the table gutted like an animal. Her intestines are scattered across the table like rope. She is still and colourless—dead. Her heart is on Lemana's plate in place of the rice and lamb; a sizable chunk is missing out of it, where she just took a bite. It swells in her throat and Lemana wonders if she should try to keep it down or let it spill back out. Julietta's head turns to her, eyes woeful, although dead and empty. Like she blames Lemana for her fate.

"Look at me," Ursedius's voice, now heavy and rough, demands. Lemana has to force her gaze away from the butchered corpse of her only friend. When she looks to Ursedius, his left eye is cavernous again, bleeding thickly, as his other one stares at her unwaveringly. "Look at what you've done."

"This isn't my fault." Lemana shakes her head weakly. "Your own vengefulness made you what you are."

"You did this to me."

"You made me!" Lemana shrieks. Her ears ring with the memory of water rushing past her head, held down to die as she choked.

"Things could have gone very differently."

They could have gone differently, indeed. Ursedius dares to look at her like it's Lemana's fault, like *she* is the one responsible for everything that transpired between them.

"You claim to resent me and yet you still cling onto me," Ursedius says, "Do you really think I can't sense my own flesh that you keep?"

Lemana's hand flies over her bag, now aware of the ever-so-subtle invisible force that tries to snatch it from her. She grabs the eye out of the pouch, the pull still drawing it away, but it's not strong enough to pluck it out of her fingers. Ursedius is not yet at his full power.

"Is this what you want?" Lemana raises the eye, showing it in her clutch.

At the sight of it, Ursedius almost jumps across the table, but manages to quickly compose himself. It's no use, Lemana already saw how badly he wants it back.

"You are right. I have found peace in carrying a piece of you with me," Lemana says bitterly, "but it might be more important to you than it is to me."

She closes her hand in a fist, the eye captured inside. Viscid fluid leaks from between her fingers as a tortured scream of pain brings her attention elsewhere, to the dark end of the table. The head chair remains empty, but the seat feels occupied. The scenery around her falters, like she's waking up from a dream, yet not quite.

"Listen to me." Ursedius reaches for her shoulder from over the table. Lemana startles away from him, but the crazed look in his eye forces her to pay attention. "Time is your ally. Use it to your advantage. Do as I did last time."

In the blink of an eye, it is all gone. The table is no longer there—Julietta, Ursedius, all of it is gone—leaving the space empty and hollow. Lemana is left sitting on the ground, the eye crushed beyond recognition in the palm of her hand. She wipes her palm on the grass to get rid of the remains of it before continuing to the centre of the labyrinth.

She has to catch him.

***

BLOCKED BY A WALL OF thick leaves and branches that wasn't there a moment ago, Bane realises he has been separated from Avgust. He has no time to react or call out his name before someone steps out of the hedge. Aleksander throws a sword on the ground at his feet, not saying a single word, his gaze demanding but his eyes somehow empty. Bane can see the exit, a cavity in the greenery behind him.

"I'm not going to fight you." Bane tries to walk away, but Aleksander won't let him. "Let me through." He attempts to carefully shove him out of the way, with no success. "The princess is in trouble, it's not the time to resolve petty feuds!" His second shove is met with a violent push from Aleksander.

Bane escapes the next lunge Aleksander makes at him and bolts to the opening in the leaves, but as soon as he reaches it, it starts closing. It only opens again when he steps back. He finds himself cornered; the labyrinth keeps him trapped.

There is no way out of it, this confinement of greens has turned into an arena for a duel he does not want any part of. And yet, if he wants to pass through, he must fight.

Bane picks up the sword. The hedges behind Aleksander braid together, closing the only way out. As if this couldn't get any worse, the sun starts beaming and the drumming headache returns to torment him. He takes a deep breath before he assumes a fighting stance, and Aleksander mirrors him in an instant.

Aleksander is the one to strike first and he strikes to kill. Each jab he makes with his sword is more venomous than the last. The advantage of both strategy and practice Aleksander holds over Bane is undeniable. He never stood a chance before, and even now, his wielding of the sword isn't much improved. If anything, all the skill he used to possess has left him completely by now.

It's a pointless fight, it's clear as day who the winner will be. The speed with which Aleksander wields his sword is impossible to keep up with. Bane trips over his own feet and falls to the ground. The sun blinds him. With his sword still pointed up in a desperate attempt to shield himself, he shuts his eyes against the light. Before he even gets the chance to try to open them again, a weight falls on top of him. Aleksander lies impaled on his sword.

Blood starts flowing down the blade, trickling down in thick beads. It reaches where his hands clutch the handle, until it coats his fingers in red. The rich smell tickles his nose, filling his mouth with saliva. Bane tosses the body off himself and slides Aleksander off his blade with force. He has taken his life.

The sword is still tightly held in the grasp of Bane's soaked hand. He throws it to the ground with a clank, but his hand is already bloodied. Bane frantically rubs it on the grass to get it clean from the blood, smearing some of it on the green blades, but it doesn't do much against the enticing smell that lingers on his skin. No matter how hard he tries to wipe it away, the blood remains, like it has soaked into him.

Bane's tongue meets the flesh of his hand and laps up the

blood that he couldn't leave on the grass. Lips meet the centre of his palm where most of it has gathered, rich glistening red. It continues to drip down from between his fingers. His hand twists and turns in desperate efforts to get his entire head between his fingers like a gluttonous animal, a snake unhinging its jaw to have a bite bigger than it can swallow. His lips trace down his index finger, all the way to the thumb, which he sucks clean.

Entranced by the taste, Bane continues until his tongue traces every last drop of liquid, until he's left with nothing but the taste of plain skin, looking for more blood where there isn't any remaining. The smell still lingers.

The leaking wound that his sword left in Aleksander's core keeps pouring out blood that only smells stronger the more Bane holds himself back. He didn't know he had moved to hover over him until he was already shoving his mouth deep into the weeping cavity, sucking out the blood as it flowed.

His teeth tear the flesh under his garments like bread. Blood fills his mouth, still warm. Bane runs the wound dry, its opening no longer spitting out anything, even when he tries to push his whole mouth in. His canines have grown, like they did last time he fed on a living being. Bane looks again to the still body of Aleksander, how utterly past life it is—paler now than before and colder after Bane drank the source of his warmth. Yet his blood continues to tease his nose, blood that is of no use to Aleksander anymore. Bane sinks his teeth into his neck. The feel of the soft flesh accompanied by the lack of a pulse sickens him, yet he ravenously continues, taking gulp after gulp of blood from the dead body into his mouth.

Even the shuffling that begins in one of the walls of his confinement can't rip him away from the cold body.

He doesn't even acknowledge it until it's too late.

***

AS THEY ADVANCED INTO THE labyrinth, Eden was already out of sight. Avgust and Bane didn't know which path to take out of the three equally uncertain ones before them. When Bane peeked around one corner, the labyrinth took him, closing the entrance before Avgust could grab him.

Avgust finds himself alone.

"Bane!" Avgust screams, but there comes no answer. He tries to breach through the newly formed, thick wall of green in front of him with no success. The branches start twisting over his arms, trying to suck him in. "Bane, stay there, I'll find you!"

Avgust turns to take one of the other pathways, only to find both of them gone. In their places are only more walls of leaves.

"Avgust," calls a voice, small and gentle. Almost out of nowhere, a group of four young women sits around a nicely arranged table full of sweets and desserts. "Come sit with us." They beckon him over with elegant gestures of their hands, giggling quietly between themselves.

"I can't. I'm looking for my sister and…" He doesn't quite know how to describe what Bane is to him, so he lets his words trail off.

"Worry not. They will join us soon enough." One girl with

brown hair and round cheeks speaks as she comes to where he is standing, a smile stretching on her face.

"Would you like some?" Another girl with dark hair and deep-tan skin holds some kind of pastry to his lips. Avgust takes a bite, tasting the sweet honey as it melts in his mouth. Her long lashes blink over her dark eyes, her top lip juts out ever so slightly above her bottom one. She looks so familiar it's almost laughable how instantaneously Avgust feels safe with her.

The other girls sing a melody, one reminiscent of that of the forest birds, gentle and faint.

"I really have to go," Avgust says.

"Where?" the girl with the pastry asks. There is a child-like curiosity in her eyes as she furrows her thick brows, tilting her head with genuine interest.

Avgust opens his mouth to speak, but he can't find the words. His mind is suddenly blank. "I don't know."

"Come, you look tired." She takes his hand and leads him to the head of the table. As they walk, one of the others places flowers on their heads. Daisies and lobelias twisted by their stems into circle crowns, as lavish and beautiful as ones made of gold and brilliants.

The girl pushes him to sit in a chair with a playful look in her eyes, to which Avgust huffs a laugh. She sits on his lap, the cut in her flowy, thin dress falling open over Avgust's legs, uncovering the bare skin of her thigh, as if by accident.

Her hand slowly brushes Avgust's shoulder, his arm moving with hers, ending on her exposed thigh. She shivers under the light traces of his fingertips. Her skin is warm and soft, so soft;

Avgust feels like if he is not careful, he will damage it. His attention is stolen by a hand that caresses his hair. She twists a curl between her fingers, her eyes transfixed on it. Avgust stares back at her. He has seen her before, but he can't place it. The answer is on the tip of his tongue when she locks their lips, firm and deep. A kiss so sudden it takes the breath out of his lungs. He gasps into her open mouth. The taste of her kiss feels dear to him, well-known and practised, yet somehow disconnected. She pulls away.

Then she hands him a cup of wine, the liquid in it tasting like pure gold to match the exterior of the richly detailed vessel. Avgust gulps it hungrily.

A whiff of death and decay pervades his lungs for what seems to be less than a second before disappearing, yet it manages to choke him. He tries to wash it down with more wine. Unexpected but overwhelming bitterness fills his mouth; unable to swallow, he has no choice but to spit it out.

In a blink, the serenity is broken. There is not a trace of the soft warm skin he had under his hands. On his lap lies a pile of thorns and branches twisted together in a shape that vaguely resembles a human. Through the gaps in the branches, a grotesque sight greets him. In the other chairs sit three corpses, reanimated as if held on strings. What was long, luscious hair a moment ago is now thin strands that hang in clumps off of the girls' scalps. Their kind eyes are hollowed caverns in their skulls, covered in translucent, rotten skin. His mind clears of its trance when the smell of decay assaults his nose again. Then just as it came, the terrifying image is gone.

"Is something wrong?" the girl made of thorns asks, back

to her lively self. Avgust can't unsee what hides underneath this mirage. He shoves her off of himself and stands on shaking feet.

"I need to go."

"Isn't everything like you wanted it to be?" she says, puzzlement written all over her.

Avgust looks to the side, the others have him pinned under their gaze. He takes a small step back, then another. They mirror his every move, stalking after him like a pack of wolves prowling closer and closer towards their prey, until his back presses against the bushes that imprison him.

Cornered with no path to take, while the girls near him slowly and methodically, Avgust takes a risk. His arms sink into the green wall behind him, pushing against tough branches that scratch his skin, body and clothes. It feels like the hedge swallows him, and for a moment he doesn't think he can make it out the other side, until a single beam of light pokes through. Soon his head breaks free, and his body follows.

The sun is a welcome feeling against his skin, but his eyes take a moment to adjust against its rays. When he blinks them open, Bane is standing before him. He looks at him startled, his body hunched over someone else's. Someone dead.

Bane's face is covered in blood down to the collar of his white shirt, the sleeves stained crimson. The man lying dead at Bane's mercy doesn't matter, all Avgust feels is safe. No rotten corpses, no swallowing hedges, just Bane and his warm eyes that have never looked more terrified.

Of him or of himself?

Avgust hesitates when he takes a step towards him, and it seems to snap Bane out of his stillness, sending him rushing up to his feet. He tries to use one stained sleeve to wipe away the blood on his face, which does nothing but amuse Avgust, strangely. Daring to move closer, Avgust can't hold himself back when he rushes the rest of the way. His arms wrap tightly around Bane, and despite the state of his clothes, he buries his face as deep as it would go into his shoulder. He breathes him in. All of the iron and dirt and sweat somehow smell like home. Avgust didn't think they would ever get to hold each other again, not like this, not at all. Tears prickle at his lash line, but he shuts his eyes so they won't spill.

"I ruined your shirt," Bane swallows thickly.

Avgust embraces him tighter. "The hedge got to it before you."

Avgust tries to look at his face, but Bane barely lets him pull away. He is still clinging to him as Avgust cups his jaw with his hands. He wants to be sure that he is real. Bane shies away from his gaze, trying to bury his face in Avgust's palm. He wants to cover his bloodied mouth, Avgust realises. So, he brings him close again, letting Bane hide what shames him in the crook of Avgust's neck.

A scream breaks the quiet. Long and strained, startling them apart. Terror fills Avgust's body.

They need to find Eden.

Avgust rushes head-first, not truly knowing where he is going, the fading echo of the scream leading him. He tries to catch it before it goes silent forever.

A path has opened up through the hedges, showing him the way to the centre of the labyrinth.

At the sight, Avgust's heart stops beating, a lump forms

in his throat. He would've fallen to the ground if Bane wasn't beside him to hold him on his feet. Eden lies dead, her hair spilled around her head like a halo. Avgust can't look at her like this. So still, no colour left in her cheeks. Hot tears run down his face and Avgust can do nothing to stop them.

There is someone else there, sitting next to Eden. A woman with long black hair. Avgust's heart sinks. Anger begins flaming up inside him.

"Get away from her!" He chokes out a shout. She looks up, confusion in her eyes, as if she doesn't know him at all. This only makes him angrier. "I trusted you! You said you were my friend, Eulalia!"

"Eulalia? You are mistaken."

"Don't lie! Do you think I am that stup—"

She stands on her feet, and he gets to take a better look at her. It *is* Eulalia and yet the woman standing in front of him cannot be more different. Her demeanour, her voice, the way she speaks to him is all wrong. She isn't Eulalia.

She keeps gazing at Eden with deep frustration, her light brows furrowing.

Eden. Avgust's eyes land on her again, and she is as she last was. Still. Cold. Colourless.

He must get away; he must find a way to reverse this. This can't be the end, Avgust won't let it be.

Part III

XXXII

Lamb to the Slaughter

DUST FLIES IN THE AIR when Avgust pulls the fabric off the mirror in his room. After having kept it covered under the sheet, seeing his reflection feels strange. It's eerie, looking at himself alone in the glass without Eulalia's presence.

"Eulalia?" Avgust waits patiently, but he is only left to stare at himself. Shirt in disarray, torn in more places than he can count, and hair frizzy and full of knots, Avgust finds himself repulsed by the state he finds himself in.

"Eulalia, show yourself!" His own eyes stare back at him, rimmed in red despite not shedding a single tear. They seem dull and void of light, but the slightest glimmer of hope prevails. "Please…"

"I'm here." Eulalia's frame overtakes his in the mirror, like a ripple in water. The strong resemblance with the woman who stood over Eden's body makes him flinch. Having seen the real thing, he now can say with confidence that the form Eulalia takes is not a true-to-life depiction, but a distant memory. Suddenly all the little differences and inconsistencies make sense. It's like Eulalia is forgetting the true version.

"Do you need something, you look in quite the distress, dear?" Her voice still feels soothing to his aches, despite what she has done.

"My sister—she..." Avgust swallows thickly, unable to bring himself to say it. "You are the only one I know who could help me."

"Is something wrong?" Eulalia's head tilts in that familiar innocent way. It irritates Avgust.

"I know this isn't your real self. You can't hide from me."

"It's true," she says, "this isn't what I look like, yet everything else I've shared with you came right from my heart."

Avgust almost scoffs. "How could I be sure of that?"

"You already are. If you weren't, you wouldn't have come to me again." She's right. "You still trust me, and you are not wrong to do so. I can help you."

"You can bring her back?" Avgust's voice breaks around the words, unshed tears stinging his eyes.

She hums.

"First, you must come inside."

"Where?"

"Step into the glass," Eulalia beckons him in, waving him closer. Avgust doesn't hesitate when he touches the mirror's surface and it ripples under his fingers, like thick liquid. He startles back and withdraws, certain this wasn't the way his mirror was a moment ago. Chancing another touch, Avgust rests his palm against the cold surface again, watching the fluid swallow his hand. He can see it on the other side, as if distorted through the surface of water.

Avgust steps in, expecting to fall into the darkness that usually frames the vision of Eulalia, but there is solid ground under him. He finds himself alone in a strange, dark endless void; Eulalia is gone when he is fully inside. He follows a faint yellow light coming through what seems to be a cracked door. When he reaches it, he is hesitant but ventures in anyway.

A narrow corridor welcomes him, at the end of it a dying fire, the only source of light in the room. Avgust isn't sure what purpose this room serves. Desks on both sides thin the path even more; on each of them are scattered shears, saws, blades and other instruments that Avgust can't recognise to name. What he can recognise is the dried blood on them. He lifts his eyes to find shelves towering above him, crawling up the walls. They must go to the ceiling, but it's too ill lit to tell. All his instincts tell him to run, but he can't. He needs to do this for Eden.

The yellow light of the fire illuminates the glass jars on the shelves, small animals float inside clear liquid, but full revulsion doesn't set in until he notices the other items on it—severed parts of what Avgust continues to hope are animals, bowls of eyes and containers with hearts. The water in those is murkier, diluted with a rusted red.

"Excuse the mess, but there's no time for tidying now." A raspy voice startles him. It's only now that he notices the hooded figure in the corner by the fire. It's Eulalia, but she doesn't look the same. The voice is different, that of a man, a confirmation that Eulalia as he knows her may have not existed at all. It has been someone else all along. Avgust goes towards him.

"What are you going to do?"

"I can bring your sister back," the figure, Eulalia he supposes, says. "Yes, yes, I can do that," he mumbles to himself.

Avgust suppresses a shiver in his presence. Gone is the welcoming aura of Eulalia and instead there's a cold unease that settles deep into his bones.

"But first we are going to have to make a deal," the figure says. "There is a very delicate balance in nature. We can't disorder that. We can't take without giving back."

"What am I supposed to give back?" Avgust asks, ready to give anything.

"Soul for soul. Life for life," Eulalia explains calmly. "For her to come back, you must take her place."

Avgust's tongue feels thick in his mouth. A chill runs down his spine, but he thinks of a life without Eden. A life where he is king. A life he'd rather not live. Eden has much more to live for than he does.

"Do we have a deal?" It frustrates him that Eulalia knows him well enough to see he already has been convinced. A hand pokes out of the cloak—rather, what's left of one. Skin clings to the bone, rotten in places, leaving gaping holes all over it. Avgust has seen that hand before. He is hesitant, suddenly remembering the dream—the hooded figure, the smell of the stale water—but what choice does he have? Avgust takes the rotten flesh in his hand, accepting his fate.

A wolfish smile glares from under the hood.

Flames turn blue and the air grows cold, as if the fire doesn't emit any warmth anymore, but instead syphons it greedily. It's like the room dissipates around them, like everything dissolves into nothing, the shelves, the desks, the jars—all gone, coated in darkness or absent all together, Avgust can't decide. The now even-dimmer flames light next to nothing. Avgust can't make out anything further than his own hands.

Turning away from the light, Eulalia takes off his hood. Avgust catches glimpses of thin, taught flesh coating a skull before it sinks into the darkness.

Avgust can only make out sounds coming from the shadowed corner, metal falls on wood and Eulalia curses under his breath. Soon he hears liquid starting to pour, not in a strong stream, but it drips steadily enough. The figure emerges from the black darkness, and for the first time Avgust is able to make out a face. Life had been drained from it a long time ago, but the wounds on the left side of his face look raw and fresh as if made just now. The cavity that his eye used to fill gapes empty. Only ill lighting prevents Avgust from seeing inside his skull. On his forehead lie thin, light hairs, few and far between— what's left of what used to be eyebrows. Even in this gruesome, half-rotten state, Avgust can see the resemblance to the woman from the labyrinth. If he was never her to begin with, they still must have some kind of relation.

"Drink."

A cup is handed to Avgust. The creature clutches his left arm to his body, as if in pain. Avgust studies the dark liquid inside, it barely fills half of the cup's volume.

"Is it poison? Is this what will kill me?"

"No. It will not kill you."

"I thought I was supposed to die."

"You will, in time, but not quite in the way you think," Eulalia says. "Now drink, we must hurry."

Reluctant but complicit, Avgust does as he is told. The liquid is thick and heavy in his mouth. It tastes stale and bitter, dry somehow.

"I never got the chance to give you my condolences for your father's passing," he says. "In hindsight, it was an honest mistake on my part, I hope we can put it behind us."

Avgust doesn't say anything. Is he expected to forgive his father's death like it's nothing? But he needs his trust, he needs this deal to succeed. So, he doesn't speak his mind.

"We have bigger things to worry about now," Eulalia continues.

Bandages come undone to reveal more bandages, ones darker, dirtier. Stench begins to spread. Despite their sickly exterior, his hands move with a steady pace unravelling the bindings. Avgust is having trouble keeping track of their motion, but something catches his eye, a fresh deep cut that runs over his forearm. It's not bleeding, but it has bled.

Grey, translucent skin starts to peek through the cloth where the rib cage is supposed to be, but under it are only more layers of bandages. One would think that if all of the bindings weren't there to hold him together, the creature would crumble to the floor. He feels the side of his body with his fingers, then Eulalia remembers to close the robe around himself better.

"I'm an old thing," he tells Avgust, as if noticing his

disgust, "time has not been kind to me."

He comes closer, the putrid smell of the rotting bandages now a burn in Avgust's nose.

"But you needn't worry about things like this." A shaking hand comes up to stroke Avgust's cheek. He can't help but flinch, remembering the last such gentle touch turned to choke him until he startled awake. "Exactly ripe and ready, dear thing."

Avgust's traitorous heart stutters under the praise.

"Beauty is a fleeting thing; it should be caught in the exact right moment, or it vanishes forever. Not all of us get the privilege."

"Is that what happened to you?"

"Yes, yet still I need to keep this body alive at a cost far greater than its worth."

Something slots into place in Avgust's mind, a taunting thought. Eulalia has something to do with the people dying in their sleep, the so-called *"plague."* This is how he feeds his body. And then a worse realisation hits him—the labyrinth. Eden's death wasn't unlike the deaths of the *"plague."* Both his father and his sister are gone at the hands of Eulalia.

"I can't help but notice," Avgust says, testing the waters, "the girl whose appearance you mirror has your eyes."

Avgust is sure he wasn't meant to see the subtle twitch of Eulalia's still-remaining eye, but it didn't escape his notice. "Maybe you should go fetch her and make a whole pair for yourself," Avgust taunts, almost too spitefully.

"You speak of matters you can't fully understand." His tone is raw and irritated. "I cannot do as I please like you may think."

"But it was you, wasn't it? It was you who killed Eden."

He does seem to do as he pleases. Eulalia's lack of response is telling enough.

"Did you offer her a deal too?" Avgust asks hesitantly, desperate to understand. Desperate to keep his anger at bay.

"No. She was already halfway gone. Her mind wasn't hers anymore."

"Why not take me? I'm the one you want, aren't I?" Avgust is sure his mind has been just as corrupted by Eulalia's manipulations. He makes for an easy target too.

"Your body is too precious to be wasted in an experiment with no definitive result. Sacrifices had to be made; it was necessary."

Avgust doesn't get the chance to ask what experiment. There's a crack of bones so loud it could've been breaking. Sharp claws dig into Avgust's shoulder, restraining him in place. The rotting hand runs down his ribs, careful and slow. Avgust feels a sharp pain, something penetrating his left side. His lungs burn, his ribcage feels like it's torn open. He chokes, trying to force his body to breathe, but out comes a wet gurgle.

This is what kills him, he thinks, but the pain feels worse than death. He bleeds through the hole in his shirt, clutching at his ribs where the pain feels most stabbing.

The floor deepens, as if the dripping water in the room has started to fill it up rapidly. Avgust is sinking before he can even gasp for air, suddenly engulfed into dark water he might drown in. Is this how he meets his end? Is this what the deal was? He fights against the current that drags him to the bottom like it's clutching at his ankles. His hands flail with the struggle to swim, but he keeps sinking. The light is gone and only darkness surrounds him. His lungs burn with the lack of air, even more so when a weak scream escapes his mouth, bursting out in bubbles. The tears he has been holding back finally spill, only to be lost into the vastness of the water.

He lets himself descend to the bottom, but he never reaches it.

XXXIII

Dust to Dust

THE DOOR CREAKED OPEN. *Almost soundlessly, the soft padding of feet approached the bed. Avgust's heart jumped in his chest where he hid under the covers, thinking it must be his mother, or worse his father. But the feet sounded bare and small where they thudded against the floor. He knew they couldn't be anyone's but Eden's.*

His blond head poked out from underneath the white cotton sheets, small hands clutching the hem.

"They let you come back?" he asked Eden, voice quiet and hopeful. She was standing beside his bed, the moon from the window made her hair shine white.

"No." She shook her head and sat on the edge of the bed. Avgust adjusted and sat up with his legs folded underneath him. "I'm too scared to sleep alone."

"Me too," he admitted.

"It's not fair. I know you didn't do it."

August's eyes snapped to her, heart leaping. The bird was already dying when he found it. Its little heart barely a faint tremor in its tiny chest. It had been beyond saving, but August still cried when it died in his hands. At only nine years old, how could they already think him capable of such violence? No one believed him when he said he didn't kill it, but of course Eden did. She never was quite like everyone else.

"I'm sorry they took you away. Do you like your new room?" August asked.

"No," she said, "it's too empty without you."

This room, the one they used to share, felt too big now without her, too. August knew it was probably not true, but the room also felt colder. Their mother insisted that Eden be moved, lest August corrupt her. She never said it like that, but the fact that she avoided looking at August now and didn't let Eden spend time with him said it for her.

"Did you hear? They are bringing you a preacher," Eden said, her eyes wide and worried.

"I heard," August whispered. "Do you know who?"

"I overheard them talking. They said they're taking him from a monastery somewhere east."

"All that trouble for what? The last thing I need is another grumpy old man," August groaned. "They have Sofron helping me with my penmanship and he is enough to deal with as is." Then, a thought occurred. "I wonder if they will still bother with that after...everything."

As much as August complained about having to spend time locked away in Sofron's study, Eden could somehow tell he would still be upset if their mother decided to forbid him from going again.

"You are still the future king, whether mother and father like it or not," she said.

With his status, Avgust supposed he could get away with a lot, but that didn't entitle him to his mother's love.

"Even if they don't let Sofron teach you anymore, you will have a new Sofron to torment soon." Eden smiled a wicked grin and Avgust couldn't help his laugh. "If they are bringing him from far away just for this, he must be important," she said.

Avgust sat up with his knees on the bed, gesturing with his hands, ready to delve into a bizarre story. "Imagine, an ancient man with a beard that reaches his toes, while somehow never tripping, sent here just for me. They call him enlightened because he lives in a monastery, but really, he knows everything because he has lived it all!"

Eden laughed, entertained. She looked at him like he was being ridiculous, yet she didn't stop him.

"Maybe he's an all-knowing prophet who has foreseen this event and has been preparing all his life just to come here." Avgust settled back onto the bed. "If he is a prophet, he will know I didn't do it."

The comforting pat on his shoulder Eden gave him wasn't enough to break him out of the sudden sombre mood, but it helped a little. She was the solid earth to his wildfire. Even when everything went wrong, he would always have Eden.

Always, always, always.

***

Light, so faint and far away, streaks through the dark waters. Slowly Avgust regains consciousness and breaks through the surface. The light is now not at all as faint as the opacity of the water has rendered it to be.

For a moment he is blinded by it but makes it to the shore

with haste. Avgust lifts himself out, crimson water weighing him down, having soaked his clothes. The sun shines bright above in the cloudless sky. Birds chirp in the distance. Warm breeze swings the tree branches ever so gently. The beautiful scene around him mocks his misery.

All his joints hurt, but the pain cannot compare to the one he feels in his ribs. Dull yet so persistent. He wants to curl up on the ground to attempt to soothe it.

Cold chills hit his skin, one after another. Avgust shivers.

Snow is falling from the sky in the middle of summer. The snowflakes hit the red waters of the Lover's Sorrow, white and crystal, before melting as quickly as they had fallen.

It's strange; Avgust can't understand how it's even possible.

Eden loves when it snows, Avgust not so much. They used to play in the snow when they were little. Avgust grew to dislike the cold and the wetness of snow with age. His sister on the other hand never lost her love for it. If it keeps falling when she awakes, he hopes it makes her smile.

The further away from the lake he gets, the less snow falls. It's nearly dusk when he reaches the castle. How long had he spent under the water?

The guards let him through, but not without strange looks at his red soaked clothes. Passing through the outer court, Avgust can feel all the eyes on him, but it's when he gets inside that someone dares to speak to him.

"Your Highness—"

"Where is Eden?" he asks, ignoring the horrified look on the nurse's face. He has no interest in knowing which aspect of his appearance prompted the reaction. If he looks how he feels it's probably justified.

"But Your Highness, I thought you were aware; Konstantin said you were together when—"

"Where is she?" Avgust cuts her off.

"Her body is getting prepared for burial." Horror washes over him. These idiots were going to bury her alive, if Avgust hadn't come back on time.

"No! They must stop!"

"I'm so sorry but—"

"No, they will listen to me!" Avgust demands. "Where is she kept?"

"In the cellars, Your Highness."

She continues speaking words of condolences, of consolation he suspects, but Avgust doesn't want to hear it. He rushes through the hallways, then through the small wooden door and down the spiral stairs into the cellars.

Eden lies peacefully on a table, wrapped in white cloth. Avgust unveils her face, so she can breathe when she awakes. He looks at her, how there's nothing troubling her now, the calm lines of her brows and mouth. Avgust hopes she doesn't resent him when she wakes to find him gone in her stead.

"*So much death, in such little time,*" a voice says from somewhere.

'*They've come to take her away*', he thinks, but he couldn't be more wrong. The voices aren't coming from outside the door of the cellars. They come from above ground.

"*It's his doing.*" Over layers and layers of stone, the conversation continues and Avgust hears it loud and clear. "*The one that's marked for evil.*"

He hears steps overhead, getting quieter and quieter with each echoing word as they fade to a distant murmur.

His knees collide with the stone floor when sudden pain blooms inside him. The inside of his chest throbs, but not with his heartbeat. A steady, even rhythm that sends him groaning in pain. Avgust fears he might vomit from its intensity. His veins feel wrung out, making him aware of every single one that runs through his body like strings meant to choke him. It *was* poison that he took, another lie from Eulalia. He takes Avgust's trust lightly.

Despite all this suffering. Despite rolling on the cold, filthy stone in agony. The excruciating pain he feels contradicts his state of mind. Eden will live. As soon as he dies, she will awake. It will all be worth it in the end. He can only hope Eden forgives him. She would have done the same in his place. Even if she doesn't forgive him, at least she will understand his actions.

Writhing on the stone floor, he thinks of Eden, how he gets to be with her in his last moments, as his consciousness slips and Avgust welcomes his death.

***

There's the wooden creak of a door, steps come closer. Avgust awakes after death. A smell rests in the air, strong and rotting.

"Did you spend the entire night here?" Bane's voice bounces off the stone walls, reaching his ears loudly. "Avgust?"

Avgust shouldn't be awake, yet he is. Something must have gone wrong.

He looks at Eden's resting form and rises to sit on the cold floor.

"She should wake up any moment now."

"Avgust, she is not waking up." Bane's voice sounds sorrowful, pitying. "She is dead."

"She will, you'll see!" His own words echo in his ears, he sounds frantic.

"The smell of her fills the whole cellar, Avgust! She is gone."

"You know not of what you speak! I will take her place, and she will take mine." Avgust chokes back a sob. His hands clutch at his chest, tearing at the skin under his bloodied shirt like he wants to reach inside his ribcage and make sure his heart ceases its beating.

Bane says nothing for a long moment. Avgust feels his eyes on him but dares not look back. He can tell that there is something on his mind, something he is stopping himself from sharing.

"Let me help you get safely to your room."

"What I say is true! You will see! When I go and she returns, you will see."

"Stop making threats on your life!" Bane says, desperation rising in his voice.

"I make no empty threats; my life has already been given away for her to begin hers again."

Bane just stares at him with something between bafflement and pity in his eyes.

"They will come to take her body away soon." He turns to leave. "Use the time left to say goodbye."

"I'll do no such thing," Avgust shouts after him. "She will awake!"

The heavy door shuts. Avgust is left alone again. He steps closer to look at his sister, to look at her calm peaceful face. Except that's not the sight that greets him. Her cheeks have hollowed, and her skin has lost all colour, turning ash grey.

Bane is right, the strong smell is coming from her. Her body is beginning to rot.

Avgust runs out of the cellars and up the spiral staircase. His heart slams rabbit-fast against his chest, and with each beat it shatters. Eden is dead.

He has been tricked.

Weak, stumbling feet take him down the corridors of the west wing until he stands in front of the mirror once more. His lonesome reflection greets him again, in a far worse state than the last time he saw his own appearance.

"Time is running out. Why am I alive, still?" Avgust croaks out. "Eulalia? Why do I still live? Why didn't you kill me?" His hand hits the surface of the mirror.

"You lied," he chokes. "We had a deal! Let me back in. Do your part, let me in!"

He bangs on the glass with more strength than he intends, his hand landing in the exact place to align with the already-existing cracks. With each hit the lines grow, running like water streams across the surface, until pieces start to crumble from the impact down to the stone floor. Frustration turns to rage. Avgust grasps the mirror with both hands, its weight, which was once great and laborious, now feels as if it were made of feathers. He tosses it aside onto the floor, glass first.

Faint pinches tingle over his hands. When he looks at them, he is met with countless little cuts all over his palms and knuckles. They begin closing by themselves right in front of his eyes, one by one until there are none left. Pale bloodstains are the only trace that they were there at all.

Bewildered yet curious, he bends to pick up a piece of glass in his hand, then makes a deep cut through the width of his palm. Blood begins pouring, then ceases in the matter of a mere moment, and a blink later, the flesh has already fastened itself shut.

Amazement can't occupy his mind for too long as he finds himself gasping for air. His ribs ache again. The deeper the breath he takes in, the less oxygen reaches his lungs. His entire body shakes with anxiety, the source of which he cannot determine. Restless, he begins pacing in circles around the room. Shivers run down his spine, as a sudden coldness washes over him.

There is a knock on the door. Avgust tries to ignore it, yet the person on the other side persists. The pain in his movements crests as he drags himself to the other side of the room. A pleasant smell fills his nose and rests on his tongue. His mouth waters.

He opens the door to see Lady Roza. There's a solemn lilt to her brows and a redness on the rims of her eyes. She is wearing a plain dress, a drastic contrast to her usual lavish gowns.

"You didn't make an appearance at the funeral. I figured you prefer to grieve alone, but I needed to see if you were alright." Her eyes roam up and down over Avgust's form. "Unfortunately, I was right to be worried, you look like death."

He just blinks at her words, cold waves still washing over him.

"May I come in?"

Avgust's mouth is too dry to form words, so he steps aside and lets her in. She passes by him with a gust of that delicious smell from earlier and suddenly his teeth hurt. It's not the usual rose scent that she favours, it's something far stronger. He swallows down gulp after gulp of the saliva that pools in his mouth, but it's never-ending.

"I think you should go," he says, strained.

She whips around to face him. "No! You're sick with grief, look at you, your skin has turned ashen."

"You can't stay." Avgust tries beckoning for her to leave but she doesn't move.

"I refuse to leave you. You need consolation."

"I need…" He almost raises his voice, but his throat aches, sand grinding against its walls. "I need rest, you should leave me to it."

Lady Roza stands so close to him. One step and he could crash into her. He can't stand the pity in her eyes, so he looks away, landing lower, his gaze fixing on her throat like he is drawn to it. Without realising that he has even moved, he is tracing his lips over the crook of her neck. She shivers under his warm breath against her skin.

"Avgust, this—" Roza begins, but she never gets to finish her thought.

Avgust's teeth pierce her soft skin as easily as taking a bite out of an apple. The small gasp that she lets escape her lips quickly turns to a scream that gradually gets drowned out by the hammering of her heartbeat. Avgust swallows hungrily, his dizziness washing away steadily as he does. The more he takes, the less her heart throbs in his ears, before he realises the screams have silenced too.

Every deep gulp renders her struggle meeker and meeker, soon she lies in his arms no different than a rag doll. Avgust's mouth drips blood in heavy streams when it unlatches from her throat. Blood slides down his chin, down to the collar of his white shirt, the sleeves stained crimson. Carefully he places the body on the ground, as if she is sleeping.

Avgust stands alone in his room, a friend's lifeless body his only company, forced to face what he has done in the still silence. Something had come over him—he didn't mean to take her life. All he knows now is that his pains have quieted. He brings his hands to his face to wipe away the blood, but all that does is smear it even more over his skin.

Another knock lands on the wood of his door, this time a familiar pattern. Avgust freezes in place, not even daring to make his presence known, afraid to face Bane after what he did to Lady Roza. No matter, Bane doesn't wait for his response before he pushes the door open.

It doesn't go unnoticed when he stops in his tracks at what awaits him in the room—Lady Roza dead on the floor, Avgust drenched in her blood. But it also doesn't escape his notice when Bane enters the room and shuts the door behind himself with haste.

Neither speaks. Their eyes stay entangled in the silence, louder than words. Bane goes to draw the curtains over the windows.

"You—" Bane cuts himself off. Avgust dreads the accusation that is sure to follow; however, when he speaks again, Bane's tone is timid. "Was I the one who corrupted you so?"

Bane always finds a way to bring the blame on himself, even when he has nothing to do with this.

"No." Avgust shakes his head. "I have brought this upon myself."

Avgust doesn't need to speak his apology to know Bane has already forgiven him for the way he yelled earlier in the cellars.

"I should be dead." Avgust fixes his eyes on the floor but quickly averts his gaze when he remembers who lies there. "I felt death."

Bane sighs, all too empathetic. All too understanding.

"I killed her," he states, staring at his own bloodied hand. It finally settles in, the reality of his doing. She is gone. He had *taken* her life away from her.

Bane doesn't call him a monster. He isn't judgemental or disgusted. His eyes look at him with love and kindness despite what has become of him.

"Let's get you cleaned up," he says and helps Avgust sit on his bed. It's a nice change from the cold floors he has acquainted himself with over the past day, but the covers might be ruined now, stained in blood and whatever dirt his clothes have picked up. Avgust can hear Bane moving the body across the room but can't bring himself to look.

Bane leaves the room briefly after that. Avgust hears him talking to the maids outside the door, requesting water to be delivered to the room.

"I don't care; you must find a way!" Bane raises his voice. It's a rare thing to hear him angry. Even when they'd argue, his voice would remain calm, often frustratingly so.

Avgust can't make out any more of that conversation, and he doesn't even try as he slips into his own grave thoughts. He finds he doesn't think of much, like there are too many things fighting to settle at the front of his mind, and instead none prevail. His eyes stare at the floor. Blood has gotten between the stones, and he watches as it flows and connects in the cracks.

"Come on." Bane's words pull him out. "Lift your arms please." Hesitant, Avgust does as he is told, and Bane peels the bloodied shirt off of Avgust's body. He covers his chest with his hands, hunching over to make himself small.

Avgust turns his head to find a bath prepared. He can sense the smell of the oils added to the basin from where he is standing. He strips the rest of his clothes at Bane's request. Instinctively, he wants to protest, afraid Bane will leave him at the sight of his bare skin, but he doesn't have the strength to say anything.

He steps into the lukewarm water inside the tub, and when he sits down it overflows slightly. He brings his knees to his chest and rests his chin on them. A single crimson tear streams down his cheek and melts into the water when it falls. Soon the entire basin is coloured a faint mahogany. He averts his eyes and turns his head the other way where Bane kneels next to the basin. His touch is gentle, timidly rubbing the cloth against his skin, as if Avgust would crumble under even the slightest bit of pressure. And maybe he's right to think so, maybe he would, maybe Avgust is a broken thing. He lets Bane lift his limbs and turn him in whichever way he needs, surrendering to his careful touches.

The wet ends of his hair stick to his back. Bane reaches forward to bring Avgust's hair to the front. For a brief moment, Bane's lips brush against his shoulder, the accidental touch brings back a memory that feels so distant now, when Bane had returned to him in a state similar to the one Avgust finds himself in now.

Avgust remembers how he found him when they rejoined in the labyrinth. The scared look in Bane's eyes, afraid of being met with fear, with rejection. Avgust wonders if he looked much the same when Bane walked into this room today.

From the way Avgust is crumpled into a small ball in a bath full of someone else's blood fighting off tears, and Bane's stoic demeanour, you wouldn't guess they share an ache. It shouldn't surprise him; Bane has always known how to endure pain.

He takes his time de-tangling and brushing Avgust's hair, before he gets to washing it. It's stained a faint red in parts, stuck together in dry clumps, which he is glad he has someone to brush out for him.

Avgust hugs his knees to his chest as water pours over him. It washes away more diluted red and fills the bath. Bane shields Avgust's eyes from the water with a hand over his brow, ever so carefully. Avgust feels like a kid.

The soap Bane uses smells pleasant, calming. He has moved to kneel behind Avgust. Hands rub his scalp carefully, foaming the soap before rinsing it again. He runs the bar over the tops of his shoulders and Avgust captures his forearms before Bane can reach for the full bucket again. Avgust holds Bane's arms wrapped around himself from behind, despite the soap he must be getting all over Bane's clothes. After a few moments, Bane escapes Avgust's grip and stands up.

"Where are you going?" Avgust hears the panic in his own voice. Having the strong urge to hide himself, he tightens the grip of his arms around his knees.

Bane moves Avgust's wet hair from his forehead ever so gently, all the care in the world gathered at his fingertips.

"I'm not going anywhere. Just outside the door."

He tries to still his laboured breaths as he watches Bane get to the door, tears threatening to spill at the thought of being left alone. Avgust hears him, better than he would have thought, as he demands the maids to bring more hot water.

The door creaks open again, and Bane returns quickly enough to find Avgust much the same as he had left him.

Using water from the last full bucket, Bane rests the rag over the edge and dips his cupped hand.

"Look up, please."

Avgust's eyes shift to his face, resting his cheek on the high of his knee.

Bane shakes his head lightly. "There's blood all over your mouth."

Avgust says nothing as he peels his face off the skin of his knees and lets Bane wash his mouth and chin with the warm water in his hands. It drips down into the basin, adding more pigment to the water.

***

Bane waits for nightfall to dispose of Lady Roza's body. He plants a letter that states she has departed to the countryside due to the immense grief that has overwhelmed her, managing to turn his otherwise-blocky letters into ones more suited to a lady like Roza. If he had been of a right mind, Avgust would have offered to do it, but the tremble in his hands hasn't subsided long enough to hold a pen steady.

Bane gets Avgust into his sleeping clothes and helps him get under the covers, tucked and warm. It's lonely sleeping alone in a bed fit for a king. He wants to call out to Bane and beg him to stay, but he knows neither of them will find it easy to sleep if Lady Roza stays with them through the night.

He listens to the heavy wooden door shutting with Bane's exit. Left alone to his thoughts, Avgust's tears finally come.

The image of Eden, dead and cold, haunts him now that he knows she isn't coming back. Her peaceful expression nothing but the last face her rotting corpse will wear. The soil will eat away at her quickly until there's not much left of her but memories.

The ache in his ribs remains a painful reminder of Avgust's own death. Death that never came. In the end, it was all for nothing.

XXXIV

The Beginning

To Avgust's relief, Bane came back to him last night. The embarrassment he felt when he found him sobbing was quickly put to rest by Bane's soothing kisses along his brow. It didn't take much pleading from Avgust to convince him not to retire to his room but to stay and keep him company.

Now, morning has come already but the fabric drawn over the windows prevents light from leaking inside, for Bane's sake. They lie together under the thin sheets, Avgust's cold foot is on Bane's calf, while Bane's fingers run through his blond curls. It feels nice to be held so gently, wrapped in someone else. Avgust feels broken, with his pieces carefully being put back together by Bane's touch. The calm caress of his hands in Avgust's hair is the only thing keeping him sane.

They haven't kissed. Avgust is afraid to want it, lest it

repulses Bane away again. He's all Avgust has left now, and if it means keeping him, he will never suggest it again.

Bane's face is peaceful, serene, like he doesn't have a single thing to worry over in this moment, other than to just hold him. It eases Avgust's mind just that little bit.

"Did you sleep well?" Bane's voice breaks the quiet of the morning, rough and unused.

"Not the worst." Avgust has not slept well in weeks, but the warmth of Bane's body in his bed was a sure relief to his mind. "You?"

"As well as I can."

The silence embraces them again, and it's a calm one.

"The woman from the labyrinth..." Bane begins to say and Avgust lifts up on one elbow to look at him, suddenly alert. "She needs to see you."

"Me?" The woman...the face Eulalia stole. "What for?"

"I don't know, she wouldn't tell me. But she did me a favour, so I owe it to her."

Avgust hesitates to ask, "What favour?"

"She took care of Aleksander, after I..." Bane swallows thickly, throat bobbing. He meets Avgust's eyes, and they both know what he was going to say. *After I killed him.*

"We'll go," Avgust says.

Avgust buries his face in Bane's neck, slotting into his embrace once more before they have to get up. He smells nice, clean, and a whiff of Avgust lingers on his skin, left from his sheets. He smells safe, like home.

A knock on the door pulls them out of their bliss.

"Your Highness, are you awake?" A maid's voice comes

through the other side of the door. "May I come in?"

"No. I am not to be disturbed," Avgust grumbles, but he says it loud enough to be heard.

"I came to tell you that the maids will be ready to prepare you for the coronation this afternoon."

"I will be preparing myself," he says sternly, "I want no one sent and no one to enter my room without explicit permission from me."

"Whatever is His Highness's wish. But I will have to send someone to bring the coronation jewels," she says.

"Tell them to leave them outside," Avgust demands. "Thank you, you can go about your work."

They listen to the maid's footsteps fade away on the other side of the door. Once she is gone, Bane shifts on the bed beside him and sits up.

"We need to go meet *her*."

***

The woman, Lemana, as she had introduced herself, was waiting for them despite the fact that Bane hadn't known where exactly he was leading them. They ended up in Starosel, in a creaky tavern Avgust had never been to before. It's mostly empty, only a few day-drinkers scattered around the tables.

"I thought my instructions were clear," Lemana says from a table along the wall when they walk into the tavern, "I only need the blond one."

Bane straightens up at her rude remark.

"I can't leave my prince without an escort," Bane is quick

to say. Avgust fights the stutter of his heart.

Her brow lifts. "Are you his keeper?"

"It is my duty to ensure his safety."

"That must complicate your romance," she says casually.

Avgust feels a cold sweat threaten to break over his skin. Bane's eyes widen and Avgust gets a horrible sinking feeling.

"Romance?" He plays dumb, masking how unsure he feels with the state of their relationship.

Bane says nothing.

She beckons them to sit across from her, unconcerned. Bane lets Avgust slide into the bench of the table first before he follows.

"I did something for you, so now you must repay me."

"What do you want? Riches? Gold?" Avgust asks.

Lemana shakes her head firmly. "I need you to dive into the Lover's Sorrow and retrieve what hides within."

Avgust looks to her in confusion, and seemingly noticing, she elaborates.

"The lake is protected. Only certain people can go in."

"Like Eulalia?"

It appears it takes Lemana a few moments to understand who Avgust is talking about. He knows Eulalia is not his real name, but he never came to learn what is.

"Like my brother, yes."

Avgust tries not to visibly react, but his mind spins. *Brother...*

"Then why not get it yourself? Aren't you and him the same...being?"

"Believe me, I've tried." Her face never betrays an emotion that isn't neutral, but her voice sounds exasperated. "We are the same as much as we can be. But not in this instance."

Avgust frowns. "If *you* couldn't take it, how are you so sure that I can?"

"Because I can feel the pull from you," Lemana states, looking at each of them. "From both of you."

Avgust mulls that thought in his head. *Pull*, she says...and somehow, Avgust knows what she means. There is a subtle pull from Bane, but an even stronger one from Lemana. Maybe it attests to power.

Bane speaks before he can. "If you feel this *pull* from us both, then can't I be the one to take it?"

"You're different. It has to be him." She points to Avgust.

"Are we now the same beings then?" Avgust asks curiously. "As you and your brother." He can feel Bane's eyes on the side of his face, but he doesn't turn.

"No," she says firmly. Her expression still remains neutral, but somehow, it's etched with cruel amusement, as if the thought is laughable. "But there is a part of him in you. That's why it needs to be *you*."

"If we are not the same, then what am I?" Avgust asks cautiously.

"My brother never gave a name to his creation," Lemana says calmly, "but I've come to learn that your people have—*vampire*."

A chill runs down Avgust's spine.

"And me?" Bane asks, sounding hopeful. "If I'm different, and it has to be Avgust, then what am I?"

"Humans may not know the difference, but I do. I feel it from within you, but I suppose there aren't many characteristics that you would find different."

"So, a vampire?"

She shrugs.

Avgust jumps at the opportunity to ask more questions.

"Why did he pretend to be you? I understand that he isn't kind on the eyes, but why mimic your likeness, of all people?"

Lemana stops to think about this for a moment.

"I'm the face he knows best, I suppose. We used to be inseparable before…" Her words trail off. She seems to fall into her own memories. "He is my brother, after all. Or was. I don't know what he is anymore."

"What happened to his eye?" Avgust asks, remembering the cavernous hole in the skull of the creature that invited him into the mirror where he finally wore his own face.

Lemana doesn't give an answer, but Avgust can tell it isn't because she doesn't know, but because she refuses to say. He moves on before she decides to leave.

"What does he plan to do?"

"I cannot know for sure, but if he has chosen you, you must be wary. Because he will be back for you," Lemana says. "He doesn't give up on his conquests easily."

"He'll be back for me?" Avgust's brows furrow. "And do what?"

"You better hope you never find out."

Avgust says nothing to that. The table falls silent. What could be worse than what has already been done to him?

"Fine. I will take whatever it is you need from the lake." Avgust swallows thickly. "But you will have to answer one more question."

"Take it out and I will tell you whatever it is that you desire to know."

"How can I know you are not lying?" Avgust demands.

"You think I wouldn't keep my word? Didn't I answer too many of your questions already?" she says, tone serious. "Shall we?" Lemana speaks directly to him as she stands, ready to go, like she's afraid he will change his mind. Bane follows to his feet.

"Your services won't be needed." Lemana lifts a hand dismissively towards Bane. Avgust bites his tongue, but his distaste for the woman spreads like venom.

"I've already told you I can't leave him without protection," Bane protests.

"I assure you, *your prince* will be safe with me."

The glaring look they exchange seems to be the only common ground they stand on. Avgust spares each of them a glance and stands with a sigh.

"Bane, I'll be fine." He rests a reassuring hand on his arm, and it snaps him out of his narrowed stare at Lemana. Bane doesn't seem convinced, but with his lips shut in a tight line and a small nod of his head, he agrees to comply with her demands.

"I will wait for you back at the castle."

Then, they part.

Avgust follows Lemana through the thicket, several steps behind her. They make their way to the lake without a single word exchanged between them. The forest allows a pleasant cover from the summer heat, which Avgust would otherwise enjoy if it weren't for the present task at hand. It takes entirely too little time, not enough to prepare himself, before they reach the lake.

It looks just the same as always—thick red waters and an eerily still surface.

Lemana gives him no directions on what he is looking for or why. He wouldn't bother asking anyway. Avgust wants to get this over with as soon as possible. Not that he is eager to attend his coronation, more that he doesn't find Lemana's company very pleasant.

Avgust approaches the shore hesitantly, the memories that resurface bringing a bitter taste to his mouth. There's no time to waste, but he finds himself hesitating. Before he gets the chance to change his mind, he removes his surcoat and shirt before diving in the opaque waters of the Lover's Sorrow.

The deeper he dives, the darker it gets. Trying to use his eyes to navigate proves to be useless. Avgust is left to rely only on his other senses, but even then, there isn't much to feel other than the cold water. Soon enough his hand hits the bottom, and he begins frantically searching. He can feel himself running out of air.

There's a pulse of energy, pulling him in like a current. Avgust's mind wanders to when he crawled his way back to life in this very lake. Fortunately, his fingers quickly find something big enough to be the subject of Lemana's interest. It feels like a big flat rock, and even if it is just that, he is willing to risk having to dive in again.

As soon as his face breaks through the surface he gasps to fill his lungs with air. Avgust tosses his finding on the ground before pulling himself out of the water. He hasn't even looked at what he had pulled out and Lemana has already taken a hold of it by the time he manages to step out of the lake. It's a broken, thick piece of stone with viciously carved writing in a language Avgust is not familiar with. Lemana looks up confusedly at him, but quickly hides her puzzlement when she realises he is studying her as well as the thing in her hand.

"Where is the rest of it?" She demands.

"This was the only thing on the bottom of that lake."

She lets a silence prolong, eyes narrowed and observing. Then, her attention is back to the stone plate for just a moment, before it's back on him like she's assessing if he's lying.

"Not what you expected?" Avgust says and does not give her the chance to answer. He can see that she knows as much about the stone as he does. "It doesn't matter. I did my part, now it's your turn."

"Ask away."

"We had a deal, he and I. He didn't fulfil his part." Avgust could have asked at the tavern, but it felt important that he asks this when he has Lemana alone. The concern on Bane's face when Avgust screamed his throat raw down in the cellars is still fresh in his mind.

"What deal?" Lemana lifts her eyes from the stone plate then.

"My life in exchange for my sister's."

Lemana looks at him in concentration for a moment, and Avgust prepares for an answer, but she shakes her head instead.

"I have no way of knowing. We aren't exactly on speaking terms."

"I see."

"If it is any consolation, my brother keeps his word if it

can be helped."

Avgust looks at her long and hard. He wants to believe it, but Eden is resting deep into the soil now and he knows rationally she isn't returning. A sliver of hope bubbles inside him, nonetheless.

"You should go, your escort awaits."

He scoffs at the unflattering nickname she used for Bane, takes his clothes from the ground and turns to leave without a goodbye.

Avgust spends very little time walking to the castle, but he can't recall walking any faster than usual. He reaches the front gates and ignores the concerned looks and the people subtly moving away from him as if afraid.

"*...and Lady Roza, no one saw her again...*" a voice says from somewhere. Avgust twists around to see who is talking, but there's no one close enough to have said it. There are servants going about their tasks, but all the way on the other side of the yard. Avgust turns back around and resumes walking.

"*'She left for the countryside,' they say,*" another voice speaks, and Avgust can tell it's coming from far away, but it sounds like they are right next to him. "*And how did she leave with no horse, nor carriage taken from the stables?*"

"*Can't be...*"

"*But it is! Ask the head groom,*" the second voice confirms, "*It's all fabricated by him and that manservant of his. God knows what happened to her.*"

In the inner courtyard, Avgust's stride calms and he walks slower to the entrance of the fortress, ignoring the two disembodied voices.

The Beginning

"*I thought Konstantin was a man of God.*"

"*Once, maybe. His faith wasn't strong enough to protect him from that demonic influence.*"

"*There he is, drenched in blood again,*" one of them says, and Avgust feels eyes peering at the back of his head. "*Look at his hair, it's the second time he shows up looking like that. He has bathed in the cursed water of the Lover's Sorrow, I tell you. He is no longer human, if he ever was to begin with.*"

Avgust looks around the courtyard past farm workers bringing in produce and kitchen staff fetching water from the well until he spots two maids hunched over a laundry basin, talking in hushed voices.

"*He turns, don't look at him!*"

"*Do you think he can hear us from that far away?*"

The two maids turn quickly, avoiding his eye.

"*You know what the blood-water does to you,*" one maid signs the cross over her chest. "*Maybe it's a blessing our good king isn't here to witness this, Heavens may he rest.*"

"*Doomed to turn in his grave as long as his son has rulership over this country. What a fate.*"

"*He was never cut out to rule. He says it himself.*"

Avgust's eavesdropping is interrupted by a loud gasp behind him.

"Avgust? Oh, look at yourself!" the queen cries, hands clasped around her mouth in shock, "Do you know what time it is?"

"Late?" A big part of Avgust hopes he missed the coronation, although he knows they wouldn't start without the crown jewel–him.

"Don't even begin. Go clean yourself, go on now."

Avgust doesn't protest when she waves over someone behind him. Another maid comes to lead him into the bathing quarters. For the second time now, he has had to watch diluted blood drip from his hair into the water of his bath.

He gets himself dressed again and leaves hastily for his quarters under the pretence of not wanting to delay the coronation any longer.

Upon Avgust's return to his room, Bane stands to his feet from his seat on the bed.

"What happened? Did the water accept you?" He studies Avgust for injuries. Bane finds him cleaner than he probably expected. "What was it?"

"Just a piece of stone. Broken, at that!" Avgust scoffs. "Hope she is happy with it."

"What is it for?"

"From the looks of it, she herself doesn't know. Makes me wonder how much of what she was telling us was a guess." Avgust sighs.

The heavy royal jewels were left neatly on a small circular table that the maids clearly had brought to his room just to have somewhere to safely put them. They were laid out atop a soft cotton cloth that prevented the gold from getting scratched by the hard wood of the table. Avgust wonders if Bane had organised the jewels himself after the maids left them, just to appease Avgust's request of not letting anyone else into his room.

"Never mind that, I need to be getting ready before they barge in here and force me."

The Beginning

"Oh," Bane says quietly, "should I go?"

Avgust takes Bane's hand without thinking. He swallows, shaking his head. Being alone right before his life is about to irreversibly change doesn't feel like a good idea.

"I have been left with no mirror and no helping hand." Avgust looks at him through his lashes, hoping he would stay.

A fond smile lights up Bane's face.

Silence befalls them. All that can be heard is the loud jingle of the jewellery. The quiet company they've kept with each other recently is pleasant. It's very unlike what their usual routine of passion used to be, but Avgust finds himself content.

The ceremonial jewels brought to Avgust's quarter are heavy and bulky and not at all to his liking. Thick golden bands and chains with large adornments of precious stones. The sceptre and orb weren't part of the jewels they trusted him to figure out by himself, but he is sure they won't fit his tastes much either.

Avgust thinks about Eden's much finer jewellery, left to rust in her untouched room. He doesn't know if he can bring himself to take them now that he knows she won't be there to willingly give them away.

Bane helps him arrange the thick bracelets on his wrists and adorns his finger with a heavy signet ring. He doesn't let go of Avgust's hand as his lips thin in concentration, or maybe concern.

"If what she said is true, if both of us are now eternally cursed, why strive for absolution?" Bane's eyes are cast down, as if he can barely bring himself to speak. "You have seen me at my lowest and still embrace me without judgment for what has become of me." Bane's hold on his hand tightens. "It's a kindness not many would offer someone like me."

"You're still you." *You're still mine. I'm still yours.*

It comes out as a whisper.

Large dark eyes shine wetly as they look at him. Avgust brings Bane into a gentle embrace.

When he finally lets him go, Bane barely moves away from him, leaving only a hair of space between them. His breath is warm on his face.

"You were married..." Avgust can't help but say, "I understand if you don't want things between us to be how they used to."

Bane shakes his head firmly, "I can't last a day not wanting you."

Air leaves his lungs in a rush. Avgust has spent a lifetime waiting to hear those words leave that mouth—Bane wants him. This is real and it isn't just one childish fantasy Avgust has spent his life longing for. Confirmation is something he never thought he would get to have. The purgatory their relationship has been with the uncertainty of what they are to each other, and the hesitance to be the first one to say it, was absolute torture. Bane has never said it before, and oh, how good it feels to hear it. To know it.

His gaze drops to Avgust's lips. A heavy sigh escapes him, a shiver of anticipation.

Solid hands draw him closer, and Avgust finally feels like he can breathe. There's no apology and there is no need for one. They want the same thing; they want each other, and words have never been their way of forgiveness.

The Beginning

Bane closes the small distance between them, and when their lips collide it's a cascade of old feelings blossoming anew as if nothing ever broke them apart. Avgust relishes the feeling of the lips he gets to claim as his, savouring them like a man starved. It's like time stops moving, like there isn't a crown waiting to fall on his head. The kiss trickles into his veins like the blood that pumps him alive, like Avgust would cease to exist without it.

It's a testimony, a vow, to all there is to live for.

Epilogue

WATER RUSHES UNDER THE FORCE of the paddle. The gondola swishes from side to side as Lemana guides it through the still canal. The nights in this city are unlike those of the quaint countryside—loud and busy despite the late hour. It will take some getting used to.

How many decades has it been since she re-surfaced from the water again, Lemana doesn't know. Clearly, it has been a while. Humanity has certainly made progress in however long it has been. She can see it in the amount of care and detail that has been put into each building, beyond just a roof over their heads.

The structures stand tall around her as she sways through the water, the façades of the newer-looking ones embellished with ornaments. The only reason for it is aesthetics. Probably influenced by the crowd of artists flocking towards this city. It's unfair to compare it to the village, but the contrast is too stark.

Epilogue

One thing Lemana can say for sure, humans have grown more vain in the time that has passed.

A kiss between two different exemplars of the vampire has set the curse in motion. Lemana got lucky finding Avgust—the object of Ursedius's interest—so easily only to discover him already in love with another vampire. His opposite match.

When the curse is triggered, life pauses and doesn't resume until all Celestial creatures return to their dome—the water. But even then, it doesn't resume as it once was. Time begins anew from the moment the curse was created. The years trickle slowly, and new life begins, entirely reset, but the mould of the previous lifetime stays in more ways than one would know. People reborn in this new life follow the mistakes they made in the past one. But some parts change, like how the time Celestials get called to life is never the same—shifted slightly forward each time. Lemana would know, having lived through three resets already.

She emerged early this time, even Ursedius hasn't awoken yet. He, of course, is the one responsible for the existence of the curse, but the last cycle had ended centuries ago. Lemana can't put her finger on why Ursedius had given her the idea to reset time again in the first place. It will delay his search for a vessel, but why would he want that, let alone beg her to do it?

Avgust is being prepared to become his next host now that Ursedius has gained new energy from all of those soldiers and villagers he drained. The human body cannot hold a celestial charge, so by turning Avgust into his own distorted version of a vampire, Ursedius is making sure it can hold him in. But now, he needs to make his way back to his new vessel in this new lifetime.

Time and time again, her mind sends her back to the labyrinth. She still cannot explain what happened. Ursedius took the bait that Lemana planted in the form of one vulnerable

Eden. But it was as if he knew it was Lemana's plan all along, so he kept her trapped in that illusion. When she arrived at the centre of the labyrinth, Ursedius had taken control of Eden's body already, and Lemana caught the tail end of the last moments before the vessel expelled him forcefully. Eden then dropped lifeless and drained as Ursedius made his escape.

Luring him into a body was easy, she just wasn't there to catch him. If only she got there faster or Eden's body was stronger to keep him in longer, Lemana would've had the chance to seize him, lock him in and finally put an end to him. But now, new questions have arisen. Why had he helped her? Why now, after so long? Lemana needs to find out what he's plotting before she kills him, or the answers die with him.

It seems for now the only information she can get will be from the stone plate. However, it's broken, and Lemana has the most insignificant piece. She has discovered it is a contract; the wording of the sentences seems to suggest so. A contract set in stone is a very primitive way of making a spell. It would explain how he has been doing magic alone all this time. Lemana was always the one that held more power, and Ursedius couldn't do magic without her. Until he suddenly didn't need her anymore, which she never quite understood.

The plate consists of a few disembodied sentences, fragmented across the rest of the missing pieces, and then the signed consent of Ursedius and the other party at the very bottom, carved harshly into the stone. From what can be deciphered from the incomplete words atop, it seems to be concerning the new vessel he is desperately searching for. Who has given their agreement to take Ursedius into their vessel, and why hadn't it worked? From what she saw of him in the labyrinth, he is definitely still bound to his own body.

Lemana must find the rest of the broken parts.

She has followed a certain pull here to this city, but it had

Epilogue

turned out to be the wrong one. Yet it's not entirely useless. It appears something has gone wrong with the reset of time and Bane is here alone with no trace of the other one. He is travelling with an older man. A vampire. Lemana can't seem to trace a pull to Bane himself, but she will make sure he survives until Avgust arrives. Because inevitably, the two will always find each other, Lemana just has to wait. They are bound to now, trapped by the curse.

And where Avgust is, Ursedius will follow.

END OF BOOK ONE

Follow the authors on Instagram
@authors.coppercobalt

Printed in Poland
by Amazon Fulfillment
Poland Sp. z o.o., Wrocław